Murder
in
Thırd
Position

Murder in Third Position

An On Pointe
Mystery

Lori Robbins

LEVEL
BEST BOOKS

To Glenn

Praise for the On Pointe Mysteries

quirky characters that characterize each of her On Pointe mysteries. I was smitten long before the end of Chapter One and can't wait for the next entry in this delightful series."—Mally Becker, Agatha-nominated author of *The Counterfeit Wife*

"In *Murder in Third Position*, ballerina Leah Siderova dances her most daring investigation yet. When an acclaimed set designer is killed days before The Nutcracker's opening night, Leah Siderova fears the crime will be pinned on her dance partner and leaps into action to clear his name. But when the body count continues to rise along with the American Ballet Company curtain, Leah finds herself in a media-storm spotlight with a ruthless killer hot on her trail.Robbins choreographs a heart-pounding whodunit that will have readers furiously flipping pages to discover the culprit. Leah Siderova's grace and grit pirouette off the page, and her chemistry sizzles with the ever-gallant Detective Jonah Sobel. Mystery lovers won't want to miss a moment of this mesmerizing performance and will be begging Robbins for another encore."—Sarah E. Burr, author of *#FollowMe for Murder* and the Glenmyre Whim Mysteries

"Lori Robbins' third book in her On Pointe mystery series begins with principal ballerina Leah atop a precarious set trying to quell her fear of heights. Later when the set collapses, the mystery and intrigue begin. *Murder in the Third Position* puts us in the backstage heart of a ballet company's production of *The Nutcracker*. While Leah and her 'Choreographers of Crime' friends try to solve the murder, mayhem occurs. This is a thriller, a whodunit with humor, and an eye-opening look into the workings of a ballet production. All combine to create a page turner that has the reader wanting more from Leah and her plucky crime solving crew."—Linda Norlander, author of the Cabin by the Lake Mystery Series

"Lori Robbins gives a master class in murder with her latest On Pointe Mystery, *Murder In Third Position*. When over ambitions set designer, Maurice Kaminsky is found dead, and ballerina Leah Siderova is almost crushed by his unstable set, she takes a grand jeté into the mystery to catch the killer before he strikes again. With wit and humor, the world of dance comes to thrilling life."—Cathi Stoler, award-winning author of The Murder On The Rocks Mysteries

"Lori Robbins has written another skillfully plotted mystery set in the competitive and uncompromising world of professional ballet, drawing the New York dance world in full color."—Elizabeth Mannion, author of *Dreaming in Irish* and *Traces of Irish*

Praise for the On Pointe Mystery Series

"In this limber yarn, Robbins, an ex–ballet dancer, deploys her tartly witty prose to offer a delicious, well-observed sendup of the ballet world...As Leah navigates atop her aching, blistered feet through the labyrinth of balletic cattiness and vanity, the author's wickedly droll skewering of professional dancers is a hoot that will keep readers turning pages.

"An entertaining suspense tale adds bloodshed to the psychological mayhem of the ballet scene."—Kirkus Review [starred review]

"From chilly New York City rehearsal days to stormy interpersonal relationships, Robbins brings to life both the intrigue and the ballet world's many challenges. As astute as the action plays out, Robbins doesn't neglect a dash of ironic wit that laces the story with personality and fun. The mystery component is just as lively as the dance company descriptions and the performances themselves.

"Robbins brings all to life with a pen that performs deftly and artistically, and this will attract both dance-oriented readers and those with little experience with the world of ballet."—D. Donovan, Senior Reviewer, *Midwest Book Review*

Chapter One

The nutcracker sits under the holiday tree, a guardian of childhood stories...
—Vera Nazarian

I've danced naked in front of thousands of people, watched a tidal wave sweep away my pointe shoes, and fallen into a bottomless pit. But unlike those pre-performance nightmares, Maurice Kaminsky's Deathtrap was all too real. And while I'd woken from many a fevered dream in a cold sweat, the perspiration I endured at our first tech rehearsal was more likely to kill me than save me.

After several failed attempts, I stepped back from a nearly vertical escalator and said what everyone else was thinking. "Maurice, your set design is beautiful, but it looks as if one grand jeté will send it crashing to the ground."

I couldn't deny that the scenery for our new production of *The Nutcracker* ballet, with its cantilevered platform and glittering gears, was dramatic, imposing, and imaginatively designed. The rickety structure, however, was without one essential element: Me.

With short, powerful arms, Maurice hauled himself onto the stage from the orchestra pit below. "Get on with it, Leah. We don't have all day." He banged the side of the staircase, as if to demonstrate its strength, but which instead caused the interior mechanism to clank and rattle in protest. The grinding gears sounded like a ride in a traveling amusement park, the kind that routinely made headlines for some horrible accident.

I took a deep breath and placed one trembling foot onto moving stairs that vibrated with the strain of my puny weight. By the time his contraption transported me to the narrow platform that loomed overhead I could barely breathe, let alone dance Brett Cameron's complex choreography.

The Nutcracker was Brett's first full-length ballet, and he feared the collapse of his career more than the collapse of his principal dancer. "Move downstage, Sugar Plum! Your solo is supposed to be the highlight of the *Nutcracker Ballet*. Not its best-kept secret."

The choreographer's indifference to me and his support of Maurice came as no surprise, although their artistic partnership was almost as fiery as their marriage.

I inched closer to the edge, but Brett continued to harangue me. "Stop mincing! You look like a scared kid creeping around the edge of the playground on the first day of seventh grade."

His middle school analogy was apt. My face burned with the same self-conscious embarrassment I endured when I was thirteen. This time, however, everyone really was looking critically at me.

Actually, it was worse than that. Nelson Merrill, a filmmaker better known for true-crime documentaries, had the cameras rolling, capturing my cowardice for all eternity. I hoped, not without reason, the day's footage would end up on the cutting room floor. The dancers were incidental to Nelson's film project, which was Maurice's life and art. Our egotistical set designer was famous for his paintings, his sculptures, and his multi-media installations. *The Nutcracker* was his first commission for the ballet. He had a lot to learn.

When Maurice realized the camera was focused on him, he dropped his combative attitude and struck a more conciliatory pose. He rested his chin on his hand, as if posing for a shorter, older, and considerably less contemplative version of Rodin's *The Thinker*. "No need to worry, Sugar Plum. I built a set of ridges into the flooring, so you can feel when you're getting too close to the edge."

The only thing I could feel was an incipient panic attack. Those cautionary ridges weren't deep enough to penetrate the hard surface of my pointe shoes, and the solo included a tightly choreographed sequence of tricky balances and turns. Unless my toes were to magically achieve the sensitivity of the title character in *The Princess and the Pea,* dire consequences were sure to follow. Those fears unfolded in a series of scary images. I could trip on the pebbled, wavy surface and fall flat on my face. I could stumble out of my pirouette and land on the stage below.

Given the state of my nerves, a massive heart attack was another distinct possibility. Medically, I would qualify as unusually young for any serious coronary event. As a dancer, however, I was closing in on ancient. And perched on that platform, I was aging rapidly.

Forgetting how sharp the acoustics were in the theater, I said, in an undertone not meant to carry beyond the apron of the stage, "Why can't Tex dance up here and let me dance on solid ground?"

Maurice clapped his hands to stop the music. "I heard that. Let me explain, once and for all, that this set design symbolizes the mood Hoffman envisioned when he wrote the original story of *The Nutcracker.* Artistic decisions are my area of expertise. Not yours."

Brett, annoyed at Maurice's intrusion into his territory, took his irritation out on me. "I don't hear anyone else complaining. And just so *you* know," he turned to toss a baleful look at his husband, "my work is an homage to Petipa's original ballet. The set design is not the star of the show." He surveyed the dancers, as if daring them to speak.

None did. Between Maurice's claim to have channeled the famous writer of *The Nutcracker*, and Brett's claim to have surpassed one of the greatest choreographers of all time, there wasn't much room for ordinary people to take a position on the matter. I didn't blame my colleagues for their silence and averted looks.

Brett signaled for the music to resume, and I threw myself with renewed determination into the role. The amount of time allotted to my variation was less than three minutes. But it took Brett and Maurice more than an hour to figure out how those three minutes would look from the audience.

The general consensus was bad. Not naked-in-front-of-an-audience bad. But not good.

When I finished, Olivia Blackwell rushed to meet me. I welcomed my friend's embrace, although both of us were dripping with perspiration. As dancers, that's our normal state.

I pulled back and searched her face. "How awful was it?"

Olivia didn't meet my gaze. "You were wonderful." When I didn't respond, she conceded, "Maybe a little shaky at times, but who could blame you? Dancing on The Deathtrap would terrify me. But you'll be great in performance."

My pulse raced faster than when I was dancing. "We have one week until opening night. Not a lot of time to get comfortable, let alone great."

She moved closer and spoke more softly. "I heard Brett is going to be the next director of the company. Neither of us can afford to get on his bad side."

I matched her low tone, although nothing I said warranted discretion. "When do you finish? Let's meet later at the Café Figaro, where we won't have to whisper."

She brushed an invisible speck from her tutu. "Um, well, today's no good. I have a costume fitting after rehearsal, and then Tex and I are going out." When I hooted, she turned pink. "We're friends. I don't want to get involved with anyone in the company."

"Don't be embarrassed. Tex is a terrific guy." And he was, especially in comparison to Olivia's previous boyfriends, Horrible Horace and Creepy Jonathan.

At the sound of her musical cue, Olivia ran with exquisite lightness onstage. I headed backstage, where I found two dancers lurking in the wings. Unlike Olivia and me, they were tall, blond, and haughty. When I approached, they fell silent in the way people do when they're talking about you. One left quickly. The other, Kerry Blair, remained. She was my understudy in both *The Nutcracker* and *Romeo and Juliet*. Despite our mutual dislike, I offered advice about how to safely navigate Maurice's set.

She pretended to yawn. "Not interested, Leah. I can dance Sugar Plum without help from you." Her lips curved in a cruel smile. "But if you need a few pointers about how to dance Juliet, let me know."

If I had an answer, the words would have stuck in my throat. Had Kerry

4

been elevated from her position as my understudy? Judging from her triumphant expression, the answer was a definite *yes.*

She put her hands on her hips and stuck out her chin. "Let's see which one of us is better at playing a teenager."

This unmistakable dig at my age galvanized me. "When I dance Juliet's death scene, there won't be a dry eye in the house. If you get top billing, there won't be a dry eye at the box office."

I didn't stick around to hear her spluttering response and instead headed to a corner of the theater, where two shadowy figures spoke in the dim light of an Exit sign. There was no mistaking Brett and Maurice, who were as different physically as they were alike temperamentally. Tall, dark-haired Brett was as lean and strong as when he danced with the San Francisco Ballet. Maurice was short and stocky, with a full head of thick gray hair.

My request was modest, because ballerinas with weak knees and scheming rivals don't have much bargaining power. "Maurice, I'm doing the best I can, but the platform is unstable and unsafe. There must be something you can do to secure it."

Brett answered, although I'd directed my request to his husband. "Leah, you've made your opinion clear. This is the set we're using. If you can't handle it, we've got a half dozen ballerinas waiting in the wings who would love to take over the role."

I'd dance on the topmost ledge of the Empire State Building before I let Kerry take my place. But they didn't have to know that. "It makes no sense to threaten me. The gears creaked so loudly, I could hardly hear the music."

Mindful of Nelson's approaching camera, Maurice became more accommodating. "Okay, of course, no problem. I'll take a look at it after rehearsal today. By tomorrow, it'll be perfect."

They marched in lockstep to the front of the house and sat in the middle of Row F. I took a seat halfway down the center section of the orchestra to watch Olivia lead the Mirlitons in their delicate dance. She was smaller than most ballerinas in the company, with dark hair and dark eyes. Presumably, management thought she looked the part. I, too, had been cast in that section of the ballet when I was in the corps. It was a good role for a young dancer hoping to get promoted to bigger and better things.

Nelson and one of the cameramen followed me. I answered his questions as briefly as possible without tipping over into rudeness. The filmmaker's constant scrutiny had placed an awkward haze of self-consciousness over the rehearsals, not only for me, but for the whole company.

He said, with a friendly look, "Is there a problem with the set? I really admire how you dance on it as if you were on solid ground."

I had plenty of experience talking to the press, most of it bad. As an award-winning filmmaker, Nelson didn't qualify as paparazzi, but I'd been burned by the media too many times to get suckered into a public relations sinkhole. "It's typical to have some technical issues. That's why we rehearse."

He gestured to the cameraman, who had been filming Olivia, to direct his lens toward me. "We need to schedule some time for a proper interview. How about now? Or I could buy you a cup of coffee or a drink after your last rehearsal. It would be nice to get some candid shots outside the theater."

I cast about for excuses. "I'm better at dancing than speaking. You should talk to the front office instead."

He stroked his chin with long, thin fingers. "I did notice no one spoke during this morning's ballet class. And your buddies Maurice and Brett don't seem to want to hear feedback from the dancers during rehearsal."

I kept my eyes on the stage. "That's how we work. It's one of the unwritten rules of ballet."

Nelson didn't need to know about the gossip we shared in the dressing rooms and behind the curtain. That's where all the stuff we didn't say during class got aired.

He peered at me through black-rimmed glasses. "Yeah, that's the kind of material I'm interested in. What else can you tell me?"

"I'd love to chat, Nelson, but now's not good. How about tomorrow morning?" I was afraid to sit before the ruthless eye of his camera without clean hair, perfect makeup, and a leotard without sweat stains.

He moved his head from side to side, unwilling to give up. "I don't want things too staged. I'm looking for the process, rather than the finished project."

I gave him the Scouts salute. "I promise to be a credible work-in-process for you. Tomorrow."

He persisted. "It won't take long. I swear. Fifteen or twenty minutes at most. We have so little time before opening night. You can't avoid me forever."

With perfect timing, Tex rushed down the side stairs from the stage and rescued me. My dance partner was without his usual wide smile and easy manner. "Leah, I hate to drag you away, but we need to work through the ending of *Romeo and Juliet*."

I leaped to my feet. "Yes. The, uh, the ending. We really should do that."

Nelson held up his hands to signal defeat. "No problem. I'll finish up with Brett and Maurice instead." He motioned the cameraman to get one last closeup. "But tomorrow, you're all mine."

I was relieved when that tense and gloomy day ended. The child dancers, who were an integral part of *The Nutcracker* ballet, exited first. Their mood was no sunnier than mine. Brett and Maurice were unaccustomed to working with young performers, and the two men's profanity sent the kids into fits of nervous giggling.

Brett towered over his small audience and said, "Anyone who thinks this is a joke can quit now. Plenty of kids would be thrilled to take your place." He brandished the cast list, and, stricken with terror, they ran off.

A red-faced mother led the charge of agitated parents, who appeared to be massing for a strike, if not an all-out war. "These are children, Mr. Cameron. Your threats and foul language are unacceptable."

Brett raised one thick, dark eyebrow. "You don't appear to understand how this works. I give the orders, and the dancers do as I say. Anyone who can't handle it can leave. We've got three understudies for each kid."

The parents retreated, muttering to themselves and each other many of the same words that had offended them a few minutes earlier. I picked my way past piles of forgotten ballet slippers and leg warmers, retrieved a moth-eaten sweater, and headed backstage.

A large gold box, tied with a fancy red bow, was outside my dressing room door. The label indicated there were two pounds of salted caramel chocolates inside, and the card was signed *A Secret Admirer*, which made me laugh. Tex always got his dance partners a small gift on opening night. He was a week early, but I was not inclined to question his timing.

I hesitated before opening the box. If it was from Tex, why hadn't he signed his name? I eyed the inscription. Perhaps it wasn't from my dance partner and instead had been dropped off by a fan. Or a stalker. I contemplated handing the box over to security to check its contents but decided against that precautionary move. If an outsider had dropped it off, one of the stage door guards would have held it for me.

Although tempted to eat candy for dinner, I resisted and placed the box on a shelf. My body needed protein, not chocolate and sugar. I rubbed down my overworked muscles, changed into street clothes, and headed toward the exit. Moments later, screeching alarms rang through the building.

I rushed to Olivia's dressing room. My friend wasn't among the half-dressed women hastily tossing on their clothes. No one knew where she was or what was happening. Nor was Olivia in the costume room, where screaming seamstresses debated making a run for the exit instead of reporting to the auditorium, as the strident commands on the PA system and our pinging texts demanded.

I reversed direction and raced back to the stage. A semicircle of terrified dancers and stagehands were all staring at Tex, who was covered in blood and standing over Maurice's limp body.

Off to one side, Olivia was sobbing. "It was an accident! He didn't do it!"

Chapter Two

Simplicity is purity, purity is beauty, and beauty may one day save the world.
—Vladimir Doukodovsky

T he scene onstage eerily echoed the last act of *Romeo and Juliet*. Maurice lay in a pool of blood that was speckled with silvery glitter from the stage set. Tex crouched next to the artist's twisted, motionless body, which was disfigured by four cruel, jagged gashes. Olivia was the third dreadful figure in the ghastly tableau. In this palace of artifice, a real-life tragedy unfolded.

Someone had the presence of mind, amid the screaming and the tears, to call nine-one-one. The medics arrived first, but there was nothing they could do to revive Maurice. The police entered immediately after and cordoned off the stage. After giving my statement, I messaged Olivia and Tex, whom the cops had questioned separately from the rest of us.

Neither responded.

Homicide detective Jonah Sobol escorted me and Kerry to the nearest exit. Given the grim reason for his presence, I wasn't surprised when he acted as if we barely knew each other. Although our collaboration on two previous murder investigations was an open secret, our personal relationship was less well known.

I stopped at the threshold. "If it's okay with you, I'd like to wait for my friends."

My desire to see Olivia and Tex wasn't the only reason I wanted to stay. It was clear, from Maurice's splayed limbs and the blood on the gears, that he'd fallen off the platform. How and why it happened was a mystery, and I burned with questions about the artist's tragic death.

Kerry foiled my plan. She nudged me aside and trained her empty blue gaze into Jonah's dark eyes. "Me too. Please, Detective Sobol. Let us stay. We're more than coworkers. We're like family."

If Kerry treated her family the way she treated her rivals at American Ballet Company, her domestic life belonged in an ancient Greek tragedy. Rage, revenge, and human sacrifice suited her calculating personality better than birthday parties and Thanksgiving celebrations.

Jonah didn't make eye contact with me. "I regret that I can't accommodate either request. I'll let you know if we have further questions."

The moment he closed the door on us, Kerry clutched the sleeve of my coat. "I guess Tex got tired of waiting for Brett to divorce Maurice and took matters into his own hands. Totally sick, if you ask me." She let me go and headed to the subway.

I sprinted after her. "You're lying. Tex is Olivia's boyfriend. Not Brett's. And even if he was involved with Brett, Tex is the gentlest person I know."

She tossed her long, blond ponytail over her shoulder. "You're as clueless as Olivia. How do you think Tex got cast as the lead in *The Nutcracker* and *Romeo and Juliet?*"

I would never admit to her I'd heard the same rumors. "Tex got those roles because he earned them. He's a great dancer, and he's getting the recognition he deserves."

Kerry's pale blue eyes widened in anticipation. "If Tex gets the boot, that could spell the end to your dreams as well. Horace is way too tall to partner you. By this time tomorrow, I could be the one giving you pointers on how to dance Sugar Plum."

I followed her down the steps to the subway, where the rumble of an approaching train muffled my sophisticated response, which was something along the lines of *that's what you think!* Kerry darted through the turnstile and was lost in the crowd.

Less than thirty minutes later, her evil gossip went viral.

After the horror of seeing Maurice's dead body, the prospect of a solitary evening was without its usual appeal. Instead of going home, I walked uptown to my mother's apartment. Barbara flung open the door, insisted I lie on the sofa, and tucked a blanket around my still-shivering body.

With her maternal instincts satisfied, she wasted no time reverting to her favorite topic. "What's your calorie count so far?"

I threw off the blanket. "That's your opening? For heaven's sake, a guy died today."

"Yes. A tragedy, to be sure. We'll get to that subject in a minute. In the meantime, if you haven't hit your calorie or carb limit, I can offer you some food. High protein. Low fat."

There is no better place to lose weight than Barbara's apartment. Although my mother is quite thin, she's been dieting since the Beatles broke up. A clinical psychologist would have a field day probing the darker corners of Barbara's psyche, but my sister and I adore her. Melissa, who teaches philosophy, survived our childhood without significant food issues. As a dancer, however, I remained susceptible to Barbara's take-no-calories approach to life.

I was feeling too bruised to eat and poured myself a glass of water. "You don't know the half of what's happened today."

She followed me into the kitchen. "I know what you texted me and what the news reports are saying, which is that Maurice fell off a platform and died. Was it an accident? Did the poor man have a stroke? Or did someone push him?"

"The police didn't say. I'm worried about Tex. They separated him from the rest of us, and he's not answering my calls. He's the one who found Maurice." I swallowed the wrong way and choked on the water.

Barbara thumped me on the back to get me to stop coughing. "I'm quite fond of that young man. If Maurice was murdered, and Tex is accused, we'll work to clear him. Assuming he didn't do it, of course. I'll call Madame Maksimova and your sister. We can start right away."

I was too anxious to sit still and paced the room. "No. The police can handle the investigation without our help."

She looked at me from narrowed eyes. "That's what you thought last time. And look what happened. I suppose you talked to that detective already?"

Tension knotted my muscles, which were stiff with fatigue. I put my foot on the counter and bent over my leg to ease the pain. Stretching had the added benefit of allowing me to avoid her penetrating gaze. "I could use a cup of coffee."

"No coffee until you answer my question. Did you see that detective today?"

"Barbara, you know perfectly well his name is Jonah. Stop referring to him as 'that detective' as if he was a minor character in an old movie you can't quite remember."

She measured the coffee and set a pot of water on the stove. "You shouldn't be so touchy. I'm concerned about you. I had hoped you'd be married by now. To a doctor, not a cop. Your track record with men isn't good."

I ignored her reference to my stalled relationship with Dr. Zach Mitchell and leafed through a neat pile of magazines and journals. "Maybe I inherited it from you. Your recent track record is also nothing to be proud of." I held up a copy of *The New York Review of Books*. It was open to the Personals column, where she'd circled three ads from literary types who were hoping to meet similarly inclined hyper-intellectuals. "Haven't you learned your lesson?"

She pressed her fingers against her forehead in an effort to iron out any wrinkles that survived her latest injections. "Ancient history. Those guys weren't at all suitable." She picked up *The London Review of Books*, which also was open to the Personals column, and tossed it into the recycling bin. "My social life is going to be on hold for the next few weeks. Your Aunt Rachel is coming for a visit. An extended visit."

I couldn't help smiling at her absence of enthusiasm. "My aunt is also known as your sister. It's nice that you'll be able to spend time together."

"When Rachel is in Duluth, we get along. But she sold her ballet school and bought a one-way ticket here. That's not likely to end well for either of us." She brushed one hand against the other, as if ridding herself of her sticky sibling relationship with Rachel. "Tell me everything that happened at the theater. I can help."

Too weary to argue, I reviewed the events of the day, as much for myself as for her.

Barbara poured coffee into two mugs and took out a notebook and pen. "Let's assume for the moment that Maurice didn't die of natural causes. Who had a motive to kill him? Who hated him, or feared him, or stood to benefit by his death?"

I warmed my ice-cold hands on the cup. "I didn't know him personally."

"C'mon, Leah. This isn't a courtroom. I'll allow hearsay evidence."

"Fine. Maurice and Brett had frequent, bitter arguments, and they tried to one-up each other at rehearsals. There were rumors of infidelity on both sides. That's grounds for divorce, not murder." I cast about for a more compelling motive. "Unless money was involved. With Maurice dead, his artwork is probably worth a lot more now."

She wrote down Brett's name and drew a circle around it. "Not necessarily. That's a common myth. Sometimes a dead artist's work will increase in value, but it's not a given."

I knew nothing about the market for fine art. "That information is above my pay grade. As for other suspects, Nelson Merrill, the filmmaker who's doing a documentary on Maurice, has the advantage of being on site. But he and Maurice were friends. No conflict between them was apparent to me. More importantly, Nelson had the most to lose. Without Maurice, his movie project is probably no longer viable. The dancers were incidental to Nelson's primary topic, which was Maurice's life and art. I don't know how he's going to finish the movie without his main character."

Again, Barbara didn't agree. "Maurice's death is the best thing that could have happened to an indie filmmaker like Nelson. You can't buy that kind of publicity. Keep going, Leah. You're doing great."

"The ballet moms didn't like Maurice, but if they were going to kill anyone, it would have been Brett. As usual, we've got over a dozen kids performing in *The Nutcracker*. Brett was cursing up a storm this morning, and the mothers were furious. Evelyn Brill said she was going to lodge a complaint."

Barbara's eyes gleamed. "Hell hath no fury like a Ballet Mother scorned.

What was Maurice's reaction? I wish I could have been there for that."

I picked at a bowl of blueberries, one of the few fruits allowed into Barbara's kitchen. "Maurice didn't say anything, but Brett threatened to yank Evelyn's kid from the production. She's a terrific little dancer and is this year's Clara. Her mother shut up pretty quickly after that."

Barbara patted me fondly. "I remember when you were Clara. We were so proud." She sighed. "Of course, at that point, we figured your dance background would look good on your college application. We didn't imagine you'd end up doing it professionally."

This was not a topic I wanted to revisit. My extremely educated parents were quite disappointed when I joined American Ballet Company after graduating a year early from high school. My mother's regret was minor, however, compared to my father's reaction. Although he said many times his heart attack was not my fault, I still felt guilty.

Barbara snapped my attention back to her. "We'll continue to investigate motive, but let's talk now about opportunity. Who was around, besides Nelson, when Maurice was killed? And how exactly did he die?"

My mother wrote crime fiction and was forever scribbling ideas for possible plot lines. I wasn't sure if she was trying to figure out what happened or was taking notes for her next book.

I stared at the table, trying to visualize the scene. "It looked as if he fell from the platform and into the gears that powered the set. His head lay at an odd angle, and he had four severe cuts, one on his face and three across his chest. Glitter from the set was mixed in with the blood."

Barbara looked up from her notebook. "What was he doing on top of the platform?"

The tears I hadn't shed earlier broke through. "Maurice promised me he'd fix the scenery. The gears were creaking, and the platform vibrated each time I jumped. I was terrified of dancing on it. Or under it."

Barbara held out a box of tissues. "So you were the one who pressed him to fix it? Who was with you when Maurice said he'd check it out?"

I wiped my eyes, but the tears kept coming. "Brett was with us, but it was so dark, there could have been others who overheard him. It's hard to tell, when you're backstage, if there's anyone in the wings."

My mother passed me her notebook and pen. "Sketch out the scene for me. Maybe he lost his balance, and the fall killed him."

As much as I wished Maurice's death wasn't murder, diagramming the scene of the crime confirmed what I already suspected. "The gears were smeared with blood, and he couldn't have fallen into them unless someone pushed him with enough force to propel him forward." I dropped the pen and covered my face in my hands. "The set was supposed to look like a magical children's toy. It ended up a murder weapon."

Barbara studied my crude drawing. "I can't imagine they'll continue to use it. Which means you, and quite a few other dancers, will benefit."

I grabbed my dance bag. "I'm the only one who has to dance on it. And that's not a rational motive."

She persisted. "Then give me a better one."

I pecked her on the cheek. "I'll get back to you as soon as I find one."

The last aerobic exercise of the day consisted of a five-flight climb to my apartment. Thanks to not one, but two surgically repaired knees, walking downstairs was more painful than walking up, but the rest of my body was never happy to encounter stress in either direction. I unsnapped three locks on the door marked 5B, tossed my bag on the sofa, and contemplated the contents of my refrigerator. Other than the blueberries, Barbara and I hadn't gotten around to eating dinner, and I was hungry. A bowl of wilting salad greens sat next to a bulging container of tofu that had long since passed its expiration date. These unappetizing choices made it easy to avoid eating until the next day. I thought longingly of the box of chocolates I'd left at the theater. Perhaps it was for the best.

I texted Olivia two more times. Still no answer. I collapsed into bed. Sleep came quickly, but it didn't last. Dreams of falling from a great height woke me more than once, and I spent half the night drenched in a cold sweat.

At six-thirty am, insistent beeping from my phone roused me from those dizzy nightmares. The first text was a directive from American Ballet Company that ordered us to report to the studio instead of the theater.

The second consisted of a line of grim emojis interspersed with red hearts and the following words: **Arriving 1pm JFK**

Gabi Acevedo, my best friend since seventh grade, was coming home. And not a moment too soon.

Chapter Three

Genius is another word for magic, and the whole point of magic is that it's inexplicable.

—Margot Fonteyn

I examined my wardrobe with as much care as an astronaut inspecting a spacesuit before liftoff. Unlike NASA's decision to garb their employees in white (so unflattering) black was the dominant color, and most of my clothes qualified as suitably funereal.

The dark hues highlighted the greenish pallor of my skin, which needed a lot more food and rest to look less ghostly. I know it was shallow of me to obsess over my appearance, but if Nelson interviewed me, I didn't want him to use my sleep-starved face and red eyes as part of a tragic story of Maurice's death. The filmmaker seemed kind, but it was his job to provide drama and mine to avoid it.

It didn't cross my mind, or anyone else's at ABC, to skip the morning ballet class. I'd sooner appear without makeup, in all my vampiric paleness, before doing that. The inescapable fact of life as a dancer was one we all knew by heart: *Miss class one day, and you know. Miss class two days, and your teacher knows. Miss class three days, and the audience knows.*

I arrived at the studio at my customary early hour. As I waited for the ancient elevator, a dozen bleary-eyed dancers joined me. A few people with healthier knees than mine gave up and took the stairs, but I was not tempted to join them. My fragile joints were one reason for my reluctance. The other was that several months earlier there had been a rather horrific murder in the stairwell, and I was not eager to revisit the scene of that grisly crime. As the crowd grew, so did speculation about Maurice's death. Olivia entered and pushed past the dancers between us to stand next to me.

My friend's phone slipped from her fingers and crashed to the ground. She grabbed it and said, too quietly to penetrate the loud conversations around us, "I can't reach Tex. I-I'm so worried about him."

I covered my mouth with my hand. "I'm worried about both of you. You didn't answer my text last night."

She toyed with her bag. "I, um, I got home late. The police questioned me for more than an hour after everyone else left. I'm sorry."

"There's no need to apologize. We're all distracted and upset. But you've been so cagey about your relationship with Tex. How involved are you with him? And what did you see last night?"

She ignored my last question to concentrate on the first one. "There's nothing serious going on between us. We've met a few times for coffee or a drink. I'm not sure how he feels about me. But I really like him. A lot."

"Tell me what happened. You know you can trust me."

She looked at the other dancers, who were carefully not looking at her. "We'll talk later." Her eyes were glassy with unshed tears. "He's the best guy I know."

When the elevator arrived, we held back and stayed in the lobby. I spoke quickly, hoping for a few private moments before more dancers arrived. "You haven't answered my question about what happened. Was Tex onstage when you got there? And what were you doing there? I thought you had a costume fitting."

She hung her head so that her unpinned hair shielded her face. "You're acting like you think Tex is guilty."

"What I think doesn't matter. Tex found the body. That automatically makes him a person of interest."

Olivia rubbed wet eyes with the back of her hand. "You're my only real friend in the company. I need you on my side. On our side."

I handed her a tissue. "I can't help you if you won't confide in me. I know Tex is smart, and funny, and kind. He's also a terrific dancer who's on the verge of getting the recognition he deserves."

Olivia wiped her eyes. "That's why I'm scared. Because he is so nice. And talented. Plenty of people would love to see him go down. Not for murder, of course, but he's given the other male dancers plenty of reason to hate him."

Her assessment was accurate. Despite Tex's sunny nature, rivals would see him as a threat rather than a friend. His meteoric rise also might explain persistent rumors about his romantic involvement with Brett. I hoped the gossip wasn't true. But if it was, it wouldn't be the first time an ambitious and vulnerable dancer traded sex for professional advancement. Usually, it's women, but men were not immune.

I didn't mention these complications to Olivia. "No matter how vicious the competition is at ABC, no one is evil enough to kill Maurice to get at Tex."

She shivered in the cold vestibule, as the door opened to admit more dancers. "He hasn't answered me, which is why I can't answer you. If he was like Horace, I wouldn't be surprised at getting ghosted. But Tex isn't like that."

"Yeah. Horace is famous for treating women like garbage." I loathed golden-haired Horace, who had all the arrogance of the Greek gods he so much resembled. A year or two earlier, we'd been casual friends. Never lovers. His brutish behavior was too well documented for me to fall prey to his calculated advances.

Olivia pulled a sandwich out of her bag and began gnawing on it. I didn't say anything about stress-eating, because my friend is one of those enviable people who can ingest thousands of calories without gaining weight. I liked her too much to hold it against her, but still, gorging on a ham and cheese sub at that early hour wasn't a good sign.

I pressed her. "Are you sure you don't know where Tex was when Maurice, er, fell?"

She used the greasy wrapper to wipe her fingers. Another bad sign for my fastidious friend. "We made plans to meet after my costume fitting. But he never showed. He texted that he had something to do and would call me later."

I thought back to the last time I saw Tex. "He was still in the theater for at least part of your rehearsal. He saved me from having to submit to an interview with Nelson. We walked backstage together."

Her face brightened. "That's the best news I've had all day. You can be his alibi."

"I wish I could help, but the men had a separate rehearsal." I didn't tell her Tex seemed agitated and had disappeared as soon as we were out of Nelson's sight. Emotions run high during tech and dress rehearsals, and there was no reason to think Tex had anything on his mind other than our upcoming performances.

The lobby again filled with dancers, and we stopped talking. Thanks to the sylph-like contours of the ballerinas, and our general willingness to get close enough to kiss, we managed to all fit into the narrow elevator. When the doors opened on the third floor, Madame Maksimova was waiting for us.

Madame M hadn't changed much in the years since I was a kid in her class. Her hair was still in a chic French twist, she still had those killer diamond earrings, and her posture, although not quite as straight as it was when she dazzled audiences across the globe, was still graceful. She kissed me on both cheeks before turning her attention to the other dancers. I gave Froufrou, the tiny dog who was Madame's constant companion, a quick pat. Froufrou, however, had eyes only for Madame.

The reason for Madame's protective stance stood behind her. Homicide detective Jonah Sobol met us with a somber look and directed us into the largest studio. As on the previous day, he gave no indication we'd ever met. His attitude didn't bother me, because our relationship was over. I never thought about him or about the last time we were together.

Olivia stood to one side as the dancers filed into the room, checking to see who was there. She appealed to Jonah. "Detective, um, can I ask you about Tex? Joaquin Texeira. I didn't see him, I mean, he's not here."

The expression in Jonah's dark eyes was unreadable, although his voice was kind. "Thank you for telling me. Now, if you could wait with the

20

others?"

The dancers removed their shoes before stepping into the studio. Outdoor footwear can damage the expensive Marley floor, and since we spend a good deal of time stretched out on it, this rule is a matter of cleanliness as well.

I also hesitated. Madame made a faint gesture with her eyebrows, as eloquent as if she'd spoken aloud. I told Olivia, "Save me a spot. And one for Tex, too."

I followed my favorite teacher into an adjacent studio. "What's happened, Madame?"

Her perfectly turned-out legs wobbled, and she placed one hand on the barre for support. She said something that sounded like *Ja volnujus*. Seeing my puzzled look, she tried again. *"Je suis tellement inquiet."*

This time, I got it. She was upset. So upset, in fact, she was having trouble with English, her third language after Russian and French.

"Madame, *s'il vous plaît*. English, please."

Her knuckles were white on the hand that gripped the barre. "Police, they take Tex in for their questioning. You must to say nothing right now. Police have told staff but not yet dancers. I not able to say more. Perhaps we meet later, yes?"

I fidgeted with my dance bag. "Is it possible Maurice's death was an accident?"

She addressed me with her affectionate nickname. "Lelotchka, we must to go in with the others. We talk more later."

I was faint with anxiety. Had Tex been arrested? He was more than my dance partner. He was my friend. "Yes. We'll talk more later." As we joined the others, I had a thought.

"Call Olga. I think we're going to need her."

I circled the perimeter of the studio and sat on the floor beside Olivia, near our favorite spot at the barre. Her eyes were wide with anxiety. I could do nothing to allay her fears. Or mine. Madame Maksimova entered a few minutes later with her usual grace, although I could see from her slow pace that the arthritic hips and knees that plagued nearly all former dancers were bothering her. The other teachers and coaches, as well as the office staff, were waiting. Nelson and his camera crew stood along the back of the room.

Jonah knew enough about our world to remove his shoes. He stood next to the piano, and although he didn't speak loudly, his voice easily reached the back of the room. "I regret to inform any of you who don't already know, that Mr. Maurice Kaminsky has suffered an accident." He paused. "A fatal accident."

Kerry, whose desire for the limelight was not limited to her professional ambition, shattered the silent tension that followed this announcement. "How exactly did he die? Are you sure it was an accident? Or was he pushed?"

Jonah didn't provide any facts we hadn't surmised. "He fell and was caught in the gears of one of the mechanical devices on the stage."

The gruesome nature of Maurice's death temporarily silenced us again, as we pictured the grinding gears of his stage set. My worst nightmare had come true for him.

Nelson lugged one of the massive portable barres to one side and signaled to a tall, skinny cameraman. "Detective, Maurice Kaminsky was a close friend of mine. I've known him since we were in college, and I'd like to follow up on Ms. Blair's question. Have you determined if his death was an accident? Or was it murder?" Nelson's thick glasses didn't obscure the greedy gleam in his eye. Like many in his industry, business would always triumph over personal feelings.

Jonah held up his hand. "First of all, Mr. Merrill, there will be no filming today." Before Nelson could register a protest, Jonah forestalled any potential argument. "You may resume tomorrow, after Detective Farrow and I have finished our interviews. As for your question regarding the circumstances of Mr. Kaminsky's death, that is still under review."

Nelson took off his eyeglasses and rubbed the bridge of his nose. "Of course. I understand completely. My crew and I are at your service." He added, as if as an afterthought, "I assume you know Ms. Siderova reported yesterday that the gears weren't working properly, which lends credence to the possibility that Maurice's death was accidental."

Jonah, along with everyone else in the room, turned to look at me. I'd done nothing wrong, but I felt guilty, as if my misgivings regarding the safety of the set design were a factor in Maurice's death.

Olivia, sensing my distress, murmured, "What was the point of him saying that? Maurice's death wasn't your fault."

She was right, but the irrational feeling of guilt persisted. "I know. But what if something I said gave the murderer the idea to kill him by using his own stage set as the murder weapon?"

She cut short her answer to listen to Jonah. He said to Nelson, "Please see me immediately after this meeting. You'll have to turn over all your footage, not only what you shot yesterday." The filmmaker inclined his head to signal agreement, and Jonah spoke to the rest of us. "That's all I'm going to say for now. Detective Farrow will be here shortly. We'll need to follow up with each of you." He murmured a few words to two uniformed police officers and left the room.

Olivia rushed after the detective. "Tex—can't you at least tell me where he is?"

Jonah remained evasive. "As I said, we'll have more to report later. Please return to the studio and wait with the others."

I was angry. Jonah should have told her Tex had been taken to the station house for questioning. Why should Madame have that information, and not us? I was burning to talk to him, but he kept those dark, inscrutable eyes averted and instructed Francie Morelli, a policewoman I knew well, to escort us back into the studio.

Francie, like Jonah, acted as if we were strangers. She waited for us with crossed arms and zero eye contact. With no other options open to us, Olivia and I joined the others.

Kerry spoke to a large group of young corps dancers. Her blue eyes were wide with excitement. "Mark my words. Maurice's death was no accident, and the police know it." She pointed to various spots around the room as if taking attendance. "Did anyone besides me notice that Tex isn't here?"

Horace held up his phone. "Of course we noticed. It's all over social media. I don't know where Savannah Collier gets her intel, but it's fierce." His next words were sad, but the intent was malicious. "Too bad about Tex. He claimed Maurice was dead when he found him, but it looks like the police aren't buying pretty boy's story."

Olivia's face burned with an angry red flush. "Do you know something the rest of us don't? Or are you jealous because Tex made soloist before you?"

He bit his lip. Despite classic good looks, his career had stalled, while Tex's star had been rising. Horace didn't argue with Olivia. Instead, with fake pity, he said, "Why you poor thing! I hope you didn't think Tex could ever be interested in you."

Horace looked my friend over, as if appraising her value. He and Olivia had been lovers, which made his next words all the more humiliating. "Sadly, dear heart, you lack the necessary…how should I say it?" He put a finger to his temple, as if searching for an appropriate description of Olivia's failings and Tex's sexual preferences. "You don't have the right kind of charm to interest Tex. As for your own pathetic aspirations, trust me, being cast as the maid in *Romeo and Juliet* doesn't indicate future greatness."

Kerry, not to be outdone in meanness, flicked back her ponytail and said to Horace, "What does being cast as the third Capulet from the right indicate?"

Horace ignored the titters and looked at her with smug satisfaction. "As your Romeo, you might want to rethink that statement."

Disregarding Francie's injunction to remain seated, we rushed past the police officer to the bulletin board outside the studio, where the latest cast assignments for *Romeo and Juliet* were posted. Usually, the dancers' names are marked as being in the first or second cast, but those descriptive categories were missing. Kerry and I were both listed as Juliet. Tex and Horace were both listed as Romeo.

A whispered voice from the crowd said, "Let the games begin."

I was distracted by my phone, which buzzed with messages. The last one on the list was from Jonah. **Meet me. 7 ok?**

My pulse quickened, as it always did at the prospect of seeing him. **Café Figaro?**

The return message read, **Too public. Your place or mine?**

I pondered a moment before answering. If we met at seven o'clock, I would have enough time to shower, but not enough time to clean the apartment, stash the lineup of drying leotards hanging in the bathroom, and dispose of the rotting food in the fridge.

I'd never been to Jonah's apartment. With a nervous flutter that had nothing to do with Maurice's death, I answered, **Yours-**

Chapter Four

I am afraid of people, because they want me to lead the same kind of life they do...
—Vaslav Nijinsky

Madame Maksimova gave us a class filled with fiendishly difficult combinations to master, both physically and mentally. Even the standard warmup exercises challenged us to reverse the order of movements. Those ninety sweaty minutes were exactly what we needed.

The rehearsals that followed were less successful, as one person after another had to leave to give statements to the police. Worst of all was the rehearsal for *The Nutcracker*, which took place at the studio instead of the theater. Horace subbed for Tex, and based on the two hours we danced together, our match didn't appear to have been made in heaven.

Professionally, as well as personally, Horace was an excellent soloist but a poor partner. The best partners take their cues from the ballerina. I prefer a light touch. Horace, however, persisted in spinning me roughly and grabbing my torso so tightly I could barely breathe.

If Tex were there, Horace and I wouldn't have been paired together. He was too tall for me, a point Kerry made repeatedly, in an audible whisper. Horace was supposed to partner her, but she had to make do with his nervous understudy, who was not nearly as regal a presence as Horace.

At the close of the day, Madame called a meeting. "Listen to me, dear dancers. We have, yes, many *difficultès*. But we must be *khrabrost*." She paused, searching for an English word that could convey her deep emotion.

"We have the difficulties, but we must to be strong. No, the right word is fierce. We must all be faithful, one to the other. Anything what you need, you come to me. *Dah?*"

Madame M commanded more respect and affection than anyone else in the company. Nonetheless, her pleas for unity were unlikely to change anything. The brutal and unforgiving nature of ballet was exponentially greater at ABC than it was at lesser companies. We fight to get in. We fight for promotion. And then we fight to hold on as long as we can, because there are hundreds of dancers who would walk through fire to replace us. Despite these feral conditions, we were, for the most part, friendly, at least on the surface. Our real competition is from within, as we battle our bodies and test the limits of our talent and drive. But not far below, rivalry, jealousy, and enmity reigned.

Outside the studio, reporters mobbed the sidewalk. Having had some practice in eluding media hounds, I ducked out through the back. There was no alleyway or outlet to the street, but I had a better chance of escaping notice if I exited from an adjacent grocery store. I ignored the stench emanating from several large dumpsters and slipped into the grocery via the loading dock. The workers stared but didn't stop me. They shrugged their shoulders, exchanged amused looks, and left me alone. Thankfully, in New York City, it's a matter of civic pride to remain unmoved in the face of either the famous or the weird.

I lingered in the canned goods aisle until a noisy family of four was ready to leave. A throng of shoppers, in hot pursuit of half-price fruits and vegetables arrayed in outdoor bins, provided additional cover.

The subway was my best option for a speedy trip home, but my heart sank as I viewed the jam-packed platform of the A train. There were more people there than the typical rush hour crush of travelers, which didn't bode well for the hapless, hopeful straphangers. Sure enough, after about ten minutes, a jarring squawk blared via the public address system. *We regret the uptown A train is not in service at this time.* Loud groans from frustrated commuters rendered the rest of the announcement inaudible.

I left my fellow riders to ponder alternate routes home and called Barbara. All I needed was a shower, a mirror, and fifteen minutes to elevate my legs before leaving to meet Jonah, and her apartment was closer than mine. She also had a closet filled with clothes far more interesting and stylish than any I could afford.

My mother answered my call, as she always did, with surprised delight, as if we didn't talk nearly every day. "Leah! Darling! I'm so happy you called. Your timing is perfect. Come right over."

When I arrived, after a hurried walk uptown, Barbara flung open the door and greeted me with exaggerated good cheer. "I have a surprise for you!"

I was disappointed when we bypassed the kitchen. Barbara's recent finds included a delicious brand of coffee beans and a surprisingly affordable bottle of Bordeaux. We were still in search of a good low-calorie, low-carbohydrate salad dressing, the Holy Grail of dietary condiments. I braced myself to admire whatever new and uncomfortable piece of furniture she'd acquired, but again, I'd incorrectly guessed. Instead, in the living room stood Aunt Rachel.

She rose to meet me. "Hello, fellow New Yorker!"

Barbara stretched her lips in a pained approximation of a grin. "Your aunt has sold her ballet school. She's relocating to the city. And she's staying with me in the interim."

"Yep. I'm back in the Big Apple." Rachel pointed to a plate filled with huge black and white cookies. "Look what I brought! Your favorite."

Barbara slowly blinked, as if in disbelief at the presence of cookies in her living room. "Rachel, you shouldn't have."

My aunt was not put off. "Let's all relax for once. It's a party." She poked my middle. "Leah, you look as if you're disappearing. Worse than the last time I saw you. It wouldn't hurt you to eat a few cookies."

Under my mother's censorious gaze, I bit into one of the cookies. It was divinely delicious. I thought Barbara was going to have a stroke.

Energized by the sudden intake of sugar, I said, "I can't believe you're moving after all these years. What are you going to do about your house?" Rachel had an enormous, quite beautiful home in a suburb of Duluth. My entire apartment could fit in her kitchen.

Her good cheer lessened slightly. "It's on the market. I love the house, but with Mark gone, it's way too big for me."

Barbara was a few shades short of compassionate. "Mark moved out five years ago. Surely something else prompted this unexpected decision."

Rachel gagged on a too-large piece of cookie and swallowed a half cup of coffee in an effort to recover. When she did, she said, "My pathetic ex-husband is getting married. To one of the paralegals at his firm. So unimaginative. That homewrecker is half his age. She should be dating our son."

Unwilling to add to her distress, we didn't remind Rachel of her oft-repeated claim that she divorced her husband because she felt stifled by the bonds of matrimony. In her less-guarded moments, she admitted to Mark's serial infidelity.

Rachel peeled the icing off a cookie. "As long as we're on the subject of former spouses, Barbara, how is Jeremy? Still married to what's-her-name? I never could figure out your relationship with him. The two of you stayed friends after the divorce, which seems odd to me. Mark and I weren't on speaking terms, even before his decision to marry that scheming woman who will never in a million years make him happy."

My mother was careful in her response. "Jeremy is doing well. I know he'd love to see you, but he's in California at the moment. With Ann."

Rachel scratched her head. "I'm surprised he's still with that spacey New-Ager. He better watch out, marrying a younger woman. She'll end up giving him another heart attack." She eyed my mother. "Are you jealous?"

Barbara narrowed her nose, a signature gesture that indicated disdain. "Of course not. His wife is completely without style or wit. I'd sooner be jealous of her vitamin pills and fish oil as I would be of her relationship with Jeremy."

My aunt looked happier. "We both have husbands who married unsuitable women."

Barbara put down her cup with an audible thunk. "Please remember that Jeremy is Leah's father, as well as my ex-husband. Instead of talking about irrelevant topics, let's get back to Leah's question. What are your immediate plans, other than crashing at my place?"

Rachel contemplated the naked remnant of her cookie before downing it in two bites. "The market is red hot in Duluth. The house is paid off, and I'm going to use the money from the sale to get a place here."

Barbara pursed her lips. "The money you get from your house in Duluth won't be enough to buy a tiny one-bedroom in the city." She made Minnesota sound as appealing as the ninth ring in Dante's Hell.

"I know. I talked to a few real estate agents and checked a bunch of online listings. I'm going apartment hunting this weekend, But there's no rush. You won't mind me staying with you, will you? With Melissa and Leah gone, you hardly need this much room. We'll be roommates. Like when we were kids."

I didn't share Rachel's sunny prediction of sibling harmony. Barbara is a writer, and she was not likely to enjoy sharing her workspace with anyone except Professor Romanova, the protagonist of her novels. My mother's relationship with her fictional characters was more interesting and compelling to her than most of the real people in her life.

Rachel brushed the crumbs from her lap onto the carpet. "Let's go out to dinner. My treat. Leah, you can fill me in on all that craziness at the company. I was friends with Maurice Kaminsky, you know. We go way back."

Aside from the fact that Rachel was quite a bit older than Maurice, I couldn't imagine my staid aunt in his artsy crowd. Her idea of a wild night was to watch two reruns of *Antiques Roadshow*. "I had no idea you knew Maurice, Aunt Rachel. And thanks for your invitation, but I have an appointment tonight. Actually, that's why I'm here." I turned to Barbara. "Traffic is a mess, and the uptown subway wasn't running. I need your shower and a change of clothes."

Barbara rose quickly. "Of course. Let's pick out something nice."

Despite the new furniture, a consequence of my mother's recent passion for redecorating, Barbara's bedroom retained its familiar, comforting smell. It was a mixture of Joy perfume, cigarettes, and her own indefinable scent. She flipped through a rack of clothes and handed me a lacy top. It was pale pink at the shoulders and darkened to a dusty rose at the scalloped bottom.

I fingered the fabric. "Too dressy."

"Not with a pair of jeans, it isn't." Although Barbara's taste in men was questionable, she was unerring in her sense of style. She took out a pair of slim, high-heeled shoes with delicate, asymmetrical straps. "I wish your feet weren't so hideous. These would work perfectly, but they're too revealing."

I, too, wished my feet weren't deformed by bunions and bruises. At least they looked good in pointe shoes. I showered, dressed, and returned to the living room in my own clunky, comfortable boots.

Barbara walked me to the door. "With whom are you meeting?"

I kissed her. "That detective."

She pulled down the corners of her mouth. "I prefer the doctor."

Chapter Five

You live as long as you dance...
—Rudolph Nureyev

I usually arrive at the subway platform in time to see my train depart from the station, but after I left Barbara's apartment, the transportation gods broke with tradition. The doors to the downtown local stayed open long enough for me to dart into the car before it took off. When I emerged, I responded to Gabi Acevedo's unanswered text with a phone call. My best friend no longer danced with the company but maintained a proprietary interest in it. During the winter months, she taught ballet intermittently, spending as much time as she could with her family in Argentina.

Gabi picked up before the end of the first ring. "The second I leave, things fall apart. I was beside myself when I heard the news about Maurice."

The sound of her accent, a blend of New York City nasal and South American lilt, cheered me. "I hope you didn't cut short your visit on my account."

She blew a Bronx cheer into the phone. "Lie to yourself, Sid. Don't bother telling me you're fine. I could feel you freaking out all the way from Puerto Madero."

Gabriela and I met at a school that specialized in educating aspiring actors, musicians, and dancers. We trained together, graduated together, and performed together. A few years ago, with bewildering speed, she got married and had Lucie. Although many dancers return to the stage after having kids, Gabi was firm in her decision to retire. We remained as close as sisters, but I never stopped mourning the loss of her steady presence.

Gabi was also the only person who called me Sid. After my parents' divorce, Barbara decided Siderova would look better on a Playbill, as well as on the cover of her own books, than Feldbaum, my father's surname. She wasn't wrong, although the change felt false to me. It wasn't until Gabi started calling me Sid that I felt more comfortable using my mother's maiden name.

I checked the addresses of the buildings that lined the street. "I'm fine, other than having to dance on the same set that was the scene of a crime. It's Tex who's got some serious problems, which is not good news for me, either."

Her voice was sober. "I got off the phone with Madame a few minutes ago. She's devastated. I had no idea she and Maurice had been such close friends. As for Tex, my social media is exploding with wild stories about him, mostly due to Savannah Collier, who's doing her usual hatchet job. Keep your distance, Leah. You don't know either Tex or Olivia well enough to make assumptions or get involved. But why are talking on the phone? Come over. Lucie is asleep, and I've recovered sufficiently from traveling with a toddler to talk in complete sentences."

As we spoke, I continued to head west. Jonah's address indicated he was practically at the edge of the Hudson River. "I'm, um, I can't make it tonight."

With the kind of ESP that best friends have, she squealed. "Is it Jonah? Are you seeing Jonah?"

I clutched my coat more closely to ward off a chill wind. "This meeting is strictly business. He probably wants to talk about who might have a motive to kill Maurice and to pick my brains about company politics."

She whistled softly, mocking me. "That's not all he wants to pick."

Gabi didn't know the full story of what happened between us. With less than one block to go before I arrived at my destination, I tried to condense a Russian novel's worth of emotion into a few short sentences. "Jonah is uncomfortable with the fact that I'm still seeing Zach, although I've explained to him that Zach and I are just friends."

Gabi met this statement with unaccustomed silence. I didn't need to see

33

her to know she wasn't buying it. I wanted my oldest friend to understand without going into too many uncomfortable details.

"To be honest, I'm also kind of uneasy about the situation. I've never been successful in managing one relationship. And with two, I ended up doing twice as badly." I spoke quickly to cut off a second derisive Bronx cheer. "Not that I have a relationship with Jonah. We're good friends, that's all."

"You and I are good friends, but you've never looked at me the way you do at Jonah. Or, for that matter, the way he looks at you." She hummed a few bars of *Swan Lake* before finishing her thought. Like me, Gabi was more comfortable with music and movement than words. "I fear you're hanging onto a relationship with Zach that's never going to work out. A relationship I'm not sure will ever make you happy. And in doing so, you risk losing Jonah."

"I thought you wanted to know about the murder investigation."

Gabi was eager. "I do, of course, *querida amiga*. The Choreographers of Crime will ride again!"

I checked my texts and realized I'd missed a message thread that began while I was on the subway. "We need a different name. The Choreographers of Crime makes us sound as if we're the criminals."

Gabi's enthusiasm was unabated. "Assign Barbara the task of picking a good name. Your mother has a way with words. I loved her last book."

"The last thing I want is to have my mother once again involved in a real-life murder investigation. I have enough to worry about, where she's concerned."

Gabi remained cheerful. "I believe you're too late to stop that particular ship from sailing. But it doesn't matter, because your love life is an equally timely topic. I hope you don't think I didn't notice how you changed the subject. How long do you want to share Zach with his ex-wife? Jonah, on the other hand, is a definite keeper."

I walked faster, as if in a race against my own insecurities. "You also thought Zach Mitchell was a keeper."

"I did. He's smart, and really good-looking, and he's a doctor. He's the whole package, and although his job is demanding, he doesn't have to put his life on the line every time he goes to work the way Jonah does. I've met him, Leah. I understand his appeal. I'd bag him myself, if I wasn't married."

I slowed as I approached Jonah's building. "I have to go. As for my romantic issues, I don't possess the emotional bandwidth to handle my dance career and one boyfriend, let alone two. Zach and I are more alike than you think, except he's limited by a previous marriage, and I'm limited by my devotion to ballet."

I didn't have the time or the inclination to explain to Gabi that the men in my life had complicated relationships, even without me in the mix. Zach's ex-wife had come between us early in our friendship and had kept me from fully trusting him. As for Jonah, his work as a homicide detective had brought us together, but on more than one occasion, had driven us apart. It was too soon to commit, especially since I had no idea if either one desired commitment, or what form that commitment might take.

I looked up at the windows of a pleasant, six-story building. "I'm at his apartment, and I don't want him to see me casing the joint. I'll see you tomorrow."

"Before you go, describe where he lives."

"Red brick, pre-war, and clean. And an elevator, which is a definite plus." I'd expected a dingy tenement railroad flat, not unlike my own.

Gabi hummed into the phone. "Sounds good, but a step down from Zach's place. If you're going to move in with someone, you can't do better than a luxury building on the High Line, with a terrace, a pool, and its own sculpture garden. Not to mention a dishwasher. I can see your dilemma."

"Save the real estate advice until tomorrow. I'm late. And I'm not dating either guy on the basis of where he lives, as long as it's not a park bench."

"Fair enough. Don't forget to report back to me."

Despite the elevator, I found myself somewhat breathless as I walked down the carpeted hallway to apartment 6E. Jonah and I had met often at Café Figaro, and he'd been to my apartment several times. This felt different.

He opened the door, and there was an awkward moment when we could have hugged or kissed. Neither happened. Maybe he was still angry after our last, painful, meeting. I followed him through the living room to the kitchen. Both rooms were immaculate and furnished in early Ikea.

I handed him a bottle of wine I'd swiped from Barbara. "Nice place. Is it always so clean?"

Jonah laughed. "Absolutely not. This being your first visit, I made an effort." He took two wine glasses from the cupboard and poured a generous amount in each. I followed him back to the living room. The coffee table was laden with the kinds of snacks I love but rarely permit myself to eat.

He moved a chair close to the table. "Why don't you have a seat?" He stood next to the sofa and smiled mockingly at me. "You don't want to get too close. I'm irresistible."

His words and attitude released the knot of tension I'd carried with me for too long. I sank into the chair. "Don't flatter yourself."

"How do you do that? How do you fall into a chair and make it look like a ballet?"

My skin grew warm under his gaze. "After hours of rehearsing Juliet's death scene, I'm an expert in collapsing into the nearest open space. It's a handy skill. You should try it."

He laughed again, this time ruefully. "I'm under no misconceptions about my talents. Or about much of anything where you're concerned."

I reached for a carrot stick and dunked it with reckless abandon into the bowl of dip. "That's good thinking. You may be a detective, but I make my living pretending to be someone I'm not. I wouldn't be too confident if I were you."

"Where this case is concerned, I'm not feeling at all confident. Farrow and I have talked to all the dancers, all the teachers, and all the office staff. Maurice wasn't a popular guy, but we don't yet have a strong motive for anyone to have wanted him dead."

I reached for another carrot. "Are you sure it was murder? Is there any way it could have been an accident? He could have put the gears in motion to test them, and then lost his balance and fell in. Or maybe he slipped."

Jonah was grim. "That possibility is off the table. According to the forensic reports, he would have had to hit himself on the back of the head first."

I struggled to appear calm, although the news sickened me. "Well, that settles the matter. Do you have a murder weapon?"

He stared at the platter of vegetables. "Not yet. We scavenged all the garbage bins and dumpsters in the area, but my best guess is that it's either still hidden inside the theater or is on its the way to a landfill. I think the killer was hoping it would look as if Maurice's injuries all occurred after he fell. Given what we know so far, we've identified two persons of interest, although we're nowhere close to making an arrest. I need information, and you can help. You've been working closely with Maurice and his husband. More closely than anyone else, other than Joaquin Texeira."

My mouth went dry. "I'm certain you're going down the wrong road where Tex is concerned. I've been partnering with him since Daniel left the company. Tex is a genuinely good person. He doesn't have a violent bone in his body. He also had no motive to kill Maurice."

Jonah ran a hand through his short, dark hair. "I wouldn't be too certain of that. We've heard Tex was having an affair with Brett. An affair they deny. But if it's true, that gives either of them, or both of them, plenty of motive to want Maurice out of the way. They could have been in it together. The husband and the boyfriend. Doesn't get simpler than that."

I took a deep breath. "Did you know Tex and Olivia have been seeing each other?"

He leaned forward. "Yes. More than one dancer shared that information. But it doesn't exonerate Tex. A relationship with Olivia might have given him a different, but equally powerful motive."

I eased open the zipper on my boots, hoping the release of pressure on my arches would stimulate clearer thinking. "If Horace is the rat who told you about Tex's supposed affair with Brett, I wouldn't give it much credence. He's furious Tex got promoted before he did, and if he can eliminate Tex, he's first in line to score the lead role in *The Nutcracker*."

Jonah was sympathetic but unflinching. "Horace may have an ulterior motive, but multiple sources confirm his statement."

I rearranged the plates of food to give myself time to think. If Horace replaced Tex as the Cavalier, Kerry had an excellent chance of taking over my role as the Sugar Plum Fairy. Did I want to reveal to Jonah my selfish, if secondary, reason for wanting Tex exonerated? I decided, after a brief internal debate, this lesser incentive wasn't important.

Instead, I said, "Multiple people can repeat a rumor without it being true. And Brett has plenty of motive without dragging Tex into it. Isn't the husband the most likely suspect?"

"Yes. Brett appears to have an alibi, but it's not enough to rule him out. CC cameras confirm that when he left, Maurice was still alive. There's no footage showing he ever returned, but we identified two malfunctioning cameras in the rear of the theater. He could have returned via one of those doors."

This wasn't much help. "They were at the back of the stage when I last spoke with them, but at some point, most of us were."

Jonah stuffed a half-pound of cheese inside a roll, eating with a sublime indifference to calories I would never know. "What was Tex's mood? He's your dance partner, and you spent most of the day with him. Did he show signs of unusual stress?"

I picked up my wine glass, put it down, and picked it up again. I didn't know if Tex's anxiety before the *Romeo and Juliet* rehearsal was a natural reaction to the pressure of his upcoming debut, or if something less obvious caused it.

"We were all stressed. Opening night is less than a week away. Tex was his usual self."

Jonah looked at me in the way people do when they suspect you're lying. "Tex claims he misplaced a pair of ballet slippers and returned to the stage to look for them. He said when he saw Maurice, he tried to resuscitate him and called out for someone to help, having left his phone in the dressing room. The stagehands and one of the cameramen, the tall, skinny one, were next on the scene. They're the ones who called nine-one-one. Your buddy Olivia arrived sometime in the middle of all that."

I reached into my bag to pull out a tiny notebook and a pen. Thanks to my erudite parents, I had yet to leave the house without paper, a pen, and at least one book. They would have died of shame otherwise. I jotted down all that Jonah told me.

"This isn't for you to make public," he cautioned.

"I know. But I think better when I'm writing." Looking up from my scribbles, I said, "There's always a pile of stuff backstage, from ballet slippers to water bottles. The murderer could have taken Tex's shoes."

"If the killer wanted to frame Tex, then where are the shoes? It's more likely they were never there to begin with."

I put down the pen and laced my fingers to avoid nervous fidgeting. "Have you learned anything suspicious in connection with the stagehands or Nelson and his camera crew? It appears they were all on site when Maurice was killed."

"We're following where the leads take us. I know you don't want to hear this, but Tex has no alibi. That excuse about missing ballet slippers isn't going to wash. He had plenty of time to start the escalator, conk Maurice on the back of the head, and shove him into the gears. As a dancer, he's quick, he's agile, and he knew how it worked."

I scratched a few doodles in my notebook. "If you take into account personality and motive, Brett is still the prime suspect. How much digging have you done into his relationship with Maurice? From what I observed, it wasn't good. Maurice's death frees him from an unhappy marriage and benefits him financially as well. Maurice was a famous artist. His works are probably worth a fortune."

"I'm not ruling anyone out at this point. Maurice and Brett have been married five years, and the only record we have of any problem between them occurred last summer at their place in the Hamptons. The neighbors called the police after hearing what sounded like a violent argument. By the time the cops got there, if they had been fighting, there was no sign of it. Maurice said they were trying to scare away some black bears rooting around the garbage cans, and several ripped-open bags seemed to confirm their story. They also complained that the neighbors were nosy nitpickers, who resented them for throwing parties on the weekends."

He picked up a file and flipped through the pages. "The Doyles were serial complainers, so no one took it too seriously."

I nibbled on a small piece of cheese but resisted the potato chips, which

I love. "I'd trust the Doyles, whom I've never met, over Brett. Although I regret speaking ill of the dead, Maurice was an arrogant guy and was tone-deaf in regard to other people's feelings. The stagehands loathed him more than they detested the jaws of the hellish contraption that killed him, and that's saying a lot. To be honest, I didn't care for him or for Brett. They were quite similar in temperament and attitude."

"Most people have admitted to not liking either guy. But again, not liking someone isn't a sufficient motive for murder. Not yet, anyway."

I got up and stretched my legs. "Relax. I'm on the case."

He tossed the file on the table. "That's exactly what I don't want. But my desire to keep you safe hasn't stopped you before, and I'm certain it won't stop you now. So I'm not going to waste my time or yours by telling you to back off."

I looked into his dark eyes, as enigmatic as ever. "Then why am I here? What is it you want me to do?"

"I want things to be different. This time, you don't keep secrets from me. You don't embark upon any devious plots that involve tailing a murderer down a dark alley. We work as a team. Unofficially, of course." His earlier levity vanished. "I can't work if I'm chasing after you instead of the killer. Last time, you were a target. That's not the case now. Let's keep it that way. Be smart, Leah."

The fatigue of the day evaporated. "Trust me, I won't take any unnecessary risks. I'll be careful." After reflecting upon our past history, however, I had second thoughts. "What about you? Will you keep me in the loop? Because if you freeze me out, all bets are off."

It was his turn to hesitate. "I...I'll tell you as much as I reasonably can. But you can't go off on your own. Otherwise, no deal. Your job is to clue me on what people are saying behind the scenes, the kinds of things they wouldn't tell me."

His request was reasonable, but the assumption behind it made me uneasy. "Does this mean you think a dancer was responsible?"

"Not necessarily. But there's no one better than you to pull together seemingly random bits of information into something that makes sense, something that makes a coherent story. A perfect example is what you told me about the stagehands. Their resentment of Maurice didn't come out at any of our interviews. Is it important? I don't know, but now I can find out. Your world isn't easily accessible to people outside it. It has its own rules that you take for granted, but that aren't available to the rest of us."

I clinked my glass against his. "I'm in. And who knows? When I retire from dance, I can start my next career as a private eye. I'm already experienced."

"I wish you'd hang out your shingle now." Pointing to his laptop, he said, "Private investigators do most of their work online. The days of staking out a suspect, or roaring off in a high-speed car chase, are over."

I pictured myself in a trench coat and a fedora. "This idea is sounding better and better. I never learned to drive, and I would never follow anyone down an alleyway if there was the slightest chance of running into a rodent of any size."

"Sounds like for once we're on the same page. I don't want the person who killed Maurice Kaminsky going after you. But I can't keep you safe if you hide things from me. Farrow and I will be at the theater tomorrow. I've also got Francie Morelli as backup. She'll alternate with Ana Alvarez."

As I bent to take a sip of wine, a lock of hair fell across my face. He put down his glass and gently smoothed it back. As had happened in the past, his touch burned through me.

His expression gave nothing away, but his hand shook slightly. "Good to have you back, ballerina girl."

Chapter Six

We are not in our bodies, but our bodies are in us...
—Ruth St. Denis

T he police cleared us to return to the theater, and the following day we had company class onstage. Brett arrived shortly after we did our *reverence*. This lovely ritual ends every ballet class. The dancers bow and curtsey as if we were onstage, but instead of receiving applause, we clap for the teacher and the pianist.

Brett's eyes were red, and his thick dark hair hung about his face in uncombed curls. "Thank you for your kind words and support." He choked up, and we looked away until he could compose himself. He cleared his throat and said, "I want to assure you that I remain committed to the vision Maurice and I shared. It's what he would have wanted."

He blinked, as if trying to remember what to do next. After an awkward pause, he said, "Please check the schedule for recent changes. The funeral is at one o'clock tomorrow, and we've arranged a rehearsal break to accommodate those of you who wish to attend."

Brett left the stage to take his accustomed place in Row F, so that he could see us from the audience's vantage point. Madame M touched a handkerchief to her eyes. Her acquaintance with Maurice predated everyone else's, including Brett's. There was an awkward silence that lasted until Brett's impatient call to tell us to begin.

I took my place in the wings as the corps de ballet lined up for the opening dance. Madame followed me. "Lelotchka, I will see you tonight, yes? We make the plan. I have had the fears, about this…this what you call it? *Mashina*? No, that not it." She furrowed her brow. "This *machine*. Mechanical thing. But I never think it would become a weapon. This is catastrophe. And tragedy."

I hugged her, careful of her brittle bones and arthritic joints. "Yes, Madame. I'll meet you tonight. Try not to worry."

It was advice I needed for myself. To my horror, Brett insisted we use the set "as Maurice intended." I waited to see if anyone besides me was willing to protest. No one was. Dancers are trained into obedience from their first class, and the precarious nature of our careers kept us that way. The adult dancers were as quiet and submissive as the children, who were waiting in the wings for their entrance. The kids stood with the same perfect discipline that had long ago been drilled into us: feet turned out, head held proudly, arms curved gracefully. The lead child dancer, Madison Brill, stood out for her serious expression and perfect form.

The parents, not having been hammered into submission by years of dance training, were less self-controlled. They whispered feverishly amongst themselves, to the exclusion of their usual cell phone gazing, and didn't give us their full attention until their kids began dancing.

Madame beckoned to Brett, and although I couldn't hear her, she appeared to be arguing with him. She gestured over and over again at the set, but he met her entreaties with a set jaw and fixed stare. I resigned myself to once again dancing upon The Death Trap. If Madame M couldn't convince him, there was little chance any of the dancers could.

The corps de ballet jumped and twirled in front of the glittering gears. No trace of blood remained, and the audience would see a stage set that looked like a giant child's toy, peopled by doll-like dancers. I blanked out my fear and stepped forward on cue. Dancing demands a completely different kind of consciousness that's difficult to explain. Without deliberate effort, I left Leah Siderova in the wings and became the Sugar Plum Fairy, who was a living embodiment of crystalline perfection.

Tex was back in his usual place. He didn't say much, and although he moved with his usual ease, his face was tense. When the music began, life outside the theater receded into the background, and we danced as if the Nutcracker's magical Kingdom of the Sweets was our whole world.

It's what we do.

Sugar Plum Fairy was not among my favorite roles. Despite the beautiful and dramatic music, the character is relatively one-dimensional. Brett, however, had put the existing choreography on steroids, and for once, I was dancing as exciting a set of steps as my partner. This was risky. Half the audience would love it. The other half would complain that the sacred tradition of *The Nutcracker* had been defiled with cheap tricks. If all of them left the theater talking about it, we'd sell out the whole season.

I was a Mouse the first time I performed in *The Nutcracker*, and one year later I debuted as Clara, the same character Madison Brill was dancing. Despite the passage of time, the excitement never abated. I looked forward to dancing with the young girl and imparting to her the same lessons a previous generation of dancers so generously gave to me.

I couldn't repress a shudder, though, as I contemplated the risk of having kids perform onstage while an unknown killer lurked in the wings. Thankfully, Francie stood guard over them, and I vowed I'd do the same. If anything went wrong, or anyone showed up who didn't belong there, I'd see immediately what the police officer might miss.

The kids weren't the only ones in need of support. Olivia's variation preceded mine, but instead of warming up, she stood as still and pale as a marble statue.

I held her by her shoulders and forced her to look at me. "I know you're upset about Tex, but this is your career that's on the line. Suck it up. If you don't go out there and kill it, there are a dozen other ballerinas who are ready to step in."

She was the picture of misery. "You think I don't know that already?"

I was relentless. "Knowing it isn't the same as doing it. Don't make me go all *42nd Street* on you."

Her posture lost some of its tension, and we chanted, in an exaggerated New York accent, "You're going out a youngster, but you've gotta come back a star!"

Olivia ran lightly to center stage and, although not in costume, daintily held up an imaginary skirt. She was the perfect picture of a ballerina. Her efforts earned her one of Madame's rare compliments. "*Chère fille*, you remind me of Gelsey Kirkland." She threw me an affectionate look. "Or my Lelotchka. Delicate and brilliant. Brava."

When the rehearsal was over, I pulled Madame aside. "I'd like to invite Olivia to come tonight. She needs us. And we need her."

Madame hesitated. "I think not, Lelotchka. I fear she has the feelings for Tex. Not so good for her to join our Choreographers of Crime. She cannot be impartial."

Her use of Gabi's term for our informal collaboration amused me, although her reluctance to include Olivia worried me. "Madame, you know Tex. Do you think he's guilty?"

She didn't hesitate. "*Nyet.* Not guilty. But still, not yet to invite Olivia to join us. Better for her she not know what we plan."

Madame put her forefinger to her lips as the last of the kids trooped offstage. She gave them her notes on their execution, and I returned to my dressing room. I craved a pop of energy from something sweet, but the chocolate box from my secret admirer wasn't where I'd left it. There aren't many places to lose things in a dressing room, and I finally found it in a basket of pointe shoes. Either I'd absentmindedly tossed it in the pile of shoes or one of the cleaners had done so.

Two pounds of candy was too much temptation for one dancer to handle. I grabbed it, neatened up the loose ribbon, and headed for the kids' dressing room. When I opened the door, the chatter and squeal of a dozen preteen girls was earsplitting, but as soon as they saw me, they quieted down.

I stepped inside. "You girls have been absolutely amazing. And you deserve a treat." I placed the pretty gold box on the makeup table. "A friend gave me these chocolates, but there's too much for me to eat alone." They giggled in anticipation. "I was hoping some of you would share it with me. Anyone here like chocolate?"

The response was deafening. I turned to Francie, who was standing at stiff attention in one corner. Poor Francie. She was not a fan of ballet. She stepped forward and inspected the elegant box with its fancy red ribbon and printed card. "Where did you get it?"

I showed her the inscription. "I have a secret admirer. Someone who knows how much I love caramel chocolates. With sea salt."

The police officer didn't look half as impressed as the kids. I slipped off the ribbon and gave the box to Madison. She peered inside, jumped back as if burned, and dropped to the floor in a dead faint.

Francie called for backup. The alarms clanged, and the girls screamed.

Evelyn Brill charged into the room. She shoved me aside and screeched, "What have you done to my child?"

Chapter Seven

The dancer's body is simply the luminous manifestation of the soul...
—Isadora Duncan

Tex was not in the theater when his blood-stained ballet slippers popped out of the box of chocolates. For ten heart-stopping minutes, I feared my beleaguered dance partner was hurt. Or dead.

Neither was the case. He was across the street from Lincoln Center, buying a large salty pretzel when the alarm went off, and he couldn't get back into the building until the police opened the doors for him. Olivia leaped to her feet when he walked inside the theater, but Detective Farrow got to him first.

We had to wait for hours while the police conducted their search. The plaza in front of the theater was cordoned off, and armed officers were stationed at each entrance. I assumed the blood on Tex's ballet slippers belonged to Maurice, but that information wasn't made public until the following day.

I was most concerned about Madison. All of the kids were upset. None were as pale and shaky as the young girl who was scheduled to dance Clara, the most important child's role in *The Nutcracker*. The boys hovered anxiously around the girls. Because they had been in a separate dressing room, they were spared the shock of what the girls had seen. They pretended to be unafraid, but their edgy movements contradicted their tough poses. I wished Madame was there to reassure them, but she was locked in a tense conversation with Jonah.

I wasn't ready to take on Madame's role, but no one else appeared willing to do so. I approached their closed group with a half-formed idea of what I wanted to say.

"Listen, all of you. I need your help."

The kids were silent, their eyes fixed upon me. Most company members didn't interact much with them, although they idolized us.

I made a sweeping gesture that encompassed the whole of the theater. "Professional dancers don't let anything or anyone get in the way of their art. I've seen you all dance. You're good. Better than good. But making it as a dancer requires more than technical skill. Your mind has to be as strong as your body."

I took a deep breath. Making speeches was not my strong suit. "Bad stuff is happening. I get that. Any of you need anything, you come to me. I'll take care of you. Can I count on you to do the same? To make this best *Nutcracker* New York City has ever seen?"

They jumped up, and yelled, "Yes! Yay!"

"Are we in this together?"

They cheered. "Yeah! We got this! You can count on us!"

Although I'd never in my life offered to high-five anyone, I put up my hand for Madison to slap. She missed and began giggling. The kids laughed and began jumping up and down, pretending to miss each other's high fives. Relieved to see them acting more like kids and less like terrified trauma victims, I looked up and was embarrassed to find the adults' eyes fixed upon me.

Tex stepped out of the shadows. "Was that pep talk just for them? Or for me as well? I won't let you down, Leah."

"I know you won't. And I won't let you down either."

Evelyn tapped me on the shoulder. "That's all well and good for you, Ms. Siderova. But these are kids."

"Not anymore, Ms. Brill. Now they're dancers."

The grisly discovery of the missing ballet slippers made the quest to find

Maurice's killer both personal and urgent. Maurice's blood was not on my hands, but the box had been delivered to me. Had the killer targeted me? Or had my dressing room presented the most convenient place to leave incriminating evidence against Tex? As a performer, I was used to having people scrutinize and judge me, but there was no way to ascertain if someone was gazing with professional interest or sinister intent. Every shadow, every sharp sound, made me jump.

My body clamored for rest, but the Choreographers of Crime were waiting for me. This group included my beloved ballet coach, Madame Maksimova, my best friend Gabi, and my sister Melissa. My mother was also a member, which in the past had proved a mixed blessing. Barbara was smart and tough, but her devotion to fictional crime often posed a distraction. The possibility of my aunt joining us was another potential obstacle to logic and clarity.

I traversed a familiar path to Madame's apartment. The interior would not have been out of place in Moscow or St. Petersburg. Each element was like a love letter to the grandeur of pre-Revolutionary Mother Russia. The ornate furniture was upholstered in red and gold silk, and heavy damask draperies fell in graceful folds to the floor. The tables and walls were covered with photographs, all in silver or gilt frames. Most were pictures of Madame in her prime dancing days. Although I'd seen them many times, her heartbreaking beauty never failed to move me.

Melissa was perched on a chair by the fire when I arrived. She put down her cup of tea to embrace me.

"Hey, sis. What took so long?"

I brought out a bottle of Madame's favorite champagne, which I'd bought at the corner liquor store. "You can thank me later."

She drew me closer to the fireplace, where a cheerful blaze warmed the drafty room. "Rest a bit. You look like you're about to keel over."

Madame, who knew my preferences well, didn't offer me tea from a silver samovar that had pride of place on the sideboard. Instead, she poured a cup of dark coffee. "Letlotchka, you should not spend the money on wine. But must admit is my favorite. We have with dinner, yes? First, as your so smart sister says, you take the break. After all, you must dance tomorrow."

She left to answer the doorbell, and when she returned, Gabi, my mother, and my aunt were with her.

Melissa said, from behind a cupped palm, "There was no point in trying to prevent Barbara and Rachel from coming, although I did try."

Gabi embraced me. My mother and aunt pointedly sat apart from each other. They didn't share the same sisterly bond I had with Melissa, or the equally close relationship I had with Gabi.

My sister left her spot by the fire and sat next to Rachel. "So nice to see you again. I hope you'll visit David and me soon. You won't believe how Ariel and Benjamin have grown."

"You want me to come to New Jersey?"

Melissa didn't let Rachel's lack of interest in her husband and kids dent her good cheer. "I'm a thirty-minute ride from Penn Station. I'll pick you up. If you don't believe me, ask Leah. It's easy."

Rachel remained noncommittal. "We'll see." With more enthusiasm, she said to Madame, "Did you know Leah became a dancer thanks to me? I was the one who told Barbara to send her to ballet school. And now look at her!"

Madame didn't debate my aunt's claim or mention the years she'd dedicated to coaching me. "That was smart for you to see my Lelotchka's talent at such a young age."

The reference to ballet lessons was a sore topic for Melissa. "You're not exactly batting a thousand, Aunt Rachel. You also told Barbara to send me to ballet class. Those were the worst two years of my life."

Rachel accepted a cup of tea from Madame and spooned three helpings of sugar into it. "I always knew you had no talent, but I figured it might make you more graceful." In the silence that followed, she made amends by saying, "Don't feel bad about it. Leah doesn't have your brains."

Barbara doesn't often lose her composure, but she made an exception that evening. "I'll thank you to refrain from comparing and insulting my daughters."

Rachel came close to cracking the delicate teacup when she dropped it onto the saucer. "What's the problem now?"

My head was pounding. The success of our investigation rested on all of us working cooperatively, which was why I didn't want my mother and aunt involved. They were capable of turning a discussion about laundry detergent into a ten-year conflict that rivaled the Trojan War in bitterness.

Melissa, the family peacemaker, intervened before Barbara and Rachel could reignite their smoldering debate over whom their parents loved more. My sister plucked the champagne from an ice bucket and said, "Let's not wait for dinner to open this." On that proposal, we were all in agreement.

She popped the cork, and immediately after, the doorbell rang again. Madame murmured, *"Le dîner est arrivé."*

Barbara patted Rachel's shoulder and said sweetly, "That means dinner is here."

Pleased to have enraged her monolingual sister into a sullen silence, my mother joined Madame in plating the food. They unpacked caviar, blini, and an array of colorful salads and placed them on the elegantly set table. The crystal chandelier reflected prisms of light on the white tablecloth, gleaming plates, and heavy, ornate silverware. Madame ladled steaming hot soup into bowls. "Please to eat now. We will be restored, and then we make the plans."

Gabi, Melissa, and Rachel filled their plates. Barbara, Madame, and I were more modest in our food choices. I wished I was the kind of person who could eat whatever she wanted, but I was cursed with a body that converted calories into real estate. I was used to ceaseless dietary denial, broken by the occasional black and white cookie or pint of dulce de leche ice cream. Salted caramel chocolates, I suspected, would no longer be as tempting.

Rachel, after packing away three blini and four slices of pumpernickel bread, said, "I left a date with my friend Victor to come here, so I'd like to get started. I wanted him to come tonight, since he knew Maurice quite well and can help in the investigation. He could give us inside info we wouldn't otherwise have." She blinked in Barbara's direction. "But your mother objected."

I suspected Barbara's opposition was motivated by her desire to annoy Rachel, but whatever the reason, my mother's conclusion was sound. "I agree with her, Aunt Rachel. We don't want to advertise the fact that we're hunting for the person who killed Maurice. Whoever it is could come after us."

Madame looked interested. "What is Victor's last name? I have been friends with Maurice for many years. Is possible I know him."

Rachel looked proud. "He's quite a well-known lawyer. His last name is Roth."

Madame said, "I know this Victor Roth. He is lawyer to famous artists. Have met him at the art galleries." She bit her lip. "Before he marry Brett, Maurice often take me to these parties. We must not to forget why we do what we do. My friend, he deserve justice."

Until that moment, I didn't realize how deeply Maurice's death grieved Madame, and how important the investigation was to her. My initial incentive was to help Tex, who had, by sheer chance, become a suspect. Madame had a compelling interest that outstripped mine. My friend was a murder suspect. Hers was a murder victim.

Sensing Madame's distress, Froufrou jumped into her mistress's lap. Their brief interaction visibly soothed both. I'd never had a pet, as Barbara refused to subject her carpet and clothing to a furry animal. Perhaps someday, I would.

Fortified by Froufrou, Madame continued her analysis. "We assume for moment that Tex not guilty. I truly think not. He have the purity of dance in him. Like you, Lelotchka. But still, cannot say for certain he innocent. Which mean we must to now figure the plan. Tomorrow is funeral. We can do much there, although must be careful. Not want to alert killer we are on case."

I took out my notebook. "Before we decide the questions we want to ask, and the people we want answers from, let's talk about the clues we already have. According to Jonah, the killer hit Maurice on the back of his head and threw him into the gears. That tells us a lot."

Rachel said, "The only thing it tells us is that someone hated him enough to murder him."

"Not at all, Aunt Rachel. It tells us the person who killed Maurice is someone he knew, someone he trusted. If it wasn't, Maurice wouldn't have turned his back, and the killer would have had to strike him in the face. The second thing it tells us is that the killer is strong. Maurice was no lightweight. His body was thick and powerful, and the killer needed plenty of muscle to shove him far enough off the platform so that he fell into the gears. A weaker person would have had to roll him off."

Barbara was pleased. "You're beginning to remind me of Professor Romanova, Leah. Well done."

This was high praise. My mother respected few people more than her own fictional character. "None of this means we change our usual strategy. We need as much information as we can get from anyone who knew Maurice, in order to figure the motive."

Melissa clinked her glass against mine. "I agree with all Leah said. I'm not going to be at the funeral, but for the rest of you, it's probably best to divide and conquer. Leah, you should interview Nelson. Let him think he's interviewing you, but in the process, get as much information as you can from him."

I nodded and turned to Rachel. "You were friends with Maurice. Make sure you mention that to the people you meet. It'll make them more likely to confide in you."

Rachel pulled at the neck of her shirt. "I didn't exactly know him personally. But I knew people who knew him personally."

This information was less surprising than Rachel's earlier assertion of friendship with Maurice. "In that case, use Victor to introduce you to Maurice's family and friends. We should also use Olivia as a source."

Madame, Barbara, Rachel, and Melissa expressed varying degrees of concern in response to my proposal to include Olivia. Gabi sided with me. "Olivia is closer to the corps dancers than Leah, and they're more likely to talk to her."

I added an extra incentive. "I'll make sure Olivia goes to Kerry Blair's party. She wasn't planning to attend, but she'd do anything to clear Tex of suspicion."

Melissa said, "You should go to the party with Olivia."

"Tempting, dear sister, but no. I have an appointment with a book and a cup of coffee. I simply can't get out of it at this late date."

She poked me. "I'm not giving up. You can't send Olivia into the lion's den by herself."

I'd ski the Matterhorn before agreeing to attend another of Kerry's parties. "I'll consider going if you come along as my bodyguard. For now, let's concentrate on the funeral and our plan of action over the next few days. Madame, you've got the office staff and all the teachers to question. They may not have been at the theater, but they know more about what goes on behind the scenes than anyone. I'll talk to the stagehands. They might have some insight as to how Tex's ballet slippers ended up in my box of chocolates."

Madame sipped her champagne. "Yes, this I will do. Also, I will talk to Bobbie York. She not fond of you, Leah, but I have the good friendship with her. She was backstage, helping with costumes, on the day Maurice die. I think too, I will get Olga to join stage crew. She can be eyes and ears backstage. Also to keep dancers safe. Union will not let her in, of course, but Olga, she have ways to manage this. Am sure Olga's friends will handle details. Will explain with Brett tomorrow."

All of us, except my aunt, cheered Madame's offer to include Olga, her powerful, six-foot-tall, tech-savvy Ukrainian friend.

Rachel was testy. "If Madame can involve this Olga person, why can't I involve Victor?"

Barbara's answer had enough acid in it to etch glass. "You're lucky we're letting you into the group."

Madame defused the situation with gentle diplomacy. "When you meet with Olga, Rachel, you will understand. We need trusted professional to assist." She patted my hand. "And speaking of professional, Leah, tell us more about the nice Detective Sobol we like so much."

Barbara looked sharply at me. "Yes, Leah, tell us more about your meeting with that detective."

There was no point in softening the seriousness of the peril my dance partner faced. "Tex is a prime suspect. That's why we're here. Unfortunately, in addition to his other problems, he's losing his battle in the court of public opinion. Savannah Collier, who did a hatchet job on me last year, is back to her old tricks. She and Kerry have been brutal, and I fear it's made some company members suspicious of him."

Gabi pounded her fist on the table. "Everything Savannah posts is a lie. I bet no one pays attention or believes anything she writes. What benefit does she get out of trashing him?"

My friend didn't understand how much social media had changed the landscape at ABC. "The administration and the board pay a lot of attention to our online presence. The negative publicity may hurt Tex professionally, as well as personally. As for Savannah, she'll get another fifteen minutes of fame, along with another ten thousand followers. What scares me is how accurate her posts are. I don't know who her source is, but it has to be someone in the company. We have to fight back by getting the kind of information the police might not think to ask. The cops know crime. We know dance. So tomorrow, we ask questions. And we say nothing about this meeting."

Chapter Eight

If dance wasn't in my life, it wouldn't be worth living...
—Paul Taylor

Olivia and I took a rideshare to Maurice's funeral, which was held at a synagogue on the Upper East Side. We wore black dresses under black woolen coats, leaving our large, brightly colored dance bags at the theater. With opening night of *The Nutcracker* looming, the dancers received only enough time off to attend the funeral before resuming rehearsals.

While we crawled through traffic, I scrolled through the day's headlines. "The mayor called Maurice a national treasure. He says solving the murder is a top priority."

Olivia didn't bother to pull up the article. "That's not good. What if his political pressure makes the police rush to judgment?"

Her anxiety was contagious. I tried to reassure her. "Jonah isn't going to do that."

She rummaged nervously through her bag and took out a protein bar. "Jonah's a cop, and he's subject to the same pressures as the rest of the police department." She stared at the half-eaten food. "Tex has been avoiding me since the murder. I don't understand it. Why would he ghost me now?"

I, too, was concerned at Tex's decision to distance himself. His reticence was making it extremely difficult for us to help him. Before the murder, Tex was a gregarious extrovert. His wide, welcoming smile, good looks, and kind nature earned him many friends, but overnight he'd turned into a loner.

"It's not personal. He's avoiding everyone. On the plus side, no one believes Tex is guilty. Not even the police."

She was bitter. "Is that what Jonah is telling you? You better be sure you're not as deluded about him as I was about Tex. What if he's using you, telling you what you want to hear, in order to get inside information about the company?"

I made myself sound more confident than I felt. "That's ridiculous. I am, of course, going to give Jonah any relevant information about the murder we manage to uncover. Isn't that the point of our investigation? To help the police find the right person?"

"What if we find something that implicates Tex?" She corrected herself. "Something that *seems* to implicate Tex. I think that's why he's avoiding me. Because he knows you and I are such good friends. And he knows you're tight with Jonah."

"You could be right. Do you think we should avoid each other? We could pretend to have an argument and see if that changes how open people are with you."

She was uncertain. "But then we're tricking Tex as well. I'm not sure I want to do that. I want him to know he can trust me."

As the car crossed Second Avenue, I told the driver to pull over. The synagogue was between First and York, but traffic had slowed to a near-standstill. Limousines and double-parked cars choked access to the street, and the traffic cop stationed at the intersection was little help. Walking would take less time than riding.

Ten painful minutes later, I regretted the decision to leave the cab. My chic new boots, with their long skinny heels, fit comfortably the entire time I was inside the carpeted shoe store. When challenged by real life, however, they began a brutal assault on the bunions of my left foot. Like many dancers, my left foot is a full size larger than my right. Those multiple turns that so delight audiences are always performed to the right, which means it's the left foot and leg that take the hit. I loosened the laces in an effort to relieve the pressure.

I ignored my throbbing toes to concentrate on Olivia. "I respect your desire to be straight with Tex, although in this case, it might be better to give more weight to the ends rather than the means. We can decide later if we want to pretend to have had a falling out. In the meantime, we each have a job to do. You extract whatever information you can from the corps dancers. It shouldn't be difficult, given the circumstances. No one is talking about anything else. I'll text you after the funeral."

She joined a group that included Catty Kerry and Horrible Horace. I continued alone, looking for Barbara, Madame, and Gabi. The added three inches of height my heels gave me didn't help much. I'm smaller than most people, and it was difficult to see over the crowd. My task was made more difficult by a strong desire to avoid the press. Luckily, there were many skinny, black-clad women wearing large dark sunglasses in attendance. I attracted no special notice from the milling reporters but did not escape Bobbie York, American Ballet Company's costume mistress.

Bobbie and I were not on good terms. I tried many times to convince her I had no interest in her pleasant, pudgy, middle-aged husband, but her misplaced jealousy continued, unabated by the passage of time. In spite of this tortured history, I hoped she would speak openly with me. Her position gave her a front-row seat, as well as a backstage perspective. Although Madame was supposed to be the one to tap her for information, I decided to take advantage of my proximity.

Bobbie scrunched up her face when she saw me. She spoke with heavy sarcasm. "Look who's here. Little Miss Sensitive. If you hadn't complained about the set, Maurice might still be alive."

"Eavesdropping again, Bobbie? You might want to think twice about advertising that fact. If the wrong person finds out you've been snooping, that could prove dangerous."

She tossed her head. "I'm not afraid of you."

I stepped closer. "Of course not. Why would you be afraid of me? I'm not a violent person. But someone else, someone who was in the theater when I talked to Brett and Maurice, committed murder. Are you sure you want to advertise the fact that you were there as well?"

Her nervous look surprised me. "What do you know, Leah? Did Brett say anything about me?"

She didn't see Madame Maksimova approach us, and when Madame spoke, Bobbie jumped and turned pale. "Madame! I, er, I was just going in."

Madame put a gentle hand on Bobbie's arm. "Perhaps you help me to seat, yes? My knees and hips, they are giving me the trouble today." Madame tilted her head and winked, as if to say, *I'll take it from here.*

Bobbie could hardly refuse Madame's request for assistance. They walked to the front of the line, and the crowd parted to let them pass. Bobbie puffed with pride at the reflected glory Madame provided. The dance critic for *The New York Times* stopped to speak with them, and a flotilla of reporters followed in their wake.

I spied Gabi crossing the street, stepping lightly past the cars blocking her way. I waved and pointed toward York Avenue. Without giving any indication, she saw me, she reversed direction, and we met in front of a prim entrance to an orthopedist's office. The Hospital for Special Surgery was close by, and orthopedists were as common on that street as wine bars and nail salons were on First Avenue. Thanks to multiple knee surgeries, I knew the area well.

Gabi caught me in a swift hug. "What time is the funeral supposed to begin? I thought I was late, but there's a million people trying to get in."

"I doubt they'll delay too much longer. And with so many celebrities who want to get themselves on camera, we should be able to sneak in without attracting attention. The mayor and the police commissioner are still talking to the press."

We walked as quickly as my foot-crushing boots allowed. Having attended several weddings at the synagogue, I was familiar with the setup. Instead of entering through the front, we passed through a wrought-iron gate to the left of the stone building and traversed a gravel path toward the half-open doors of a side entrance.

From behind a large oak tree, a voice with a honeyed Southern accent hailed us. I pretended not to hear, but Savannah Collier followed us, cameraman in tow.

She spoke with suave authority. "I'm Savannah Collier, and I'm here with Leah Siderova, the dancer who was so intimately involved with the recent spate of violence at American Ballet Company. We are at the funeral of renowned artist and set designer, Maurice Kaminsky. Ms. Siderova, tell us in your own words what led to this epic tragedy."

There was no place to hide. If there had been, I would have gladly taken refuge in a snake pit. Well, maybe not snakes. Definitely not rodents. And no bugs. If I had to submit to torture in order to avoid talking to Savannah, dinner with my parents, my stepmother, and any of my mother's recent boyfriends qualified as a suitably excruciating swap.

Because the garden was visible from the street and surrounding buildings, I resisted the urge to poke Savannah in her little, upturned nose, which unquestionably had been surgically rearranged to form a more aesthetically pleasing addition to her blandly pretty face. She'd briefly been a dancer with American Ballet Company. When she realized she would spend her entire career dancing in the back of the corps de ballet, she quit and left for theoretically greener social media pastures.

It wasn't a bad move, from a financial perspective. Many accomplished dancers spend years trying to get promoted before they end up on the unemployment line. It's not easy to reenter the job market when the highlights of your resume are an online high school diploma and an eating disorder.

Savannah avoided that pitfall by securing a clerical position with ABC, but her love of the limelight didn't end with her dance career. She parlayed her considerable talent for self-promotion, as well as a gift for social media, to transition into a job with a popular morning news show. Someone more generous than I was would have forgiven her for trashing me as a means to elevate herself. It's theoretically possible I may someday be able to think of her without raging resentment. But probably not in this life.

I looked into the camera lens and ignored Savannah's calculating gaze. There was no point in muttering "no comment." She'd hound me to the ends of the earth, partly because she wanted a good story, but mostly because she loathed me for living the life she wished she had. I pitied her, but not enough to overlook the pain and humiliation of her relentless trolling and trashing.

Dancers are trained to discipline their bodies, and I used that self-control to keep myself physically still and composed. Fidgeting on camera makes you look guilty, and Savannah would use any excuse, including a spurious analysis of my body language, to discredit me.

I ignored the pain in my feet and stood as tall as a person of rather small stature can. "The loss of this great artist is a tragedy. Like all the mourners here today, I'm grieved by his death."

Savannah relished her temporary power over me. "Is there nothing personal you have to add? This is a tragedy for all of us who knew Maurice personally, as well as professionally."

To my knowledge, Savannah had never met Maurice, but honesty wasn't her strong suit. I turned away, but like a lepidopterist with a prized butterfly, she refused to let me go without piercing me with a few more pins. "Our sources tell us it was your fault Mr. Kaminsky was at the theater so late, and that you were the one who complained the machinery wasn't working properly. You must be devastated at the role you played in his death. Can you comment for our viewers?"

Gabi tilted her head and gave me warning look, to remind me to think before speaking. "I have no knowledge of how Mr. Kaminsky met his death, nor do I know why anyone would seek to harm him. And now, you must excuse me. I'm here to pay my respects."

Savannah persisted. "Your dance partner, Joaquin Texeira, has been named as a possible suspect, and evidence against him was found in your possession. What can you tell us about that so-called coincidence?"

I caught my breath, overcome with fear. Who was feeding her information the police hadn't released? And to what end? Gabi moved behind Savannah, raised a fist, and punched the air three times. She was telling me to fight back.

With renewed calm, I said, "I can tell you that Tex is unquestionably innocent. He's an artist. Not a killer, in any sense of the word. For example, he would never destroy an innocent person's reputation in order to make herself look important." I hoped that by switching to a feminine pronoun, I could make it clear I was talking about Savannah herself.

She visibly gulped and turned bright red. Gabi and I walked away, but not fast enough to miss hearing her response. "If you're just joining us now, ladies and gentlemen, that was Leah Siderova, who was on the scene immediately before and after Mr. Kaminsky was killed. Some of you may remember her from the last time violence struck American Ballet Company. Stay tuned for further developments in this baffling case, where the brutality of ballet spilled over into murder."

Chapter Nine

The most essential thing in dance discipline is devotion...
—Merce Cunningham

The funeral service was a nontraditional blend of speeches, music, chanting, and singalongs. Although the rabbi exhorted the audience to participate, the off-key sounds that emerged from my willing but flawed vocal cords appalled even me. Gabi didn't evince discomfort at hearing me mangle the opening bars to "Somewhere Over the Rainbow," but Barbara and Rachel were not as tolerant. When we got to the part about wishing upon a star, my mother flinched, and my aunt poked me with gratuitous force. I got the message and started mouthing the words. My third-grade music teacher, who feared I would ruin her highly emotional staging of "I'm Proud to Be an American" taught me this trick.

Throughout the speeches, a stream of pictures showed Maurice, from birth, to bar mitzvah, to his wedding with Brett. Maurice's artwork was interspersed with personal photos. There were many images of his paintings, sculptures, and collages. A host of photos featured his set design for a recent Broadway production of *Hamlet,* for which he'd won a Tony. Understandably, there were none of his scenery for *The Nutcracker*. I didn't know Maurice well, but the photo of him at age five, smiling ear to ear as he opened a box of crayons, had everyone in the audience, including me, reaching for the tissues.

I couldn't see the faces of his family and close friends, who had filled the first few pews before the rest of us were allowed into the sanctuary, but from my vantage point in the rear I was able to identify many of New York City's glitterati, as they swanned their way down the aisle to the front.

Barbara gave me a knowing look as a gaunt, platinum blond woman with an angular bob and spiky leather boots approached the lectern. "That's Charlotte Dankworth, the art dealer. She has galleries in London and New York."

Rachel whispered, with complacent pleasure, "Victor invited me to her reception later tonight. Lots of famous people are going to be there."

I craned my neck to see around the people in front of me. "Which one is Victor?"

Rachel pointed to the left of the lectern. "He's in front, next to where Charlotte was sitting. They're dear friends. I told you how close he was with Maurice and Brett. Victor said Brett is completely devastated."

I opened my mouth to ask her to wangle an invitation for me, but she shushed me as Charlotte began speaking.

The art dealer articulated her words in a posh, almost-British accent that would make a headless chicken sound intelligent. She spoke at length of her long association with Maurice and included many details of his most famous works.

I put my mouth to Barbara's ear. "Charlotte's speech sounds more like an advertisement for her gallery than a eulogy. I bet Maurice's work is going to be worth a lot more now. Maybe Charlotte's the one who killed him."

Barbara frowned. "I doubt she was able to enter the theater unnoticed. She's a rather striking woman."

This was true. Charlotte's pale hair and sharp features didn't lend themselves to covert maneuvers. "She might not have done it herself. She could have arranged to have him killed."

Although I directed my words to Barbara, Rachel answered. "You shouldn't be so suspicious, Leah. It's unseemly."

"We're conducting a murder investigation. The whole point is to be suspicious of everyone."

She cocked her head at my mother. "I hope, Barbara, you're not going to be as distrustful as Leah. It's time you got over your skepticism of Victor. He's well-known and well-connected, and I want you to drop this unreasoning prejudice you have against him."

The woman in the pew behind us let out a furious *Hush!* that was many decibels louder than our whispered conversation. Chastened, we settled in to listen to the rest of the service. In the process, I gained a new appreciation for Maurice's life as well as his art. I was most interested in listening to Brett, because as Maurice's husband, he was the prime suspect. But Brett did not speak.

The memorial service ended with an emotional appeal from the rabbi, who urged the audience to return for regular services on Saturday. He also pitched the all-new Singles Club (better than JDate!) The noted opera singer Anna Firenzi led a rousing chorus of "Climb Every Mountain" for the recessional.

Rachel, who was eying the crowd, waved and called, "Yoo-hoo! Victor! Over here."

Barbara muttered, "He looks like Frankenstein's monster."

I let out a most unladylike sound in my attempt to swallow a laugh. Although Victor was without a neck bolt or green skin, he had the monster's requisite stature, black hair, and square head.

Victor kissed Rachel's cheek and said to my mother, "Ms. Siderova, it's a pleasure to meet you. I've read all your books, and I'd love to get to know you better."

It was clear from my mother's pleased greeting that her objections to Victor Roth were unlikely to continue. "Why, thank you, Mr. Roth. I'm well acquainted with your work as well. But please, it's Barbara. And this is my daughter, Leah."

He gave me a warm, slightly damp handshake. "I'm a big fan of the ballet. And of you."

Rachel edged between us. "Not many people know this, Victor, but I'm the one who started Leah in ballet. Her whole career is thanks to me."

He smiled, revealing large white teeth. The toothy grin made him look more like a wolf than like Frankenstein, as in *The better to eat you with!* variety.

Victor gestured to a waiting limousine. "I fear I must leave you, ladies."

Barbara said, "Please visit us sometime. Dinner, perhaps?"

Victor took her hand. "I would be delighted if all of you could join me tonight. Charlotte Dankworth is having a reception in honor of Maurice, and I'm certain she would be happy to have you come."

As soon as he was out of earshot, Rachel said, "Nice work, Barbara. I wouldn't have introduced you if I knew you were going to crash the party."

My mother was all innocence. "I don't know what you're talking about. But I'm starting to understand why you like Victor, and I'm looking forward to getting to know him better."

Rachel muttered, "I'll bet you are."

I looked from my mother to my aunt. If the two of them spent their time vying for Victor's attention, the party invitation would be a wasted opportunity. "Charlotte's reception will give us access to a lot of people who were close with Maurice and Brett. I know this is a high-class crowd we're going to be hanging with, but that doesn't mean one of them isn't the killer."

Barbara pinched my arm. "Since when do you use phrases like 'hanging with'? Professor Romanova would not allow any of her students to use an obscenity like that."

I admired my mother's dedication to writing but had come to loathe her habit of using fictional characters to score points. "Since when do I have to worry about offending a character you invented? It's bad enough you've raised me to talk like an elderly English teacher. As for Victor, let's reserve judgment until we know him better. Tonight is the perfect opportunity to do that."

Barbara said, "This is an ideal setup for my next book. I'll use a fictionalized version of Victor as a red herring in *Homicide and Hamlet*."

I kissed them goodbye. "Call me later with deets about tonight's party. I have to get back to the theater." Barbara got the joke and didn't scold me for using a slang word that would have been anathema to Professor Romanova.

I took a last look at the thinning crowd. Jonah and Detective Farrow monitored the departing mourners from a few feet away. No one appeared to take much notice of the police officers, except for Savannah, the poisonous reporter, would-be influencer, and my personal nemesis. I expected her to attempt another forced interview with me, but she waved away her camera guy before approaching Jonah. His expression was neutral. Hers was flirtatious. After a moment, they withdrew into the side garden, to the same spot where she'd ambushed me into giving her an interview.

I re-entered the synagogue and eased open a door that let out onto the gravel path where Savannah and Jonah were talking. I was too late to hear the entire conversation, but it wasn't difficult to infer the content of what I'd missed.

Jonah said, "Seven is perfect."

Savannah answered in an accent so sickly sweet, listening to her posed the risk of a diabetic coma. "I'm *so* looking forward to seeing you again."

I slunk away. Gabi was waiting for me. She gave me a quizzical, sidelong look. "Did you get what you were looking for?"

I kept my face averted. "More than I bargained for."

The wait for a rideshare was long, and I stepped into the street to scan for an unoccupied taxi. None appeared until Barbara helped us out. She had a gift for making cabs materialize. This included rainy days during rush hour. It was another of her talents I hadn't inherited.

I settled back in the seat and eased my aching feet out of my boots, which could have served as an instrument of torture during the Spanish Inquisition. With some reluctance, I answered Gabi's insistent questions regarding Jonah.

"There isn't much to say. Nothing that relates directly to our investigation, anyway. I did learn that once again, I've made a fool of myself. I really thought Jonah was, well, interested in me. As a woman and not merely as a means to gain inside info on the company. Olivia was right about him."

"Olivia isn't a good judge of men. Didn't she date Horace?" Gabi pulled a chocolate bar out of her pocket and broke it in half. "Here. This will make you feel better."

I hesitated. It's not easy to be close friends with two women who can eat without guilt and shame, but this appeared to be my fate. The decision to accept the candy was a tough call. Chocolate always gives me a lift, although its restorative properties did not include repairing a broken heart.

"Take it," she ordered. "This is an emergency. You can't dance if your feet hurt *and* you're miserable."

I mentally added the calories in the chocolate bar to the calories I'd ingested earlier. Constant practice had made me adept at adding three-digit numbers in my head. The resulting number was low enough for me to eat the chocolate without swallowing a ton of remorse with it. As we traveled with distressing speed through a series of yellow-to-red lights, I told Gabi about the conversation I'd overheard between Jonah and Savannah. I couldn't have shared how I felt with anyone else.

"When I went to Jonah's apartment, it felt intimate. We mostly talked about the murder investigation, but he acted as if he wanted more than a professional partnership. And then, I overheard him making a similar arrangement with Savannah." I burned with the thought that this woman, who had done her best to destroy my career and reputation, was going to have a romantic evening with Jonah. I felt betrayed. Humiliated. Hopelessly gullible.

Gabi was measured in her response. "I understand how you feel. But I think you should wait before you jump to conclusions."

I added *bitter* to the list of uncomfortable emotions. "What's the point in waiting? Jonah knows all about how Savannah plotted against me. If he thinks he can use us by playing one against the other, he's dead wrong."

Gabi puffed out her cheeks with exasperation. "You have no idea what Jonah is up to. For all you know, he's going to tell you about his meeting with her. If he doesn't tell you about it, we can revisit the topic."

I watched a crew put up Christmas wreaths, although the holidays were still weeks away. "I'm not expecting anything from Jonah, other than some loyalty. If nothing else, we're friends. I thought I knew him, but if he's attracted to that airbrushed airhead, I will lose all respect for him. Good riddance."

Gabi persisted. "On the subject of romance, you still haven't said a word about Zach. What's the status of your relationship with him?"

"If I knew, I would tell you. Zach says he wants a committed relationship, whatever that means. But I don't know why we're talking about my pathetic love life when we've got a murder to investigate. An innocent guy's life may be hanging in the balance."

Gabi didn't answer immediately, and when she did, it was without her former assurance. "It frustrates me that I'm so distant from the action. If I were still dancing with the company, I could help a lot more. So I'm counting on you. Has Tex been any more forthcoming? It's going to be hard to help him if he won't help himself."

I rummaged in my purse for a few bills to give to Gabi for my half of the fare, but I had no cash. I sent the money via a cash app, and her phone beeped with the message. That done, I said, "What if Tex isn't protecting himself? What if he's protecting someone else?"

Gabi's eyes grew wide. "I did hear he was having an affair with Brett."

The cab pulled up to the curb so sharply, I had to brace myself to keep from hitting my head on the partition. "I doubt Tex would endanger himself for Brett's sake. I'm worried he's covering for someone else."

She grabbed my arm to stop me from leaving. "Olivia? You think she's guilty?"

"Of course not! But she was on the scene. Maybe Tex thinks he might implicate her by saying he saw her. If that's the case, I have to stop them from playing the part of self-sacrificing, star-crossed lovers."

Gabi bit her lip. "Listen, girlfriend: I'm liking this situation less and less. Forget Tex. And Olivia. You need to protect yourself. That box of chocolates didn't go to one of them. It was left for you."

Chapter Ten

The candid camera is the greatest liar in the photographic family...
—Lincoln Kirstein

After a grueling day of rehearsals, muscles I didn't know existed came to life in unpleasant ways. By the time I got home, even my head hurt, a consequence of the choreographed falls in Juliet's death scene. My body wanted complete rest, a grilled cheese sandwich, and two cupcakes. Chocolate chip cookies dipped in vanilla ice cream would also have been acceptable. My brain was similarly starved, but I had little time to recharge or refuel. Resisting the comfort of the sofa, I sat in a straight-backed chair in my tiny kitchen and concentrated on a plan of action for Charlotte Dankworth's upcoming reception.

With virtuous intention, I retrieved my notebook. The neatly penned names of potential suspects in Maurice's death sparked no insights, not because I was tired and hungry, but because I was distracted by the memory of seeing Jonah with Savannah. I wasn't jealous. If Jonah was the kind of guy who could be seduced by a backbiting celebrity-influencer-wannabe like Savannah Collier, he was welcome to her.

The contemplation of murder suspects faded into the background, replaced by memories of the last three men in my life. My track record, like my mother's, wasn't good. One former boyfriend broke up with me via text message during the company's European tour. To his credit, he had the decency not to update his social media with pictures of his new girlfriend until the following day. I will discourse no further about this avowedly commitment-phobic man, other than to note he married within a year of breaking up with me.

More recently, my relationship with Zach had migrated from a torrid tropical zone to a far more temperate climate. His complicated attachment to his ex-wife kept potentially passionate feelings in check, at least on my side. I won't deny some distress over the situation, but that emotion came and went without excessive sorrow or painful gnashing of teeth.

Which brought me back to Jonah. The decision to put our relationship on hold was his. When he unexpectedly stopped by my apartment, bearing a bouquet of my favorite flowers, I was not alone. Although Zach and I were having coffee, not sex, the situation was…awkward. And now, I had no option other than to accept the unpleasant truth that what Jonah did in his free time was none of my business. Although Gabi suggested Jonah's interest in Savannah might be professional, and connected to his investigation into Maurice's death, his words suggested otherwise. I was not jealous, a fact I may have mentioned already.

I gave up trying to formulate a calculated plan for the evening and called Barbara. "Are you alone? Or is Victor there?"

She sounded distracted. "He's not here yet. I'd love to chat, but I simply cannot decide what to wear. If Maurice's friends and family were sitting shiva, or holding a wake, that would be easy. But tonight's party has me baffled. It would be frightful to be under-dressed and even worse to be over-dressed."

I tossed the take-out salad that was supposed to be my dinner into the fridge. "I have no idea what you should wear. But when you're done, pick out something for me. On a far more important topic, however, how close is Victor with Charlotte Dankworth? Did you get any interesting details from Rachel?"

Barbara ignored all of the important parts of what I needed to know. "Sorry, darling, but after I get dressed, I have to persuade your aunt to wear something approaching twenty-first-century style."

"You have more clothes than Bloomingdale's. I need you to think about what we're doing, as opposed to how we look."

The silence from her end lasted so long I thought we'd been cut off. After my third *hello?* she answered. "Leah, stop shouting at me. I'm thinking."

I put the phone on speaker and hunted in my closet for shoes, the one item I could not borrow from my mother. She said, after a few more minutes of deliberation, "It's no use. I can't think until I resolve this potential fashion disaster. We'll figure out a plan of action when you get here."

"If Victor gets there before I do, tell Rachel not to confide in him. Remind her we're planning a murder investigation. Not a bar mitzvah."

My mother is nothing if not stubborn. "I was quite favorably impressed with him. This cloak-and-dagger routine might not be the most productive approach."

I locked my door and headed downstairs. "Maurice is dead. Tex is under suspicion. The killer hid evidence in a chocolate box that was in my dressing room. Everyone is guilty until proven innocent."

When I arrived at Barbara's apartment, I did my makeup and pinned my hair into place. The next item on the evening's agenda was to find something to wear that wasn't a leotard, tights, or in need of dry cleaning. Inside my mother's walk-in closet, which took up a third of her bedroom, she had three cocktail dresses on display.

I fingered a pale pink dress and another in dark blue chiffon. Before I could give the matter sufficient thought, Rachel barged in. "Wear the black one. And don't worry about keeping Victor waiting. He texted me his apologies. He's running late and will meet us there."

Rachel wore a gray silk shirt over black pants that fit reasonably well. She didn't meet my mother's exacting standards, but few people do. When I complimented her, she raised her shirt to show me the safety pin at the waist of her tight pants. "If I end up getting stabbed and dying of sepsis, it will be your mother's fault."

Barbara, of course, was perfectly turned out in a knee-length, high-necked silk sheath. I stepped into a strapless black dress and tugged at the top. "Are we going to a funeral reception or a cocktail party?"

Barbara handed me a matching cropped jacket. "We'll find out soon enough."

Most of the guests at Charlotte's Central Park West apartment looked familiar, not because I'd met them, but because they existed within, or on the margins, of fame. Although I knew the names of many, I could claim a personal acquaintance with very few. As a principal ballerina, I'd attended many elegant parties where the dancers were the star of the show and as recognizable to the guests as artists, actors, and socially prominent rich people. At Charlotte's reception, however, I went unnoticed, a not unpleasant change from the spotlight.

The clinking of a knife against a glass silenced the buzzing in the room. Charlotte spoke slowly and distinctly, giving weight to each word in a manner that forced close attention. "We're here to celebrate Maurice Kaminsky's life. Not his death. It's no exaggeration to say this extraordinarily talented man will live forever through his art. We're all united in grief, none more so than his devoted husband, Brett Cameron."

Charlotte wiped an invisible tear from her eye and drew Brett closer to her side. She was grave but composed. Brett, however, looked pale and ill. She gave him a reassuring look and then continued, "It's rare that a marriage of hearts is also a marriage of art. And now, let us honor our dear, departed friend, who died much too soon, with a moment of silence."

She bowed her head and closed her eyes. I kept my eyes open and surveyed the somber faces around me. I wasn't being disrespectful. My goal was to learn all I could about Maurice's life. That was how I would honor him. Not with silence, but with action.

After about fifteen seconds, Charlotte resumed speaking. "As we all know, no one loved a party like Maurice." A few people chuckled at this. She raised her glass. "So let's remember him the way he'd want to be remembered. With joy." She took a ceremonial sip. "And with wine."

Given permission to party, there was a general move toward the bar and the food, and I began my quest to learn details about Maurice's life beyond what a Google search could tell me. This was not an easy task. Despite the large number of people in attendance, it was a rather clubby gathering. With nothing more promising to go on, I set my sights on three members of the Franklin family. They were generous donors to many arts organizations and had recently bankrolled an American architecture installation at the Metropolitan Museum of Art.

Mrs. Franklin, and her younger son, starchitect Melville, regarded me with stiff politeness, and after a murmured excuse, ditched me. Jonathan, the older son, remained. I cloaked my dislike with a friendly handshake, and he pulled me in for an unwelcome kiss, which he aimed at my mouth. I turned my head but was unable to dodge his full-body hug.

I resisted the urge to wipe my cheek clean of Jonathan's damp imprint. After offering a few standard condolences, I asked, "Were you and Maurice good friends? I know so little about him, outside the short time we worked together on *The Nutcracker*."

This line of questioning didn't interest him. "Nah. Barely knew the guy. My mother owns a few of his paintings, which was an excellent investment. When Maurice won a Tony last year, the value of his stuff doubled."

For someone who knew nothing about Maurice, Jonathan was well-informed. "How about Brett? Were you friendly with him?"

He seemed baffled by the question. "Why would I know him?"

His ignorance shocked me. "Brett is choreographing the new production of *The Nutcracker*. I thought, since you were still on the ABC board, you might know him."

Jonathan's face cleared. "Oh yeah, *that*. Honestly, I've kind of stepped back from my responsibilities at the company. Too busy with the real world these days." He looked me over with insulting thoroughness. "I may have lost interest in the ballet. But not in ballerinas."

Having hit a dead end with Jonathan, I moved away to pursue a more fruitful line of inquiry with someone else. Jonathan had other ideas. Bucking the riptide of my indifference, he stuck to my side like a barnacle. He held my bare arm with sweaty fingers and regaled me with tales of his real estate prowess.

Waving a glass of scotch, he became pensive. "Let me explain about me and my wife. She's not sensitive. Not like you."

I wracked my brain for a graceful way to stop him before he indulged in any marital revelations. In desperation, I waved to Nelson, who joined us and spared me from having to listen to Jonathan's complaints about his wife. I'd been avoiding Nelson since he began filming but was delighted when he cut short any further disclosures from my former boss.

Nelson ignored Jonathan. "Leah, I'm going to apologize in advance for bringing up business at this sensitive time. But it's a stroke of luck for me that you're here. I was going to film Charlotte, but I can't pry her away from her guests."

Jonathan, with the arrogance of old money, appeared unaware of Nelson's prompt for him to discreetly take his leave. He simply stood there, his eyes blank and his mouth slack. After a moment, he said, "Hey, don't I know you?"

Nelson looked amused. "Yes. I'm a director."

Jonathan's face turned red. "You—I recognize you now. You're the one who made that movie about me and my father! Why, I oughta—"

A tall thin woman of exceptional loveliness interrupted. With a charming apology, and more diplomacy than was characteristic from someone so young, she said, "Jonathan, your friends will have to do without you for a few minutes. Charlotte is looking for you." The woman nodded to Nelson and me. "So sorry to interrupt, but you know how it is. My husband's a popular guy."

Jonathan, with grudging courtesy, said, "This is my wife. Leonora."

She acknowledged the introduction before drawing him into a group that was far too merry for a reception in honor of a dead person. When they were a safe distance away, I said to Nelson, "Jonathan described his wife as unfeeling and insensitive. Now that I've seen her, though, she seems much too nice to be stuck with him."

Nelson threw back his head and guffawed. "Leonora has to stay married to him for five years as part of the prenup in order to get any money, post-divorce. Let's see how nice she is a few years down the road. He's not smart enough to realize she's probably documenting his extracurricular activities."

I tried not to stare. Jonathan's weak chin, bulging eyes, and arrogant air were only partially offset by his rich man's tan and expensively tailored clothes. "Why was he so angry with you?"

Nelson winked. Without his black-rimmed glasses, he looked much younger. "An occupational hazard. I did an exposé on his family's holdings in the Bronx after a big fire broke out in one of their buildings. It was an ugly story, but it didn't dent their standing in the crowd they run with. The Franklin family's financial support of half the city's institutions was more than enough to ensure they'd end up on their feet." He tossed back the rest of his drink. "As you may know, arson cases are my specialty."

I didn't know that, but Nelson was uninterested in further conversation about Jonathan. He beckoned to his cameraman. "Eddie here is going to set things up for us. I'll ask Charlotte if we can use her library. It's got several of Maurice's paintings on the walls, which would be a great backdrop."

The cameraman looked as if he'd had more alcohol than his skinny frame could handle. I doubted he could film anything more challenging than a stationary cup of coffee.

I didn't answer Nelson directly. "Let me think about it. In the meantime, why don't you tell me how you came to do the project on Maurice. Don't you usually do true crime?"

Nelson motioned to a passing server to bring us another round. "Yeah. I specialize in cold cases."

Eddie wavered a bit as he drained his glass. "We were all set to cover the serial killer case in LA, when the boss here decided New York City was a better idea." He exchanged a glance with Nelson, one I couldn't decipher. "It should be interesting since we're now characters in the story we're filming. I thought we'd have to do without our signature ending. That won't be necessary now."

I was reluctant to admit I hadn't seen any of Nelson's movies, and thus didn't understand Eddie's reference to their signature endings, but I made a mental note to watch at least one of their films.

"I see your point. You came here to do an art documentary, but you ended up with a murder case."

Eddie leaned against the wall for support. "You got that right. Which reminds me, Boss, we've got footage from the funeral that includes half the people here. I'll follow up with them as well."

Nelson took Eddie's empty glass. "That won't be necessary. I'll take care of it. And don't bore Leah with these kinds of details. She doesn't need to know how the sausage gets made."

Eddie winked at him. "Sure thing, Boss. I won't give away any of your secrets."

Nelson, annoyed that the server he'd signaled for fresh drinks had yet to acknowledge him, headed to the bar. "I'll be right back."

I steered Eddie to a chair and scooped some cheese and crackers onto a plate for him. The guy needed food far more than another drink. He wasn't quite as skinny as Nelson, but he'd had more alcohol than he could handle. As Eddie noisily ate, I said, "Nelson told me he specializes in cases of arson. Did you work on the film he did on the Franklin buildings?"

Eddie spoke around a mouthful of food. "Yeah, I did. Nelson's kind of obsessed with that crime. His college sweetheart died in a suspicious fire, and he never got over it."

"What made him decide to do a documentary on Maurice?"

Eddie wiped his mouth and said, "Nelson and Maurice have been good buddies since college. He wanted to help Maurice, whose career had hit a dead end. But like you said, now we've got our very own murder. That's Nelson for you. He's always been a lucky guy."

He looked out the window. It was a moonless night, and the view of Central Park was shrouded in mist, other than small pools of light around the street lamps.

"A few days ago, I would've said all I wanted was to get back to Southern California." He scraped the toe of his shoe against the floor. "But, uh, I met a girl. A woman. When we got here, I couldn't wait to get back to Cali. But New York is looking pretty good right now."

His shy pleasure touched me. "That'll do it."

Eddie went on to regale me with stories of film shoots and the famous people he'd met. He had a self-deprecating sense of humor that was starkly different from the mantle of privilege the other guests wove about themselves. It was a relief to talk to someone so down to earth. If he were doing the interview, instead of Nelson, I would have been much less wary. The older man's easygoing manner didn't obscure his sharp, judgmental eye. Despite Nelson's friendliness, he made me nervous.

When Nelson rejoined us, I looked at my phone and opened my eyes wide, as if astonished at what the screen revealed. "Unfortunately, I'm past my due date. It's later than I thought, and with opening night coming up, I have to conserve my energy. I'm going to thank Charlotte and say a few words to Brett before I leave. Have you seen them?"

Nelson pointed to the windows that framed the balcony where our elegant hostess held court. Madame, Bobbie, and two members of the ABC board of directors were among the group.

"Charlotte's over there. Not sure where Brett went. Can't blame him if this was all too much for him. Poor guy."

I patted Eddie on the shoulder. Although we were close in age, he seemed much younger. "Good luck with your new girlfriend. New York's a great place to fall in love."

Chapter Eleven

Art is an investigation...
—Twyla Tharp

The throng of people at Charlotte's party continued to grow. I withdrew to a relatively quiet corner of the living room and tapped a few cryptic notes into my phone. Something in the information I'd gotten from Nelson, Eddie, and Jonathan didn't fit, but I couldn't figure out what it was.

My mother was mildly annoyed when I interrupted her tête-a-tête with Victor Roth. A tiny crease in Barbara's forehead tipped me off to her displeasure. She rarely furrowed her brow, as she believed it made wrinkles.

"Leah, did you know that Victor and Maurice met as undergraduates?" Barbara looked up at him from under her lashes. "It's a testament to your friendship with him that you've stayed in such close touch with each other. I'm so sorry for your loss."

I was about to ask the lawyer if he'd also been friends with Nelson, when he said, "There isn't more than three degrees of separation between most people here. My connection with Charlotte, for instance, goes beyond a mutual friendship with Maurice. It began professionally, when one of my partners represented her in a dispute with an artist. She invited me to one of her shows, and we became good friends. As you can tell from this apartment, her taste is impeccable."

"Yes. It's quite impressive. Almost a gallery in itself." Barbara craned her neck to see around the bottleneck of people at the bar. "But where is Brett?

I don't think I've seen him since Charlotte's speech."

Victor, who was much taller than either of us, checked out the room. He caught Charlotte's eye, and she charged in our direction, heedless of those who stood in her path. She kissed Victor on both cheeks. "Victor, darling. Thanks so much for coming."

"Dear Charlotte. You are a saint for doing all this." His placed his large arm around her bony shoulders and introduced us.

She patted her stiff, blond hair. "Don't be absurd, darling. It's the least I could do for one of my oldest and dearest friends. I'm delighted you could come. I know it means the world to Brett. He's shattered by Maurice's death."

Barbara said, "Is Brett still here? I wanted to offer my condolences."

The art dealer started when Barbara spoke, as if a piece of furniture had answered her instead of my well-dressed and beautiful mother. "I believe Brett is in the library. He needed some downtime after the service and the funeral. Perhaps I shouldn't have had the reception tonight, but the gallery is booked solid for the remainder of the year."

My aunt, bearing a plate filled with enormous shrimp, squeezed herself between Barbara and Victor. "This apartment is stunning, Charlotte. It must have cost a fortune. I'm looking for a place myself." Rachel waved a shrimp, and we moved back to avoid getting splashed by a spray of cocktail sauce. "Though it does seem a bit cold. Reminds me of a fishbowl, but without the colorful pebbles. You should get a few pillows for the sofa. Warm things up."

Untroubled by Charlotte's glare, my aunt continued to offer design advice to the elegant gallery owner. "I suggest adding something a little more traditional. I'm not that into modern art myself. Never could understand what all the fuss was about." She picked up another shrimp by the tail. "But ask me anything you want about ballet. I'm an expert on that. I'm the one who gave Leah her first ballet lessons. Her whole career is thanks to me. Not many people know that."

Charlotte was nearly as tall as Victor, which enabled her to effortlessly look down her nose at my aunt. "What makes you an expert on both ballet and art?"

Rachel was so eager to explain, she didn't notice the red cocktail sauce on her plate dripping onto the white carpet. "I used to dance myself but gave it up when I got married. When my cheating ex-husband and I moved to Minnesota, I opened a ballet school. *Very* successful. And now I'm back to where I started. But, like you say, I'm an expert. Do you know someone who could use my talents? I wouldn't charge much."

This was too much information for our hostess, who murmured something inaudible before abandoning us. Victor and Barbara exchanged amused looks and laughed.

Rachel looked sideways at my mother. "What's so funny? What did I say?"

Barbara was careful not to hurt her sister's feelings. "Nothing that wasn't clear and honest. And I love you for it."

Despite winks, raised eyebrows, and subtle jerks of my head to telegraph my desire to get Barbara alone, I couldn't pry her from Victor's side. Defeated, I left them and wandered around the penthouse. I eavesdropped on some uninteresting conversations, swapped my wine for water, and took in the clouded view of Central Park. Glass in hand, I circled the room, admiring Charlotte's taste and style. As Rachel noted, the apartment was furnished with bone-chilling minimalism. Decorated in shades of white and gray, the pale walls and furniture made the colorful works of art even more striking.

When Charlotte saw me examine the largest of the paintings, she stood beside me and said, "It's a deLoomis, of course. His work is so mature, it's hard to believe he's twenty-three years old. Did you know he won the same prize that launched Maurice's career? I foresee a bright future for that young man, and a smart investor will get in on the ground floor. Are you a collector?"

I leaned closer to examine some of the exquisite details of the painting. "I wish I was in a tax bracket that would finance a deLoomis. If I was, I'd want this. I guess I'll have to settle for a cheap poster of it."

Charlotte sniffed loudly, as if either the painting or I offended her olfactory sense. "I don't sell knockoffs. Though we can hardly stop imitators from infesting the internet with copies."

I was embarrassed and hastened to make amends. "I was joking. I, er, I meant that I admire the painting." I swept my hand to include the entire wall. "Trust me, I would steal the original before I would buy a fake."

This was not true. All of the art in my apartment was either a poster or a cheap reproduction. I did, however, own a series of photographs, created by a student at the School of Visual Arts, for whom I'd posed at no charge. Unlike deLoomis, she had yet to make it big.

Charlotte's icy glare showed no sign of melting. I mentally cursed myself for making jokes with a woman I didn't know. Talking to people with no sense of humor is worse than listening to those same people explain what a great sense of humor they have.

She turned away from the deLoomis painting to more closely inspect me. "Wait a minute, yes, I do know you. You're that little, er, that dancer."

I bit back a sarcastic response. "Yes. Victor Roth introduced us. I'm Leah Siderova."

"Yes. That's right. I think I may have mistaken you for someone else. You dancers all look alike to me." She regarded me as dispassionately as if I were one of her paintings and spoke as if checking off boxes on an invoice. "Small head, long neck, big eyes. And skinny. Though aren't you a little on the short side for a dancer?"

Although dance companies are famous, or infamous, for choosing dancers based on body type and facial features, it's not pleasant to hear other people comment upon your lack of individuality. My coping mechanism for dealing with stressful situations is to leave my real self behind and adopt the persona of one of my fictional roles. I fixed upon Myrtha, from the ballet *Giselle*, as my alter ego. Myrtha is the Queen of the Wilis, a relentless and powerful figure.

I returned her gaze with the implacable glare Myrtha uses to condemn men to death. "Dancers are as unique as paintings. Attend one of ABC's performances, and you'll have no trouble figuring out who's who."

She cared too little about me to register offense. Her eyes roamed the room, having gotten bored with examining my undistinguishable face and body. "Dear Victor. He is delightful. And I suppose your mother is that romance writer?"

I again reminded her that Victor had introduced us less than fifteen minutes earlier. "My mother, Barbara Siderova, writes crime fiction. She's really rather well-known. To people who read."

My answer, once again, didn't make much of an impression. "Is she? I never heard of her. Such an odd last name."

I was about to explain the meaning behind my last name when a beautiful woman swooped between us, in a swirl of perfume and gin. Her elegant dress and haughty expression matched Charlotte's.

Charlotte honored her with a double air kiss. "Sloane, darling! So glad to see you!" She swiftly followed the happy words with a sober look. "Though devastated that it's for such a tragic reason."

The art dealer flicked a glance in my direction and said, "Have you met Lila, um, the er, dancer?"

I turned around to check if a fourth person had joined us, before realizing Charlotte had again forgotten my first name, as well as my odd last name.

After a brief, shocked, glare, Charlotte's friend pretended she didn't know me. I didn't blame her. Sloane Mitchell was not interested in discussing our shared interest in her ex-husband. Neither was I.

The two women amiably gossiped and namedropped while I waited for the opportunity to break into their mutual admiration society. As the minutes ticked by, I grew impatient.

"So interesting to hear about your new place in the Hamptons. Sounds marvelous!" With no attempt at a logical segue, I continued, "All of the dancers at ABC are devastated by Maurice's death. Do either of you have any idea who could have done such a thing?"

They looked at me with as much horror as if I was the one who'd killed Maurice. Patches of red appeared under Charlotte's dead white makeup. "No, we do not."

As I had no desire to remain on her A-list, I persisted. "There are a lot of people here. Do you know if any of them had a history with Maurice? Maybe a competitor? Or an estranged lover?"

Charlotte didn't throw her drink in my face, but she jiggled the ice in it as if assessing its value as a projectile. "Maurice didn't have any enemies. I don't know what it's like in your world, but mine is supportive and close-knit."

Sloane lowered her chin and looked meaningfully at Charlotte. "Dancers." She said the word *dancer* the same way most people say *serial rapist*.

Charlotte was quick. Much more perceptive than Sloane, who appeared unaware of why I was pumping them for information. "If you're here, Lisa, on a mad quest to find someone who had a motive to kill Maurice, I think you'll have better luck looking closer to home."

If we continued to talk, there was an outside chance she would eventually remember my name, but I was willing to forego that possibility. Instead, I checked my wrist, although I wasn't wearing a watch. "I'd love to stay longer, but we dancers have to get up early. Thank you so much for inviting me."

With a gesture at the art that lined the walls of the apartment, Charlotte became again the gracious hostess and businesswoman. "You can take one of my cards on your way out, should you ever find yourself in the market for something truly unique."

Sloane lifted one disdainful shoulder in lieu of saying goodbye. She and Charlotte threaded their way back to the bar, and I looked for a place to sit. For the second time in less than twelve hours, my feet suffered the fashionable indignity of sky-high heels. If I didn't heed the warning pain from my bunions, they would surely take revenge by keeping me awake all night and tormenting me at rehearsal the next day.

Victor appeared at my elbow. "You look tired. Can I get you anything?"

I stifled a yawn. "A chair would be nice."

He steered me toward an angular white loveseat. Pointing to my empty glass, he said, "Let me get you something to drink. Or would you prefer some coffee and dessert?"

"Thanks, but it's past my bedtime. I'm going to rest my feet and then get going."

He frowned. "It's started to sleet. I'll call a cab for you and let Barbara and Rachel know you left."

I looked out the window. The railing of the wraparound balcony was slick with ice. "Thanks, but I can handle it."

I didn't yet have a good read on Victor. He seemed nice enough, but he was too close to my list of prime suspects for me to feel at ease in his presence, and his wolfish look made me wary. Victor Roth was a prominent lawyer. He had no motive, no means, and no opportunity to kill Maurice. That didn't make me trust him, though. Not with my mother, not with Aunt Rachel, and certainly not with inside information about our murder investigation.

He closed the large gap between us and said, "I saw you talking to Charlotte. Don't judge her too harshly. She's got a good heart."

I handed my empty glass to a passing server. "That's the side of her she shows to you. She was less taken with me."

"You have to get to know her better. She's first and foremost a business-woman. You have to be tough to make in the art world, and she's done it all on her own. I respect her for that."

I was cynical. "Is that what this party is all about? A chance to do business?"

Victor remained genial. "She's on the make. Who isn't? No one goes to these things without trying to capitalize on it. We're here to see and be seen."

I was in no position to question the ethics of conducting business at a funeral reception. My primary motivation in attending Maurice's memorial was to get information on his killer, a goal that wasn't entirely unselfish.

Victor left me, presumably for greener networking pastures, and a cheerful group of young guests drew me in. They recognized me from the life-sized posters outside Lincoln Center and hailed me with an enthusiastic friendliness that was a stark contrast to the general air of indifference I'd encountered from all but a few predatory men.

Jonathan's wife, Leonora, was at the center of this welcoming group. She looked as if she could have been a dancer herself. She asked me what I knew about Maurice's death. Placing delicate fingers on her husband's arm, she said, "You'd think Jonathan, who is on the board of directors, would know more about it. But he knows less than I do."

Jonathan disentangled himself from her grasp. "You'll have to excuse Leonora's ghoulish interest. She used to fancy herself a dancer." He appeared oblivious of his wife's blush.

I was quick to reassure her. "I'm not surprised to learn you have ballet training. I was thinking myself you looked like you could be a dancer."

Leonora was pleased. "Too tall. I ended up a model. Not as much fun, but better money."

"That's for sure." I looked more closely at her delicate features. "I saw you, or rather, saw your picture in the paper last weekend. Ralph Lauren, right?"

She nodded. "That was a good gig. Though the jobs lately are far and few between." She pulled back the skin on her neck, although it showed no signs of sagging. "I'm getting old."

In response to her eager questions, I told her, as if it was privileged information, exactly what had been reported in the newspapers and online. She patted her eyes, which were damp with emotion. "I met Maurice at a photo shoot we did at Charlotte's gallery a few years ago. Everyone from the agency is simply devastated."

I gave her a sympathetic look. "Same here. Although I didn't know him well. Did you?"

She moved closer. "Friend of a friend. The word on the street is that the honeymoon between him and Brett was so over. That's why I was surprised when I found out they were collaborating on this dance project." She raised her eyebrows. "You know, of course, what went down over the summer."

Jonathan gave Leonora a warning look, which she ignored. "Brett and Maurice's marriage wasn't going through a temporary rough patch. It was more serious than that. Huge arguments, bad enough that their neighbors called the police. I know for a fact they were getting a divorce." She briefly placed a forefinger across her lips. "You didn't hear it from me, of course."

Leonora pointed across the room to a tall, blond dancer I knew all too well. "Horace is the friend who told me about the divorce. He models in the off season, which is how we met, at a shoot in the Hamptons. He certainly is a charmer. But don't forget to keep what I told you on the down low."

I promised aloud not to tell anyone, and added a silent rider, *Except for my Choreographers of Crime and the NYPD.*

Before leaving, I again reviewed the conflicting information each conversation yielded. Charlotte believed Brett and Maurice were happily married. Leonora contradicted that rosy assessment by providing details about Brett and Maurice's impending divorce. Jonathan said the value of Maurice's artwork had increased, but Eddie and Nelson claimed the opposite was true. It wasn't much, but I didn't have enough energy to continue. The room was hot with the press of many bodies, and the crowd of people grew so dense I couldn't find either Barbara or Rachel. I texted my mother a goodbye and, with some difficulty, located my coat.

In the gilded, softly lit lobby, a uniformed doorman rose from his perch behind a highly polished desk. "Let me get you a cab. It's pretty icy out there."

The doorman walked outside and across a few feet of pavement. He stepped off the curb and into the street. Squeezing between double-parked cars, he raised a whistle to his lips. Thanks to each of those moves, he was safely beyond the point where he would have been crushed by the body that fell sixteen floors and hit the ice-slicked sidewalk in a swift, brutal, fraction of a second.

Most of what happened immediately after was a blur, which was why I couldn't tell the police how long it was before Tex exited the building to arrive at the scene of the crime.

Chapter Twelve

I am haunted by the need to dance...
—Anna Pavlova

A dark shadow, a faint vibration, and the muffled scream of the doorman. That was all that penetrated Charlotte Dankworth's well-insulated building. With no understanding of what occurred, I hurried to assist the doorman. He pushed me away, retching violently into the street. I jumped aside. Only then did I realize the dark missile that fell from the sky was Eddie, Nelson's cameraman. My knees buckled, and the last thing I remembered was falling against a fire hydrant. The world around me started spinning and then went dark.

Much of what transpired after that shock unfolded as a slow-motion, surreal dream. When I opened my eyes, Tex was by my side. He sounded as if he was speaking from a great distance. I stared at the sidewalk, immersed in a kind of out-of-body experience. My brain wasn't yet ready to process what I'd seen. I didn't know where I was and wondered, with a calmness that later baffled me, if I was dead. Full consciousness didn't emerge until after someone kindly removed me from the sidewalk and placed me on a sofa in the lobby. I was vaguely aware of a doctor's gentle touch. My eyes felt as if heavy weights were keeping the lids closed.

A warm hand pressed against my forehead. "Don't get up."

I squinted to bring the face that hovered above me into focus. The reassuring voice and hand belonged to Dr. Zachary Mitchell.

He waved off an approaching EMT. "I'll take care of her."

In response to the medic's surprised look, he said, "I'm not on duty. Just happened to be passing by."

I rubbed my eyes. "If you're not on duty, what are you doing here?"

He looked across the lobby. I followed his line of sight to where a police officer was questioning his ex-wife. Turning back to me, he said, "Sloane called. But that's not important. We can talk later. The important issue is that bruise on the side of your head. You need to get to the hospital where they can do a better job of checking you out than I can do here."

I flexed my arms and legs and conducted an internal reconnaissance mission. Other than a banging headache and a few bruises, I was fine.

"Thanks, Zach. But dancers instinctively know how to fall without suffering serious damage. Please, take care of someone who needs you more than I do."

He turned me on my side and examined my head. "Thanks for the update. But you conked out on a fire hydrant. You could have a brain bleed. Do you feel dizzy? Nauseated?"

I had more immediate concerns on my mind than questions about my health. "My mother. Can't find her."

Like the magician she is, Barbara materialized out of thin air. "I'm here, Leah."

I clutched her. The memory of Eddie's fall flooded back, and again I felt faint. I pressed one hand against my chest to quell the hysteria that wanted to come out. My tears would do no one any good, least of all Eddie.

"Leah! Leah!" Rachel frantically waved her arms at us. In her haste to get to me, my aunt bustled past Sloane and Charlotte, knocking them out of her way and into a marble pillar. She was haggard with shock. "Eddie fell. People said he'd been drinking heavily. He went out on the balcony to get some fresh air and toppled over the side."

She leaned on Barbara, who wasn't looking any too steady herself. Clutching her stomach, Rachel said, "The floor of the balcony and the guard rail were covered in ice. Eddie—he lost his balance. That's how he f-f-fell." She pulled out a wad of tissues to blot the flow of black, mascara-hued tears.

I struggled to stand. Barbara put one arm around my shoulders and the other around my waist, but her attempt to support me was unequal to her strength. I stumbled back onto the sofa and put my head between my knees. I couldn't stop shivering. Zach picked up a metallic blanket that had slipped off my shoulders and wrapped me in it.

Another voice emerged from the surrounding chatter. It belonged to Jonah, but he wasn't addressing me. "Can she talk?"

Zach answered. "She seems to be okay. Shock, mostly. But she's got a good-sized bruise. Possible concussion. More importantly, I want to rule out a brain bleed."

I fingered the lump on the side of my head. "No hospital. I'm already feeling better."

Jonah turned his back to Zach and bent down so that we were on eye level. "Don't be so stubborn. The doc here wants you to go to the hospital. And so do I. But if you're up to it, I'd like to ask you a few questions first, when what happened is still fresh in your mind."

Zach edged Jonah aside. "Let me take care of you, Leah. Mr. Sobol can wait."

As I struggled to sit without wobbling, Barbara said, "Jonah, uh, Detective Sobol. I agree with Dr. Mitchell. You do your job and let him do his."

Officer Francie Morelli intervened. She corralled Barbara and Rachel, as well as Victor, who'd been hovering in the background. With a firmness of purpose that brooked no dissent, she led them, along with as many people as could fit in the elevator, back up to Charlotte's apartment.

Sloane broke free from the officer interviewing her and descended upon our uneasy threesome. "Zach, thank God you're here. You can't imagine how awful this has all been. Please, darling, let's go home." She took his arm with a possessive air.

Jonah raised his eyebrows at Zach. "Yes, Dr. Mitchell. If there's no one else that needs medical attention, you should take your wife home. I can follow up with her tomorrow."

Zach didn't lose his polite, professional demeanor. Nor did he correct Jonah's deliberate reference to his former spouse as his wife. "Leah, after I drop Sloane off at her place, I'll come to your apartment. It shouldn't be long before I'm free." He ticked off a series of potential symptoms and made me promise to go to the hospital if any emerged. Sloane grew impatient and tugged at him.

He gently pried Sloane's thin, elegant fingers from his arm before walking away with her, as he'd done multiple times in our brief history together. Their divorce was final. But their relationship? That was far from over.

Jonah and I were finally alone, if you didn't count the all the people still milling about the lobby.

My tongue felt thick in my mouth. "What are you doing here?" My brain had cleared enough to remember he had plans to meet Savannah.

He searched my face, as if to ascertain I hadn't suffered any cognitive impairment. "Are you sure you're okay? Obviously, I'm here because I got the call about Eddie. What are you doing here?"

Looking at the beautiful people lingering in the lobby, I said, "I was asking myself the same thing. I don't belong here."

A smile broke through his grim expression. "That wasn't a philosophical question. I meant it literally. You're a witness to Eddie's death. Take your time. I hate doing this, Leah, but anything you can tell me now, while we're at the scene, will help."

A river of tears, which I'd kept dammed up to that point, suddenly broke through. "I-I didn't understand what happened or know what I was seeing. I was in the lobby. I saw a shadow and heard a thud. Eddie missed hitting the doorman by a few feet."

Jonah listened intently. "Before that, when did you see Eddie last? And who was he with?"

I thought back to my conversation with Victor, as well as the one I'd had with Leonora, Jonathan Franklin's beautiful wife. How long had each lasted? "I saw Eddie about a half hour before I left the party. I don't know who he was with or where he went after that. You might want to question the bartender, or one of the servers. Or Nelson Merrill, the filmmaker. He was with Eddie for a good deal of the night."

I tried to visualize the party. "Charlotte's place is huge, with a big dining room and living room, plus a foyer that was large enough to qualify as a separate room. The apartment is a duplex, with a wide staircase, and there were people hanging out on the steps as well. There were so many guests, though, it was impossible to easily track anyone. But I don't recall seeing anyone on the balcony."

Jonah wrote with tense, short strokes. "I haven't been upstairs yet. Let's get back to Eddie. How did he seem? Anxious? Upset?"

I spoke around a painful lump that had taken up residence in my throat. "He seemed fine, other than that he'd had a few drinks too many. But he wasn't staggering around or slurring his words. We had a really nice conversation." Dreading the answer, I asked, "Do you know if it an accident? Did anyone see it happen?"

He put his notebook away. "No witnesses. The last anyone saw him he was in the library, not the main room, and no one remembers if anyone was with him." He dropped his professional mask and looked into my eyes. "You told me a dancer knows how to fall gracefully, but that doesn't make you immune to a concussion. Or worse. Your doctor friend is worried about a brain bleed. Get checked out at the hospital. We can continue this tomorrow. My team will be at the studio first thing in the morning."

I held his arm. "Answer me. Off the record. Was it an accident?"

He rubbed his forehead. "Can't say. Given the fact that his death so closely followed Maurice's, I'm not inclined to think so. Especially when you consider their close working relationship."

I choked, thinking about Eddie's longing to return to California and his shy revelation about his new girlfriend. "I can't think of a single person who could have wanted that nice guy dead."

Jonah waited, as if debating whether or not to speak, before saying, "Then think harder. I'll follow up with you tomorrow, Leah. If you're determined not to go to the hospital, spend the night with your mother. I'll wait for you to call her. I told Morelli to get her statement first."

Cold chills ran down my back. "Do you think the killer might come after me?"

He didn't hesitate. "Yes. If Eddie was murdered, and the killer saw you talking with him, then yes. I do think you could be a target. Which means that everything we talked about other night is off the table. No more investigating for you. You have to step away. Leave it to me."

I didn't answer.

Jonah was insistent. "This killer operates in public places. There is no safe space for you to investigate." He stopped to check his phone. "One more thing. Did you contact Tex tonight? Tell him to meet you here?"

I felt sick. What, or who, had brought Tex to Charlotte's party?

He pointed to my handbag. "I'd like to see your phone."

"Do you have a warrant?"

The corners of his mouth twitched, but he refrained from any obvious show of amusement. "I can get one. Or you could trust me that this is important. Show me all the texts and calls from this evening."

He instructed me to scroll through the messages. I'd missed many texts from family, friends, and, as it turned out, Zach. Jonah skimmed through them and stopped when he got to a funny selfie Olivia sent from Kerry's party. Without comment, he sent it to himself.

His return to inscrutability exasperated me. "This might be easier if you told me what you're looking for."

He enlarged Olivia's picture. "Keep away from your friend Tex."

Cold chills ran down my back. "Tex is innocent. I'm certain of it."

"I know you're upset. In shock. But think about it. Tex's appearance at the party puts him squarely at the scene. If you're right, and he's innocent, then the killer is going to great lengths to pin the murders on him. But if Tex is guilty, he'll use any means possible to keep suspicion from falling on him. That includes using you, or your friend Olivia, as cover. Don't fall for it, Leah."

I didn't argue the point. Nor did I follow his advice to spend the night with Barbara. I needed the peace and quiet of my own apartment. My nerves were at the breaking point. Victor ordered a car, and we drove in near silence, broken by my aunt's sobs. The driver brought me home first. Victor waited in the vestibule of my building, at the foot of the stairs, until I was safely inside.

Zach texted as I walked upstairs, and when I didn't answer immediately, he called me. "I can be at your place in ten minutes. Let me take care of you, Leah."

I unlocked the door and fell onto the bed, too tired to move. "I can take care of myself, but I appreciate the offer."

He persisted. "We've hardly seen each other lately. How about dinner? I'll make reservations someplace special. You love Indian food. I'll take you to Masala Magic."

We agreed on a day and a time. This meeting, I decided, was going to be different from all the others we'd had. So often, I'd resented Sloane's intrusion into my relationship with the handsome doctor, but Zach's close ties to her could prove useful. Sloane would never confide in me, but if I could persuade him to pump her for information, I might be able to gain the kind of insight I'd hoped to get at Charlotte's party.

Given the long and tortured day I'd had, sleep should have come quickly. It didn't.

Chapter Thirteen

Dancers are never alone onstage. Our teachers are always with us...
—David Howard

Tex didn't return my messages until the morning. I was so relieved to hear from him, I nearly dropped the phone into the sink when the screen brightened with the words: **Meet me b4 class?**
I dried my hands and tapped, **LC diner ok? In 45**

He answered with a like. I showered in record time and got to the diner near Lincoln Center precisely forty-five minutes later. The shabby restaurant isn't actually called the Lincoln Center Diner, but given its close proximity to the performing arts complex, it might as well be. The owners catered to performers, audience members, students, and neighborhood people. The servers treated their customers with a signature New York City attitude that combined extreme efficiency with a bottomless cup of sarcasm.

Tex was seated in a booth when I arrived. In front of him was an untouched plate filled with eggs, bacon, toast, and hash browns. I leaned over to hug him, but he stiffly resisted the embrace. The waitress brought coffee. She knew me too well to bother cluttering the tiny table with cream, sugar, or one of their tombstone-sized menus.

I looked up at her. "Thanks, Rita. Nothing else for me."

She didn't miss a beat. "Breakfast is the most important meal of the day. Would it kill you to eat an egg?"

Rita was right, and I was starving. "You win. Two scrambled eggs."

She took my order and nudged Tex's plate closer to him. "Eat up, buddy.

You look like you need it."

He swallowed with visible effort, and she relented. "Lemme get ya something else." When she returned with my eggs, she brought a large blueberry muffin for Tex. "On the house, kiddo." She brushed off his thanks, grabbed a pot of coffee, and began refilling cups, regardless of the diners' desire for more caffeine.

Tex held up his phone. "Explain to me what this is all about."

On the screen was a message: **Need you asap-leah**

I couldn't make sense of what he was showing me. "That's not my number."

He flicked to the next screen, which had Charlotte's address on it, as well as another message that purported to be from me, saying someone had stolen my phone.

Tex's face was stiff with anger and fear. "If you didn't send it, then who did?"

My mind was racing. "Where were you last night?"

"Before I got to the murder scene, I was at Kerry's party. With a million other people. What's going on, Leah?"

The cold dread that had taken hold of me since Maurice's death intensified. "I have no idea. But I'm going to find out." I took out my notebook and jotted down the phone number from Tex's phantom caller. "Tell me all you can remember about Kerry's party. Omit nothing. Who was there, when they were there, what people were doing."

He leaned back and closed his eyes. Like many dancers, he was better at remembering images and movement than conversations. After a minute, he sat up, grabbed my notebook, and began jotting names. When he finished, he tossed it back to me.

"Now you know everything the police do. I hope you can make good use of it. I sure as hell can't. Kerry shares an apartment with two other dancers, and the place was packed. People came and went, and it was too crowded to know if anyone left before I did. I didn't think I'd need an alibi. Or that I'd be asked to provide one for anyone else."

I studied the names. Tex's list was mostly comprised of company dancers, along with a few members of Nelson's camera crew. "We don't know yet what piece of information will end up providing the evidence we need. Tell me what happened after you got the text."

He stared down at the table. "The message sounded urgent. I ran all the way from Kerry's place to Charlotte's. The doorman let me in. When I got to the party, I couldn't find you. Nelson thought you were still there. But your mother said you'd left. I must have just missed you. It was late, and I was wiped out. I figured I'd pack it up and go home." He put down his fork with a trembling hand. "I thought it was a prank. Some joke."

"Yeah. Under other circumstances, it would seem to be a prank, in which case my first instinct would be to tag Horace. He and Kerry have played mean tricks like that before. But I don't think that's what happened."

I didn't doubt Tex's innocence or his veracity. Nonetheless, I made a mental note to confirm his story with Barbara. If there was a way to do so discreetly, I'd also check with Nelson and Horace.

"I send you a box of chocolates, and someone sticks my ballet slippers inside. I go to a party and end up at the scene of a second murder." He buried his face in his hands. "It's like I've been cursed."

His words reminded me of another open question. "When I got the box of chocolates, I wasn't sure you were the one who sent it. You usually wait until opening night."

He looked up. "You were having such a hard time up on that platform. I thought a present from a secret admirer would cheer you up."

I was ashamed of doubting him. "We'll figure this out, and together, we'll make dance history on opening night. Brett's personality may be vile, but his choreography is spectacular."

Tex stretched his lips in a weak imitation of his usual bright smile. "I'm happy you're so optimistic, but I can't ignore the fact that the police questioned me for hours last night. I don't know what to do."

Unlike a thousand other questions he could have asked, the answer to this one was easy. "You eat your breakfast. Then you take company class and rehearse, preferably without dropping me in the middle of our pas de deux. Leave the rest to me."

Madame was in her usual place when Tex and I arrived at the studio. Neither Brett nor Nelson was there. Whether they were detained by the police or by their shared grief, no one knew. Olivia was last to show up, moments before the first pliés. No one questioned the administration's decision to forge ahead with a full day of work. It's what we do.

At the end of class, as we were on our way to check the schedule, Madame stopped us. Her low-pitched, Russian-inflected voice filled the room. "Please to wait, my dancers. I want that you should think with most care about children. They not know about Eddie. Not to tell them, please. We act happy, like we all fine. Official statement has been sent to parents, and they will talk to children. Information must not, my dear dancers, come from you."

Kerry waved her hand, nearly knocking over Olivia, who ducked in time to avoid getting conked on the head. Knowing Kerry, her aggressive hand-waving was probably deliberate. With her blond hair and pale skin she looked like princess, but her ruthless personality was better suited to a dictator of a repressive nation. For once, though, her words were appropriate to the situation. "Madame M. The kids are asking questions. They must already know what happened to Eddie."

The faces around me were grim. Eddie had been a favorite among the children, bringing them hand puppets and sneaking them candy. He'd impressed them as well with his collection of gaming cards, his love of Harry Potter and his unwavering allegiance to Hufflepuff.

Horace forgot to be nice to Kerry, his new partner in *Romeo and Juliet*. "Surely, you can figure that one out. If a kid asks you anything, tell them Eddie left to do another movie."

I exchanged glances with Olivia, who covered her mouth to hide her amusement. Horace's suggestion that we lie to the kids was absurd. They all had cell phones, and most were obsessed with TikTok. Madison Brill had her own YouTube channel, managed by her indefatigable mother. It was likely they knew more than their parents.

Madame was diplomatic. "That thinking come from good heart, Horace. But best not to lie. Best to say you not know and children must practice their dance and not to worry."

This pleased both Kerry and Horace. Madame was a born diplomat. The State Department should appoint her as the ambassador to the United Nations. She was that good.

My beloved teacher had one last word for us before admitting the kids into the room. "Email has been sent to parents, and I will talk with them separately from children." She winced as she stretched her arthritic knees. "Please to remember: There can be no *Nutcracker* performance without little ones. Ballet company depend upon *Nutcracker* to stay in the good finances. America not like other countries. Need to make the money here. Why government not fund our art and pay dancers? This I do not know. But is fact of life."

Madame was not exaggerating the financial importance of the upcoming season. ABC, like most ballet companies, depended heavily upon the revenue that our annual holiday performances provided. We doubled down on our schedule to capitalize on *The Nutcracker's* popularity. As an additional monetary bonus, attendance at the school's open classes soared every January. Like me, many kids who saw *The Nutcracker* during the holiday season fell under the spell of ballet and began dreaming of when they too could perform on that stage.

Madame had one more piece of advice. "We must also look to keeping children protected in their bodies too, yes? I not think they in any danger. But we stay careful of them and of each other. Not to take chances with safety. Best idea is not to be alone."

There was unanimous agreement from the assembled dancers. If any of us harbored different feelings, it wasn't apparent to me. We left the studio filled with renewed purpose and reported to our individual rehearsals. The kids trooped into the classroom we vacated, led by Francie. In a most welcome development, Olga brought up the rear.

The burly woman crushed me in her embrace. "Lelotchka! So happy to see you." She clapped a hand over her mouth and lowered the volume of her booming voice, which nonetheless remained loud enough to make the windows dance in their frames. "We talk later, *tak*? Make the plans."

For the first time since Maurice was killed, my worry about the kids abated. With Madame's trusted friend Olga there, no harm could come to them.

On the surface, nothing changed. But the atmosphere was subtly different, and we lost the easy camaraderie that builds before a big performance. The police interviewed us one by one, interrupting rehearsals and generally keeping us all on edge. Although Eddie's death wasn't in the morning news cycle, it was a trending topic online. The internet exploded with conspiracy theories, and scores of talking heads weighed in with dubious stories and sensationalist accusations.

Traditional news media outlets caught up by the end of the day. Reporters again staked out the sidewalk outside the studio and the theater, and no one was safe from their relentless questions. Dancers who hadn't made their social media accounts private learned the perils of public exposure, as streams of DMs, some of them quite abusive, poured in. The hosts of television and radio talk shows, whose usual topics centered on political outrage, overnight became experts on dance. People who sounded as if their last dance experience was at Dolly Dinkle's School of Ballet rolled out timeworn, and often false, clichés regarding ballet's toll on young people's bodies and psyches.

Savannah Collier, who as a former dancer did qualify as an expert, posted ghoulish tweets that went viral, but the photos she shared disturbed me more than the text. Other than the shots from Maurice's funeral, the pictures were taken inside the studio and the theater, which meant we had a spy in the company. If it wasn't a dancer who gave them to her, the most likely person was a member of Nelson's film crew.

Despite my distaste for Savannah, I didn't wish her any harm. But plenty of others did, including Brett, whose loud, angry reaction penetrated the glass walls of the office. The anxious parents, who were riveted to the news feeds on their phones, barely glanced up, although Brett's favorite vocabulary words, the ones that had caused them such fury a few days earlier, were clearly audible.

My first rehearsal of the day included a dozen other dancers. Olivia was not one of them, as she was scheduled to work on her demi-soloist role in *Romeo and Juliet*. For her sake, I was glad she had a more interesting and high-profile assignment than the one played by the ballerinas that surrounded me in a precise semicircle. They had little to do, other than look pretty and festive. Many swallowed yawns as they stood in B plus position, one foot turned out, and the other crossed neatly behind. I couldn't remember all the names on Tex's list of people who'd attended Kerry's party, but many at that practice session had been there.

While the corps dancers maintained their stiff posture, Tex and I practiced the dramatic pas de deux that is the climax of *The Nutcracker*. Dancing in the studio instead of the theater meant I didn't have to work around the distracting scenery onstage. The outside world melted away, and I made my first entrance not as Leah, the bruised witness to Eddie's death, but as the serenely gracious and elegant Sugar Plum Fairy.

The elation that moving through space gave me faded, as I watched Tex's labored rendition of his variation. Stress robbed him of his usual elastic grace and ease. His pirouettes were rushed and off balance, and his typically light and airy jumps appeared leaden. In the middle of our pas de deux he flubbed the lift, which further flustered him. Instead of soaring into the air, I ended up earthbound, in an awkward, unscripted embrace, as he grabbed at my waist to keep me from falling. This happened twice. On our third attempt, he managed to hoist me over his head, but we didn't win any points for style. Horace watched from the side. Tex's rival radiated contemptuous pleasure.

Brett arrived halfway through the rehearsal. I waited nervously for his usual sarcastic comments, but he remained wordlessly grim throughout our duet. His restraint was probably due to nervousness about opening night. Without a fully functioning Cavalier, the choreographer's much-anticipated premiere would fall on its candy-colored face.

Tex was far superior, in terms of technique and charisma, than the other two dancers slated to perform the role. He was also best-suited to partner me. In a pinch, I could dance with the alternates, but the mismatch, in terms of height, made that pairing a last-ditch option.

Although Brett maintained an attitude of pained forbearance with Tex, he didn't extend that courtesy to the weary women in the corps de ballet. "Ladies! Your arms are supposed to overlap in third position. They're drooping like dead flowers. And quit wobbling, you two in the back. Are you dancers or drunken sailors?"

He walked over to the unlucky twosome and showily surveyed their slender bodies from the rear. "If you were less bottom-heavy, you wouldn't have that problem."

Compared to his worst tirades, these criticisms were relatively mild, although telling a dancer she has to lose weight is never pleasant. People unfamiliar with our world might assume from the dancers' stoic reactions they were immune to Brett's insults. But those assumptions would be wrong. We're trained to keep our pain private. When thwarted or challenged, athletes can grunt, swear, and throw things. Dancers are different. Showing effort or emotion is a sign of weakness that's bred out of us at an early age.

We stood at attention as Brett berated the unhappy targets of his anger. The choreographer was clearly broken over his husband's death, and the dancers were an easy outlet for that ache. Brett's grief was probably made more painful by the fact that he and Maurice had worked together so closely on the *Nutcracker*. The rehearsals were a daily reminder of that loss. In deference to his sorrow, there was none of the typical teasing and easygoing banter on the sidelines that day. Our mood reflected our own misery, as well as the choreographer's.

During the break, I approached Tex, who sat apart from the rest of the dancers. If anyone needed the old *42nd Street* pep talk, it was my beleaguered partner. The iconic words never failed to ignite Olivia and had become our inside joke for tough times.

He stopped me with a raised hand. "I know what you're going to say. I'm sorry about the lift. Don't worry. In performance, I'll be fine. We've pulled it off a thousand times, and we're a great team onstage. But you have to do something for me."

I took off my pointe shoes and rubbed my aching feet. "I'll do anything to help. And don't worry about the lift. Happens to the best of us."

He held up his phone without showing me the screen. "Talk to Olivia. Ask her to back off. She's a nice kid, but I have enough problems right now."

My heart sank. "I don't know how involved the two of you were before Maurice died. But you should be the one to tell her you want to break it off. You're not in the sixth grade. Man up, Tex."

He turned his gaze to the middle of the studio. Horace had taken advantage of the empty space to reel off a series of turns, which he executed with speed and precision. A gaggle of young dancers clapped when he was done, and he gave them a fake-humble bow.

I jiggled Tex's arm to get his attention. "Don't do this. You're not like Horace. He should come with the kind of warning label found on cigarette packs. Something along the lines of him being deadly to ballerinas' emotional health and well-being."

Tex bent double over his outstretched legs and pulled at his feet. "You're right. I'm not like Horace. That's why I don't want to involve Olivia in the mess I'm facing. I know she means well. Please do me this favor. You're her friend."

I was not eager to get in the middle of Tex's complicated relationship with Olivia. The most likely outcome was they would both end up resenting me. "Olivia is one of the kindest and most loyal people I've ever met. You could use a friend. Someone you could trust. I'm sure you know how much she cares about you."

He looked at me and through me. "If she cared that much, she'd respect how I feel and leave me alone."

During my next break, I stopped by the kids' studio, where Madame was overseeing their progress. The parents were lined up on the benches in the hallway outside the classroom, elbowing each other in an attempt to see through the one-way glass.

Evelyn Brill grabbed my arm with aggressive force. When she wasn't posting videos about Madison, bragging about Madison, or nagging Madison, she knitted. This constant exercise must have made her fingers unusually strong. Her intensity unnerved me.

She put her mouth to my ear. I tried to pull away from the unsolicited intimacy, but she held tight. "Who is that—that woman?" She loosened her grip to point at Olga. "She looks dangerous. I've told management I don't want her near my child. Especially now. I don't trust her."

I shook myself loose. "That is Olga Shevchenko, the woman who would lay down her life to protect your kid. But don't annoy her. She doesn't like most adults." The last part of what I said wasn't true, but I didn't want the angry mother to harass Olga.

Evelyn aimed her phone at Olga and snapped a picture. "I have my eye on her. And on you."

My large Ukrainian friend, seemingly unaware of Evelyn's hostility, bounded over to us. "Lelotchka! We are allies again, with the big plans, no?"

I spoke in an undertone. "It's not a good idea to talk about this now."

Olga's answer made me ashamed of underestimating her. Her sunny façade hid a steely intelligence, and she was as smart as she was strong. With a gentle gesture she drew me aside, to an alcove in the hallway.

"No, my dear little friend. I think you wrong about that. Best not to keep too quiet about why I am here. Olga need people to know children protected by me. Bad guys stay away if they know they not stand chance." She thumped her chest. "No harm to them with Olga here." She gave me a wink and pointed to Evelyn. "That lady, she not like me. She ask all kind questions."

I glanced at Madison's mother, who was watching us with undisguised interest. "That's Evelyn Brill. What did you tell her?"

Olga exhaled with a sound that was part grunt, part snort. "I tell her I live in Brighton Beach. That I work for good guys." She winked again. "Most of the time. Must pay bills!"

I laughed at Olga's impish rejoinder. The Brighton Beach section of Brooklyn where Olga lived had so many people from her homeland, it had come to be known as Little Odessa. Things weren't all borscht and blintzes in this heavily Ukrainian and Russian outpost, though. It was also a center of the Russian mob. I had no clear knowledge of what Olga did when she wasn't engaged in helping Madame and me. She once described herself as a cleaning lady. Neither she nor Madame, to whom she was devoted, ever explained in any detail the kinds of cleaning that required Olga's specialized services.

She grasped my hands, cracking the bones. "Madame say you must rest tonight. She worried about you, Lelotchka. But we meet tomorrow."

I flexed my fingers and hugged her. *"Dah."*

Chapter Fourteen

My ballets belong to my dancers and to the public...
—Maurice Béjart

An unusual amount of activity inside the glass-walled main office drew my attention, as I waited for the elevator at the end of the day. Bobbie was there, along with her team of seamstresses. Her face was red, and she looked angry, but this was typical for the passionate costume mistress. Brett looked as if he was on the verge of a nervous collapse. Jonah didn't appear to see me, but my phone buzzed with a text from him. **Café Figaro in 15?**

I was exhausted and had long since sweated off my makeup, but the promise of new information was too tempting to pass up. I tapped **Ok** and headed to one of my favorite places in the city.

Mrs. Pizzuto ushed me in with her customary enthusiasm. She led me to a table in the back. "Detective Sobol told me to save your usual place."

The room, as always, was full. A few of the customers did a double take when I walked by, which wasn't uncommon at the Café Figaro. The walls were lined with photographs, most of them of me. Several years earlier, I posed for Mrs. Pizzuto's daughter as part of a portfolio she submitted to the School of Visual Arts. The kid had talent. She got a full scholarship, and I earned a place as an honorary member of the family.

Mrs. Pizzuto patted me on the shoulder. "I like that man of yours, Leah."

"He's not my man, Mrs. Pizzuto."

She frowned. "He should be. What's taking so long?"

"No comment."

She threw me a pitying look and left to tend to her customers. With the amount of time before Jonah was due to arrive down to three minutes, I hastily repaired the ravages of the day and previous night. I smoothed some color on my pale, chapped lips and released my hair from the pins that kept it nailed in a tight bun.

Mrs. Pizzuto returned with a double espresso and two glasses of water. She also had a plate of pignoli cookies. "Fresh out of the oven."

The scent of sugar was intoxicating. And, for me, toxic. "Thanks, Mrs. Pizzuto. But opening night is less than a week away. Get back to me when you start serving celery sticks."

She put the plate on the table. "These cookies taste better than celery. They're Detective Sobol's favorite."

She was as inexorable and predictable as the tides. I compromised by eating one and pushing the rest to the opposite side of the table. Free of the cookies' distracting fragrance, I reviewed the notes on my phone, crosschecking them against handwritten observations penned over the last few days. So much had taken place in such a short time I hardly knew how to organize my fractured thoughts, let alone a plan of action.

Mrs. Pizzuto reappeared with another steaming cup of coffee. "Look who's here!" She gave me a knowing look.

Jonah sat down. "Thanks, Mrs. Pizzuto. These are my favorite cookies."

She looked at me and beamed. "I told you so. I'll get you a cannoli to go with them." She stepped behind a gleaming counter to fill a crisp cylinder of dough with heaping spoonfuls of thick, creamy, chocolate-flecked filling.

Jonah had dark circles under his eyes. He hunched over the table, drank some coffee, and ate three cookies before leaning back to survey me. "Thanks for meeting at such short notice. I was worried about you. How's your head?"

Eddie's horrific death had made me forget about my injury. I felt for the lump, which was not as painful as it looked. "It's getting better. Nothing to worry about."

He reached across the narrow table and brushed back my hair to examine the bruise. "I'm so sorry you had to go through this, Leah. I promise not to keep you long, but I need whatever information you can give me."

I clasped my hands to keep them from trembling. "I'm not sure I can tell you anything you don't know, but I'll try. Brett spent most of his time in the library, away from the main room. Charlotte said the party was too much for him, which makes sense, since the place was packed. Jonathan Franklin and Nelson argued, but it was a one-sided debate. Jonathan hates Nelson for a movie he did that investigated a fire in one of the Franklin family buildings. Eddie worked on the film, but Jonathan didn't mention him."

I checked the list in my notebook. "Nelson agreed to do the movie about Maurice as a favor to his old friend. Most of the time, he does true crime, mostly cold cases. According to Eddie, Nelson never got over the death of his girlfriend, who died when an arsonist set fire to her dorm room, but that was years ago. The thing that pops out at me is that Horace, like Tex, started the night at Kerry's party but ended up at Charlotte's. Were you able to identify the person who messaged Tex?"

"Burner phone. If Tex is innocent, someone's going to a lot of trouble to make him the fall guy. The chocolate box with the bloody ballet shoes seems to suggest that the person trying to pin the murder on him is a company member. Would anyone, other than a dancer, know they could fold up so small? I sure didn't. An added complication is that you didn't open the box until two days after you got it."

The coffee cup slipped from my fingers, and half the liquid splashed onto the table. "I didn't think much about it at the time, but the ribbon was loose, and the box wasn't where I left it. That proves someone tampered with it after Tex dropped it off. Is it possible the murderer's goal is to destroy Tex? That he's the real target of this violence?"

Jonah rubbed his eyes. "Tex could have set himself up, along with plausible alibis that appear to exonerate him."

He ate the last of the cookies, and Mrs. Pizzuto placed a cannoli on the empty plate. "Mrs. Pizzuto, will you marry me?"

"I'm a married lady." She lifted her eyebrows a full two inches in my direction. "Not like some people."

I don't often blush, but my face did get rather warm. Avoiding Jonah's eyes, I said, "Did you get any usable fingerprints off the chocolate box?"

"Tex's, Francie's, the kid's, and yours." In response to my exasperated look, he said, "There's also a few we haven't yet identified. I'm not at liberty to say more."

"Who are your prime suspects? I need names, Jonah. Names and possible motivation."

He took out his notebook. "There's plenty of motive to go around. From a monetary perspective, Brett benefits most. He's set to inherit a bundle, aside from getting most of Maurice's artwork."

"What about Charlotte? Won't she benefit as well?"

He frowned. "The benefit to Ms. Dankworth isn't as clear. Theoretically, the dramatic nature of Maurice's death, and the fact that his works are now finite, should elevate the value of his art. On the other hand, he's no longer around to increase the number of items that could be sold."

Jonah's assessment was similar to Barbara's. This came as no surprise. Although my mother's writing career engulfed her in intense relationships with fictional characters, she was razor-sharp in her dealings with the real world.

I gratefully accepted another hit of caffeine from Mrs. Pizzuto. "Last night, when I asked you who could have a motive to kill Eddie, you annoyingly told me to figure it out. Do you think it has to do with something he might have seen or filmed?"

"Yes. Which means the second murder was a coverup for the first and not part of the original plan. But that still leaves more questions than answers." His voice became more urgent. "I don't know if the person who killed Eddie planned to do so before the party. Or maybe Eddie said something, knowingly or not, that made the killer suspect he was a threat. That's why I need you to think carefully about what he told you and who might have overheard him."

I related as much as I could remember from what transpired at Charlotte's party. "Leonora Franklin, Jonathan's wife, told me what we all suspected, which was that Brett and Maurice were planning a divorce. Eddie confirmed Maurice's problems with his career."

I stopped to recheck my notes. Something didn't fit, but I couldn't figure out what it was, and said, "Eddie had a new girlfriend. Someone he really liked. Do you know who that was?"

Jonah put down his pen. "We'll have to do this more often. Unfortunately, I have to get back to work. Farrow and I are going through all the footage Eddie and the rest of the camera crew filmed."

I stayed seated. "You didn't answer my question about Eddie's girlfriend."

"I know."

I kept my temper. "If you won't tell me who she is, then tell me where you were last night. You were at the crime scene minutes after it happened."

I was curious to see if he would admit to meeting Savannah. I wasn't jealous, of course. Merely curious.

Jonah didn't return my gaze. Instead, he turned to a large photograph on the opposite wall. It was one of the pictures Mrs. Pizzuto's daughter had taken of me. I preferred the studio portraits, where I wore an immaculate costume, with perfect makeup and my hair cemented into a neat bun. The one he chose to study was taken in Central Park on a chilly day. I was dressed in a ratty tutu, my hair was loose and messy, and my eyes looked too big for my face. Although I didn't like the haunted expression she'd captured, I knew it was Jonah's favorite.

I grew impatient. "Are you going to answer my question or not?"

"I was with Eddie's girlfriend last night."

Few answers could have startled me more. "Savannah? She was Eddie's girlfriend?"

He opened his eyes in mock surprise. "Why did you ask me where I was when you already knew?" He signaled Mrs. Pizzuto for the bill and said, "Let me offer you some professional advice. If you're going to eavesdrop, make sure your reflection isn't visible to the person you're tailing."

I dug in my purse for cash. I didn't have enough money to cover my part of the tab, which thwarted my plan to toss a few bills on the table and stalk out. It's not as dramatic a gesture when you have to ask for a preferred cash app.

Despite that minor detail, I maintained my dignity. "Thanks for the information. I know you're busy, so I won't keep you any longer."

He sat back and crossed his arms. "I don't know why you're angry. Interviewing people is part of my job."

My mood was not conducive to detached, psychological analysis. "I'm not angry. There are few people I dislike more than Savannah, but if you took advantage of her to interrogate her, that is completely unethical. Was she aware that your interest was purely professional? Or was it more personal than you're letting on? She's attractive, if you like that type of woman."

He grinned. "You can relax. We didn't have sex. Not one kiss. All business. No pleasure."

My teeth clenched at the thought of him kissing her smug face. "You're quite the gentleman. I'm sure your mother would be proud."

Jonah dropped his amused attitude. "I noticed your doctor friend was at the crime scene almost as quickly as I was. It must be nice to have so personal a physician."

I hadn't called Zach. It was Sloane who had summoned him, but I was too irked to clarify the situation. "Zach and I are friends. Nothing more."

"Then I'll ask you the same thing you asked me. Does the good doctor understand your relationship status? Because from what I observed, it didn't look that way."

Chapter Fifteen

The creative process is not controlled by a switch...
—Alvin Ailey

I left the Café Figaro angry, edgy, and hungry. I stopped by the corner deli for supplies, but again, I was thwarted. Mr. Kim, who owned the store and never failed to save me a stash of my preferred brand of sugarless candy, had none.

He was apologetic. "Sorry, Missy. Maybe tomorrow. Maybe next week." He pointed to the freezer in the back of the store. "But I got your meals. Better to eat food. That candy no good for you."

He was right. I picked out a few low-calorie, zero-taste microwave packages of theoretically Indian food and brought them to the counter. Mr. Kim was one of my favorite people in the neighborhood. He rarely left his tiny bodega, and it was a point of pride to him that during the worst weather, including hurricanes, blizzards, and blackouts, his door was always open. When I most needed a friend, he helped me out, leaving his beloved perch behind the counter to make sure I was safe.

More difficult than the trek up to my apartment was the next chore of that trying day. I texted Olivia, half-hoping she wouldn't answer. Three dots danced in response and then died. She phoned a few minutes later.

Without preamble, she said, "Did you talk to Tex?"

I peeled itchy athletic tape off my knee and did a few easy stretches. "He told me to tell you he can't get involved right now. That he has to figure things out for himself."

In response to her silence, I said, "My advice is to give him some space. The police suspect him of murder, he's preparing for the biggest performance of his career, and Horrible Horace is breathing down his neck. One false move, and it's Horace who makes his debut at the Cavalier, and Tex who goes back to the corps."

My motives were not completely selfless, and Olivia deserved the truth. "My career is as much at risk as Tex's. If anything happens to him, Brett might also replace me. Kerry is a much better match for Horace. Both are tall, blond, and gorgeous. Central Casting couldn't find two dancers who look more like Sugar Plum and her Cavalier."

When Olivia didn't break her silence, I checked to see if she was still on the line. The seconds continued to tick by. "Olivia, is there something you're not telling me?"

Her voice trembled. "I was in the wings, on the opposite side of the stage, when Tex came in and found Maurice's body. So I know he didn't do it. He couldn't have. Maurice was already dead when he got there."

My pulse quickened. "What else did you see?"

She sounded miserable. "I didn't see anyone other than Tex. The police questioned me over and over. But that's all I know."

I grabbed my notebook and sketched a rough outline of the stage. "Nice try, but you couldn't have seen Tex from the opposite side of the stage. The scenery would have been in the way. Come clean, my friend. I hope you didn't lie to the police in an effort to clear Tex."

Again, that maddening silence. "Olivia. You have to be straight with me. Without the truth, I can't help you or Tex."

I grabbed an instant meal, tossed the package into the microwave, and waited for the chime of the timer to signal dinner. "You're not thinking clearly. I don't blame you. I also haven't been thinking clearly. Tex must have seen something or heard something. Maybe Tex doesn't want to talk to you because he doesn't want to implicate you."

She was indignant. "He couldn't possibly think I had anything to do with Maurice's murder."

My heart raced. "I know that. He knows that. The police don't know that.

And Tex may be seeking to protect you from the killer, as well as the police."

Her voice was thick with emotion. "What are you planning? And don't try to put me off. I saw you and Olga whispering. What are you not telling me?"

The microwave beeped three times before I heard it. "Sit tight and trust me. I'll let you in as soon as I can convince the others."

Olivia didn't hide her resentment. "Why should I trust you when you don't trust me?"

With anyone other than Olivia, I would have dropped the call. But we were friends. Good friends. I didn't want to add to her pain, but I couldn't overlook her attempt to obscure the truth. Her motives were good, but her approach was not. "It's going to be tough to convince the others they should include you in our investigation if you're not willing to trust us with the truth."

She sounded as if she was crying. "That's so unfair. They don't want me? Screw them and screw you."

The following evening, the Choreographers of Crime, with the exception of my sister, again met at Madame's apartment. Melissa was a victim of the capricious and mysterious New Jersey Transit train system. Although she'd promised to arrive early, her train was stuck outside Penn Station.

Rachel wagged her finger. "I hope Melissa gets here soon. We could use her brains."

As if to console me for my missing sister, Froufrou jumped onto my lap. I pet her silky fur, and she rewarded me by promptly falling asleep.

The dog's steady breath and warm body helped me stay calm. "With Melissa or without her, we have to get down to business. But before we begin, I want to once again request that we include Olivia."

I recounted most of my conversation with her to them but left out the part where she lied. I didn't want to waste time defending her.

Olga was quick to respond. "I say yes for poor girl. We must include."

Madame M's opposition surprised me. "Lelotchka, I not like to go against your wishes. I think we give Olivia job to do but not full confidence in what we plan. Is for her safety. Can we do the compromise?"

I was unsure of how that would work. "Olivia wants to protect Tex, but in doing so she could be exposing herself to the killer, who may see her as a threat. Without our support, she's on her own. Let's not forget, she was at the scene of the crime seconds after Tex."

Olga said, "I watch over Olivia like strong hawk. Lelotchka, you must talk to her and do as Madame say. Let Olga take care of situation."

The doorbell rang, and Barbara and I went with Madame to help her carry the food. Madame does not cook. In her words: "I not ask chef to run rehearsal and she not ask me to run kitchen."

I wasn't much better than Madame, as I used my oven as a repository for extra leotards and tights. The stovetop was sufficient to boil eggs, brew coffee, and heat soup. I'm not completely helpless in the kitchen. My microwaving skills are top notch.

To my great joy, Melissa came in on the heels of the delivery guy. She hugged me tightly. Leaving the others to set the table without us, my sister drew me aside. "Bernie, we need to talk." Bernie was the code name we used when we plotted together.

The tension that knotted the muscles in my neck and shoulders eased. "Whatever it is, I'm in."

She spoke quickly. "We've got way too many people going around in their individual circles. You and I need to figure this out. And quickly. I couldn't sleep last night, worrying about you. I told David I was going to stay with you, so we can plot all night long if we have to. I hope that's okay?"

Tears sprang to my eyes. I was struck, once again, with how wonderful it was to have Melissa as my sister. "That sounds perfect. And in case I haven't mentioned this recently, I love you."

We took our seats in the dining room. The last time we sat around the table, we put aside discussions about the murder. This time, Madame said, "You all must pardon these not good manners. But Lelotchka, she have strenuous time in rehearsals, and we must quickly make plan so she can rest."

After some debate over details, I summed up our conclusion and theories. "If Tex and Olivia are, as I believe them to be, innocent bystanders, that leaves Brett as the most likely suspect. As Maurice's husband, he had the most compelling motive, both personally and financially. As for our other suspects, Charlotte Dankworth might benefit financially from the increased value of Maurice's artwork, but not to the point of committing murder. Nelson Merrill had close ties to Maurice and Eddie, but he didn't benefit. Their deaths were an unqualified loss for him and his film."

Melissa shut her eyes, which is how she got her genius brain cells to leap into action. After a moment, she sat up and said, "I agree that Brett has the best motive, but it's too early to dismiss anyone. There are others, besides Charlotte and Nelson, who might have had a compelling reason to want Maurice dead."

I put a glass of cool water to my forehead, trying to fend off the exhaustion of the day. "I'm not crossing anyone off the list. If we can't come up with a strong enough motive in the present, we should look to the past. Nelson got his start in documenting crime stories when his girlfriend died in suspicious fire. There might be something in that. Victor and Jonathan are around Maurice's age, have known him for years, and are in the same social orbit. They might have some connection."

Gabi pushed a mound of rice and some vegetables on my plate. "What possible connection could there be between an art dealer, a filmmaker, a lawyer, and a real estate mogul? And what would motivate any of them to act after so many years have passed?"

Barbara said, "They don't all have to connect. One intersection might be all we need. As for the passage of time, someone could have been harboring vengeful feelings that stayed dormant for years, until something triggered him or her into action. That happens in my book *Homicide and Hamlet*."

Rachel said, "If my sister can put aside her fictional stories, I think we should explore Charlotte Dankworth's history with Maurice. We can visit her gallery and invite Victor to come with us."

Gabi was put out. "What am I supposed to do? I need a job."

Melissa said, "Can you get off work for the next few days?"

My friend brightened. "Yes. I teach advanced ballet in the morning, but I can get a sub for the afternoon classes."

Melissa put her arm around Gabi and said, "Madame, meet your new assistant." She turned to the rest of us. "With Olga responsible for Olivia and the kids, that leaves Madame without protection. She's got to have someone with her at all times. Who better than Gabi, who knows the dancers and can also help with rehearsals?"

Madame nodded her approval. "Melissa, you have the brains. Excellent idea it is you have."

My sister regarded each of us in turn. "The closer we get to the killer, the more dangerous it will be for Madame, Olivia, and Leah. Let's not forget that a lot of the evidence points to a dancer as the guilty person. Today's meeting should begin with how we're going to keep them safe."

Barbara tapped her fingers on the table in a nervous dance. "Leah is still without an assigned protector." She leaned over to squeeze my shoulder. "Don't you worry. I'll stick to your side and keep you safe."

Rachel, not to be outdone, said, "Me too. I'll come too."

This was getting out of hand. Having my mother and aunt in constant attendance was likely to end in me protecting them instead of the other way around.

I pretended to mull over Barbara's offer. "I appreciate your willingness to put yourselves in danger to protect me, but Jonah will have half the police department at the theater. You and Rachel will stick out like sore thumbs, since I'm a little old to have my mom and aunt babysitting me."

My whip-quick mother didn't need one second to come up with a solution. "There are two dozen parents sitting in the audience watching rehearsals. No one's going to mind one more."

Rachel added, "Make that two more. And I can help! After all, I'm a former dancer, and I taught for many years." Her cheeks were pink with excitement. "I didn't know there were any job openings at the company. I think Madame should use me, instead of Gabi, to help during rehearsals."

Sometimes the bonds of familial love can feel more like a stranglehold than an embrace. That was one of those times.

With an apologetic glance at me, Melissa said, "This idea will work if Barbara and Rachel stay in the audience and don't interact or interfere with

Leah or the other performers. They can question the parents, who may have information on what went down on the day Maurice was killed."

I was not thrilled with my sister's plan, but it did make objective sense. Barbara and Rachel needed no theatrical skill to act like two meddling ladies. "Start with Evelyn Brill. I don't like her, and I suspect you won't either. She's brash, abrasive, and like a caricature of an ambitious ballet mother. But she's smart and observant. Not much escapes her."

Having achieved a workable compromise, Melissa and I headed home. Walking up five flights of stairs was a lot more fun with my sister than it was when I was by myself. She exaggerated her breathlessness and pretended to pass out on the third-floor landing. We laughed uncontrollably, and it wasn't until Mrs. Pargeter, in apartment 3A peeked disapprovingly from behind the chain lock that we were able to compose ourselves sufficiently to get to the top.

I dropped my heavy bag the minute we got inside and filled two glasses with water. When I opened the fridge for a wedge of fresh lemon, my sister looked disapprovingly at the contents inside. "Are you serious? There's nothing in here." She held up a plastic container. "Here's an important safety tip: Lettuce is supposed to be green. This is probably crawling with salmonella."

I opened the cupboard and took out a bottle of wine. "The important items are in good supply."

We got into sweats and wooly socks and settled in as if we were still kids, and the topic was the latest boy band and not murder. Melissa took out her laptop and started strategizing.

I fell asleep.

Chapter Sixteen

I may not dance your dances or speak your language...
—Maya Angelou

The smell of freshly brewed coffee woke me up. Melissa handed me a cup and said, "I'm taking an early train home so I can finish some work and spend time with the kids. You're on your own today, but starting tomorrow, I will be your shadow. Do you remember anything of what I told you last night?"

"Not exactly." I looked out the window at a scrubby patch of brown weeds in the back of the building. When the landlord advertised an empty apartment, she included "backyard" in the slender list of amenities. This was an optimistic appraisal at best.

Melissa was forgiving. "I didn't think so. I left you detailed instructions and emailed the others what they need to do."

I tried not to show my impatience. "We need concrete clues. Like fingerprints, or secret compartments, or bloodstained hankies. All this psychological detection is getting us nowhere."

"You're not wrong, but you're not right, either. That other stuff you're talking about, the footprints and DNA evidence? The police have that covered. We've got different strengths that, in the end, will lead us to the killer. And when we find who committed these terrible acts, the police and the lawyers will handle the rest."

I opened the door to my newly clean refrigerator. "I'll do my best. But I'm concerned about Rachel. I've seen tropical storms that were more subtle than she is."

She finished wiping down the counter, which I thought was clean, but apparently didn't meet her high sanitary standards. "Don't worry so much. I explained things to her in a way I think will work."

I drank some coffee, which, thanks to her Melissa-magic, was far better than any cup I'd ever made. "Did you pit Barbara and Rachel against each other? Because the only thing that will work is having them vie for some imaginary prize."

"I told them if they said the wrong word to the wrong person, they could get you killed. I believe that will do the trick. It has the added advantage of being the truth." She dragged a heavy garbage bag to the door. Judging from the smell, the rotting food that lived in my fridge had found a new home. "Take a cab home after rehearsal. Don't go anywhere or do anything. I'll call you tonight."

"I might be late."

She took my chin in her hand. "What are you not telling me?"

I squirmed away. "Nothing important. Or dangerous. I'm meeting Zach after rehearsal."

She drew her brows together. "I like him, and Barbara adores him, but I thought your relationship with Zach was over. When did you see him last?"

I pulled a pair of clean tights and a leotard from the oven. "After Charlotte's party. He called and invited me to dinner. We're still friends. No big deal."

In response to her skeptical look, I admitted, "I do have an ulterior motive, aside from friendship. Zach's ex-wife is close with Charlotte. I'm going to ask him to pump her for information. I'd go directly to the source, but I doubt Sloane will agree to a girls' night out with me any time soon."

Melissa took out a broom and dustpan. "I have to think about this. It doesn't seem ethical to play on his feelings for you."

Her criticism was uncomfortably close to the one I'd leveled at Jonah regarding his treatment of Savannah. "You have my permission to discuss the ramifications of this moral dilemma with your students. But two people are dead. And the killer has tried to frame an innocent person. We're not talking about some ivory tower philosophical problem."

She dropped the broom and picked up her phone. "I'll call Dad and discuss it with him."

I grabbed her hand. "Do not call Dad. You and he will spend the next two months debating the ethics of a harmless dinner with a friend. I spent my entire childhood a prisoner of what Kant would do or say. This is a time for action."

She put her phone down. "I can't call him yet, since he's three hours behind us. But you should call him. He said he hardly ever hears from you."

"I promise to call him, but I don't promise to tell him anything about our investigation. I'm worried about his health. In an ideal world, he would divorce Ann, leave LA, and come back to New York, where he belongs. You've seen him behind the wheel of a car. I shudder to think of him navigating the freeway."

She picked up her bag and kissed me. "If we had a year or three, we could discuss our parents' relationships. But I have to go. I'll text later. In the interim, I'll tell you the same thing I told Rachel. Saying the wrong thing to the wrong person could get you killed."

When I got to the theater, several dancers were taking turns on stage and filming each other. I'd been lagging in my social media posts, so I joined the line. Self-promotion had become the bane of my existence, and posting occasional cheery selfies with other ballet dancers was no longer sufficient to sate the digital demand. We now had to blast daily updates on how wonderful we were, including the days when we felt somewhat south of perfect. Not doing so was risky. More and more, the managers at ABC scrutinized our online popularity as part of whatever metric they used to assess our value to the company.

The more content we provided, the more followers we got, the higher our profile. After Maurice's murder, the administration suggested a brief hiatus from the more blatant forms of self-promotion, but most dancers went back to feeding the publicity monster a day or so later. Post-funeral posts included dedications to Maurice, which ended up garnering even more attention.

I warmed up while I waited my turn. When the stage cleared, I handed my phone to the dancer behind me. I wasn't ready for fouettés, the turns in which one legs whips around and spins you. I opted instead for some showy hops on pointe and ended with a series of piqué turns. To my surprise, I did four revolutions in the last one and finished with a flourish. This accomplishment earned general acclaim.

Five dancers followed me in quick succession. Brett interrupted the sixth, calling for us to take our places in the complicated last section of the ballet. I stepped onto the moving stairs, locked my right leg in an arabesque pose behind me, and stared fixedly into the wings. Thanks to many hours of practice, I'd become, if not comfortable, at least not frozen with fear when I had to dance on the platform. Nonetheless, I couldn't escape a pervasive, creeping anxiety that had dogged me since Maurice was killed.

I wasn't alone in the fight against a growing sense of dread. People had begun to speak of the production as cursed. The sense of camaraderie that never before failed to unify us in the days leading up to opening night was missing, and we scrutinized each other with uneasy watchfulness.

Lives spent onstage are precarious. We're all one injury, or one birthday, away from the unemployment line. This fear partly explains dancers' superstitiousness. Unlike actors, we never tell each other to break a leg. Instead, we say *merde,* which, given the current situation, was increasingly apropos. We also have our individual quirks. Some dancers clutch special tokens or mutter words that are magical to them. Live performances are unpredictable, and these rituals give us the illusion of control.

The music stopped sixteen counts into my solo. I waited on the narrow platform and practiced to the music in my head, trying to block out Brett's argument with the conductor. As their debate over tempo dragged on, the dancers relaxed out of their poses. The musicians in the pit chatted quietly. The kids, most of whom were seated on one side of the stage, fidgeted and whispered. Madison and Ethan, however, were perched above the rest. I couldn't see them from my position atop the platform, but from the audience's perspective, they would appear to be floating on a glittering cloud.

Nelson, with a new assistant in tow, took advantage of the lull to talk to the kids. It was his first appearance at ABC since Eddie's horrific death. He looked ten years older than the last time I saw him. Watching him shoot from multiple angles, I thought about Jonah's advice to think harder about a motive for Eddie's death. Perhaps the killer believed incriminating evidence had been captured on film.

My mouth went dry. What if Nelson, and not Eddie, had been the intended target the night of Charlotte's party? The night was dark, the two men were similar in build, and Nelson hadn't been wearing his signature glasses.

Jonah surely knew Nelson might be in danger. But did he know Nelson was back at work? The spotlights suddenly brightened, and I could see nothing beyond the perimeter of the stage. Ignoring the music, which resumed at a spitefully funereal pace, I raced down the stairs.

Brett yelled, "Sugar Plum! Get back up there right now!"

I called out into the dark audience, "Be right back."

Francie was in the wings on stage left. Reluctant to ask the police officer to abandon the kids to watch over Nelson, I searched in the shadowy backstage area for Olga.

I grabbed Kerry. "Find Olga and get her here asap. She's probably in the audience with Madame."

Kerry waved her hand to keep me away. "Tell her yourself. I'm your understudy, not your slave."

I packed as much urgency as possible into a whisper. "This is so important, I'm asking you for a favor. Do it. Now."

With a show of annoyed reluctance, she exited, hopefully, to do as I asked.

I clambered back up the platform. Despite the delay, the Kingdom of the Sweets scene unfolded with relatively few technical glitches. Tex was steadier, the corps de ballet sharper, and the kids more confident. I didn't cover myself with glory, but I didn't embarrass myself, either. Olga arrived as the Waltz of the Flowers began. I told her to guard Nelson, which helped me concentrate on my dancing and not on potential threats to life and limb.

We took our final poses as the music ended in a stirring crescendo. The parents, who had seen the ballet dozens of times, clapped, none louder than Barbara, who was in an aisle seat. Rachel threw in a few loud whistles.

Tex and I gestured gracefully to Madison and Ethan as the lights around the adult dancers dimmed, and a spotlight glowed above the kids. The curtain came down, and I hurriedly took my place for the first round of bows and curtseys. These were choreographed as precisely as the ballet itself. Depending on how much applause we got, the curtain calls could go on for many minutes. In my opinion, too many minutes. Management insisted the audience would feel cheated if they didn't get to clap until their hands were raw. The closing bows, however, had to wait. Brett insisted we begin again, starting with my variation. Some dancers retreated to the wings, and others scrambled to take their places onstage.

That's when the lights went out, and the screaming started. People rushed madly about the pitch-dark theater, trampling each other in their fear and confusion. I held my arms in front of me to protect my face and inched toward the back of the stage. Someone violently pushed me, and I stumbled into the back curtain. My heart was pounding, but I made no sound as I felt my way to a ladder that led to the aerie where Madison and Ethan had been sitting. I climbed the hidden stairs and called their names. But they were no longer there.

Chapter Seventeen

Dance it and breathe it and be it...
—Wendy Whelan

When the theater went dark, we didn't know if the power grid in the entire city had gone down, or if the outage was confined to Lincoln Center. Several cool-headed people opened the side doors, although fading daylight from the alleyway did little to illuminate most of the theater. The dancers didn't have their phones, but the stagehands did. Tiny dots and shallow beams flicked through the black space. Disembodied voices cried out for help. People rushed madly about, crashing into each other and shrieking when they made contact.

Frozen with indecision, I crouched atop the glittering stage set, where Madison and Ethan were supposed to be sitting. If I remained where I was, and a predator climbed up the ladder, I could escape only by leaping off. My fear of heights was, for once, appropriate, as a fall would almost certainly end my dance career.

While I pondered an exit strategy, faint vibrations shook the structure, and I became dizzy and lightheaded. I clung to the railing, trying to persuade my body I was still on solid ground. Although tempted to descend, I feared greater peril from the faceless mob below. A twisted ankle or broken bone would put me out of commission for the entire season, possibly longer.

I ran my hand over the ladder. The top section fit snugly into a deep notch, but it wasn't bolted in place. If anyone tried to climb it, I could flip the ladder and send a potential attacker crashing to the ground. Secure in the knowledge I could protect myself, I decided to stay put. Let someone else find the two missing kids. Madison and Ethan weren't my responsibility.

Except I couldn't do it. As the daughter of a philosophy professor, I couldn't act without thinking of what Kant or Aristotle would do. I was no genius. My sister, who followed in my father's footsteps, had that distinction. But I was certain no moral philosopher would sanction a decision to abandon defenseless children. With my father's lectures about moral dilemmas ringing in my ears, I let ethics overtake logic and left my relatively safe space to search for the kids. As I reached the bottom, a male voice cried out in pain.

I yelled, "Where are you? Are you hurt?"

The voice groaned but did not answer. With terrifying suddenness, Tex came from behind and grabbed me. "I've been looking for you. We don't know who's out there or what's going on. Let's get out of the way, before someone gets hurt."

I feared his panic and struggled to escape his crushing grip. "Someone is already hurt. He sounded as if he's behind the scenery. You find him, and I'll look for Madison and Ethan. Every second counts."

Tex refused to let me go. "Too dangerous. I'm afraid you'll get crushed. Follow me."

I had no desire to once again leave the safety of Planet Earth, but he insisted we climb the steps of the motionless escalator. The open sides of the steep stairway made the trek to the top perilous, even when the lights were on, and I trembled as he pulled me higher. I struggled to free my hand from his and tried to make my pleas heard over the din.

He didn't slow down. "Stop fighting, Leah! You have to trust me. I can't protect you from this mob."

When we got to the top, I forced him to stop. "Get on your hands and knees." I brushed his hand against the floor. "Use those ridges to stay safe. They'll keep us from falling off."

He patted me on the back in soundless assent, although there was no reason to keep quiet. The pandemonium below provided plenty of cover. We inched our way across the platform, above the screaming crowd. I was uncomfortably aware that the sharp gears that ended Maurice's life were beneath us.

Tex snaked his arm around my shoulders and held me in a viselike grip. I wondered if he, too, was afraid of heights, for he leaned into me so hard I feared tumbling off the platform. I pushed him away, and in that moment, a spotlight from overhead illuminated us. Tex relaxed his hold.

He was trembling. "Thank God that's over. Let's get out of here."

I flexed my shoulders to ease the soreness in my neck. "What came over you? You scared me."

He was remorseful. "Sorry about that, Leah. I guess I hit the panic button pretty hard. All I could think of was that I had to keep you safe, and I couldn't do that when people who outweighed you by a hundred pounds were running blind. I don't know what I'd do if anything happened to you. Thanks for being my emergency buddy." He embraced me again, this time more gently, and we rejoined the knots of terrified people below.

Like the rest of us, Evelyn Brill was in shock. Unlike the rest of us, she could not stop yelling. Flailing her arms, she shouted Madison's name with increasing hysteria until the physical limits of a human larynx reduced her voice to a hoarse barking. She ran down the center aisle toward the stage, flapping her arms. The rest of the parents followed her lead. I scanned the people still in the audience and those onstage. It was impossible to discern who was there. And, more importantly, who wasn't.

I was worried about Barbara and Rachel but was more concerned about Madison and Ethan. My mother and aunt were adults. Madison and Ethan were kids. I left the parents to search the theater and headed toward the maze of backstage corridors. Unlike Madison's frenzied mother, I remained silent as I flung open one door after another.

All the kids, except for Madison and Ethan, were in a single, large dressing room. Francie was with them.

The police officer was on her walkie-talkie. When she was done, I pulled her into the hallway. "Madison and Ethan. Where are they? Have you seen them?"

"They're still missing. Wait here with the kids. Lock the door. Barricade it with chairs, and don't let anyone in. That includes their parents."

This job was not a good fit for me. Although Rachel took credit for my dance career, the main reason my mother enrolled me in ballet was I couldn't sit still. Now that I was an adult, that impulsive need to move was mostly disciplined. But with Madison and Ethan in danger, I could not sit quietly and wait.

I ran in front of Francie to stop her. "Find someone else to sit with them. I-I want to help you find the missing kids. You don't know the backstage area. I do."

"Negative. You'll be safer here." She bolted down the hallway.

The kids, who were quiet when I arrived, all began talking at once. They took out their phones, texted with nervous fingers, and yelled at each other to shut up.

I clapped my hands three times, as Madame would do. Not quite as quickly as they did for her, the kids responded with a measure of calm.

I started small. "Each of you is to call or text your parents, if you haven't done so already."

One of the boys raised his hand, as if we were in school and not in a locked dressing room waiting for rescue. "We've talked to our parents. Officer Morelli had us call them. We're trying to reach Madison and Ethan. They're not answering."

I kept up a cheerful front. "I'll find them. But I need my phone, so we can stay in contact. My dressing room is right down the hall. Lock the door after me, and don't let anyone in."

The same boy said, "What if it's our parents?"

I wiped cold perspiration from my forehead. "No. Officer Morelli said not to let anyone in. Not even your parents. Not even me unless you hear the secret code."

They leaned toward me, thrilled with this new game.

"First, I'll knock six times. Listen carefully." I hummed a short melody, rapped four slow knocks, paused a moment, and then executed two more, slightly faster. "That's the rhythm of the music in the Waltz of the Flowers." They nodded, their eyes intent. They knew the tune as well as most kids know "Jingle Bells."

I was pleased with their concentration. "After I knock, stay silent and don't open the door until you hear me say *merde*. That'll be our secret code. And don't text or call anyone except your parents. Can I count on you to do this? Because—" The next words caught in my throat.

A half-dozen kids were breathing too fast, in short, shallow gulps of air. Their terrified faces told me they intuited what I didn't want to say. A tiny girl pressed against my side, seeking a comfort I couldn't provide.

She said what I was thinking. "Or we could die."

I stroked her hair. "No one's going to die, and nothing bad is going to happen. After you lock the door, use one chair to wedge under the knob. Pile the rest to form a wall."

I gently put the girl aside and showed them what I wanted them to do. "Barricade yourselves in. Don't make any noise. If someone does manage to get through, arm yourselves." I pointed to the dressing table, where blow dryers, makeup jars, and hairbrushes stood in neat rows. "Throw first. Run next. Ask questions later."

The tiny girl said, with more assurance than I expected, "We know what to do. We practiced lockdowns a million times in school." Her voice broke. "Could—could you please find Madison and Ethan?"

I tried to project an air of confidence and strength, although I have neither of those qualities in abundance. "I'm on it."

When I left, I listened for the click of the lock and the sound of furniture being dragged across the floor. The sounds inside the room assured me the kids were following my directions.

I raced to my dressing room and retrieved my phone. The screen was lit with messages, which I ignored. None was from Olga, the only person I knew, other than the police, who could take down a killer. With a flash of inspiration, I texted Bobbie York, our combative costume mistress. She responded immediately, because I lied to her. Even in moral philosophy, the ends sometimes justify the means.

Bobbie arrived, out of breath and shaking violently. "What happened to the costumes?"

Ignoring Bobbie's fusillade of questions, I said, "The costumes are fine. Come with me. Your job is to keep the kids calm and safe. They'll fill you in." I dragged her back to the kids' dressing room. They opened the door after I gave the secret code.

I didn't waste time changing out of my pointe shoes or undoing the dozens of hooks that bound Sugar Plum's tight pink tutu to my torso. With no better place to stow my phone, I stuck it in the bodice, where it pressed uncomfortably against my chest.

Before leaving, I searched for something, anything, I could use as a weapon. These are in short supply in ballerinas' dressing rooms. With no better option, I fixed upon a photograph of Tamara Karsavina, prima ballerina of the Imperial Russian Ballet and later, of Ballet Russe. With apologies to her sacred memory, I removed it from the wall and smashed it against the floor. I wrapped a long, sharp shard of glass in a leg warmer to protect my hand.

I was dressed as the Sugar Plum Fairy, but I needed a more aggressive role model to inspire me. A character pitiless and violent and without the fear that made my hand tremble. Although rodents of any kind terrify me, the Mouse King in the *Nutcracker* had the requisite determination and ferocity. With the tune of his battle music pounding in my head, I grabbed the glass shard more tightly.

The hallways echoed with the sound of my pointe shoes against the floor. Other than that clacking, it was eerily quiet. The byzantine floor plan made it impossible to see if there was anyone ahead of me. Or behind. I stopped twice, thinking I heard footsteps. But when I whirled around, no one was there.

At the end of one hallway was a door that bore a tarnished sign: *Custodial Staff Only*. Breathless with fear, I peered through the keyhole and then pressed my ear against the cold metal, uncertain of what to do next. There was no reason to think the kids were imprisoned in the broom closet, other than the fact that they didn't seem to be anywhere else.

I took out my phone to call Jonah and nearly fainted when he answered, not electronically, but in person. He clapped a hand across my mouth to muffle my shriek.

He dragged me into an adjacent room and whispered into my ear. "Stay here. Don't move or speak. Lock the door. I'll let you know when it's safe."

I did as he said. After taking the same precautions as the ones I'd advised the children to do, I strained to hear what was going on behind the thin partition.

Jonah's voice came through loud and clear. "This is the police. Come out with your hands up."

Chapter Eighteen

What does dance give you? The freedom to be who you are...
—Arthur Mitchell

From behind the locked dressing room door, I strained to hear what was transpiring in the hallway. The only sound, after Jonah's command to whomever lurked in the next cubicle, was a faint murmur of voices. No gunshots. No crashing in of doors. I wiped sweaty fingers on my tights. With one hand, I turned the doorknob with excruciating slowness and peered into the hallway. My other hand tightly gripped the shard of glass.

Jonah and Olga stood close together. She was speaking in a feverish combination of Ukrainian and English and had one arm wrapped around Madison and Ethan. The kids looked scared but were otherwise unharmed. The rush of relief that coursed through my body was so intense I dropped the piece of glass on the floor, where it shattered into dozens of shiny splinters.

They jumped back to avoid the broken glass. Madison and Ethan broke free from Olga's protective hold and surprised me with a hug.

Jonah was as matter of fact as a mail carrier dropping off a package. "Leah, please escort the kids back to the theater. Madison's mother is waiting for them. We'll speak later."

I wasn't happy about leaving him before learning anything about the bizarre episodes that had brought us to that point, but I didn't argue. Madison and Ethan had seen enough of the ugliness that had plagued ABC since Maurice's death. I walked the kids back down the hallway, which no longer felt so menacing.

Madison wrapped cold fingers around my arm. "Why were we in the broom closet? When the lights went out, me and Ethan were scared. Then Miss Olga grabbed us and said we should hide so no one in the crowd could trample us."

Ethan scoffed. "I wasn't scared. All those grownups were screaming like a bunch of scaredy cats, because they were afraid of the dark."

Madison dropped my arm and registered her objection to being grouped with grownup scaredy cats, and they argued all the way back. I tried to slip in unnoticed, but Evelyn Brill yelped and rushed toward me with the heedless speed of a runaway train. Tex stepped in front of her, again saving me from harm.

She crushed her annoyed daughter to her breast. "I was worried sick about you! Where did you go?"

Madison rolled her eyes and gave the classic kids' answer. "Relax, Mom. Nothing happened." She struggled to escape her mother's choking embrace. "Why did the lights go out?"

Evelyn didn't loosen her hold. "Mr. Cameron said there was some kind of electrical problem. It's fixed now, but they're letting the kids leave early." She delivered her next remark to the ceiling. "I can't take much more of this."

I left Evelyn to walk in circles and complain to the unresponsive heavens and looked for Brett. He was behind the scenes, yelling at the stagehands. They were no more impressed with the choreographer's emotion than Madison was with her mother's. I wondered where Brett was when the lights went out.

Madison had more maternal attention than she wanted, but Ethan was alone. I drew him aside. "Are your parents here?"

He crossed his arms. "I'm not a child. I'm twelve years old, and this is my third *Nutcracker*. I don't need a babysitter like some kids."

His poise amused me but not enough to make me forget he was a vulnerable kid. "Get your phone and call them. They're probably worried to death."

We walked back to the boys' dressing room. He grabbed his phone out of a canvas dance bag that had a picture of a guy hanging from the edge of a cliff and the words *OMG Point Your Feet!* printed in big red letters.

Ethan grimaced at the line of messages, which was longer than the one that crowded my screen. "I guess some loudmouth made a big deal about the blackout. Give me a sec to text my mom." Before he finished tapping, the phone rang with the *Star Wars* tune for the Evil Empire.

He answered with bored patience. "Yes, I'm fine…Stop yelling, Mom…I'll be home soon…Yeah, everything's cool, but I'm starving. Can we have pizza for dinner?" He looked up at me. "See? It's all good."

Despite my impatience to get back to Jonah and Olga, I was reluctant to leave him. "Is your mom going to pick you up? You should wait with Ms. Brill and Madison."

He was more tolerant with me than with his mother. "I live three blocks away. And believe me, I can take care of myself." His face turned pink. "But if you're scared, I'd be happy to take you home. I, uh, do you like pizza?"

I was touched. "Thanks for the offer. But my mother is here somewhere, and I need to make sure she's okay."

With a gallant air, he told me, "Any time. It would be my pleasure."

I didn't rejoin the adult dancers. Despite Ethan's protestations of independence, I remained uneasy about leaving the boy to himself.

Evelyn, with Madison in tow, took charge. "Ethan, I called your mother and told her we're taking you home." Anticipating his response, she said, "No arguments, young man. Come with me."

He didn't lose his aplomb. "Sure thing, Ms. Brill. If you're worried about going home alone, I'll take care of you and Madison."

The harried mother grasped at her daughter, who deftly evaded her clutches and stood next to Ethan. Evelyn said, "That's brave of you, Ethan, but Mr. Brill is on his way. He's coming in the car and will escort you to your door."

Madison scowled at her mother. "Aren't you coming with us?"

Evelyn sliced off each word with the ruthless precision of a sushi chef. "I'm not going anywhere. Daddy will take care of you. Someone has to sort out this mess. And to make sure it never happens again." She turned to me and said, with barely disguised distrust, "I'll talk to *you* later, Ms. Siderova."

An eternity would pass before I voluntarily entered into a conversation with Evelyn again, although I did have a brief flash of sympathy for her. Three minutes of being responsible for a bunch of kids frazzled me. I couldn't imagine what a lifetime of worrying about one's own kid would be like.

Olivia and Tex blocked me in my attempt to slip away. She threw her arms around me. "Where did you go? We were terrified when you disappeared."

Tex was equally concerned. "I tried to find you, but Officer Morelli stopped me. And you didn't answer your phone."

With an apologetic look, I brushed them off with a "Sorry—later!" and sped back to where I'd left Jonah and Olga. Tex grabbed at my tutu to slow me down. The force of his grip ripped the stitching on a border of tiny crystals. I was shocked. Despite the emotions this bizarre day inspired in all of us, grabbing tutus is simply not done. We can't even sit once we're in costume. Each one costs a fortune.

I tapped Tex's arm, and he released me. "I know you're stressed. So am I, but you have to relax. I need to take care of something, and I can't do it with you. Go back and see to Olivia. You're still friends. You owe her that much."

He looked at his hand, as if it had acted without his consent. I gave him a nudge and said, "Go."

I walked to the end of the hallway, but Jonah and Olga were no longer there. Feeling a bit silly, I checked to make sure no one was watching before entering the broom closet. It was filled with cleaning supplies, a ladder, and not much else. My timing in real life needed more of the precision I possessed onstage.

Disappointed in my quest, I rejoined my fellow dancers. Those of us who were still in costume stood in the aisles, and the rest sat in the first few rows of the theater. I circled around them and stood in the back.

Francie leaned against the partition that separated the orchestra pit from the audience and explained that a simple malfunction caused the lights to go out. She told us not to worry and that the problem had been resolved. The police officer's brief account satisfied no one.

Kerry's sharp voice cut through the chatter. "Officer Morelli, is there anything else you can tell us? I think having the lights go out was extremely suspicious. We were scared to death. Was anyone injured?"

Francie kept her eyes fixed on the back wall of the theater. "No one, other than Nelson Merrill, was hurt." She raised her hand to quiet the immediate outcry that followed this announcement. "There's no need to panic. Nelson's injury isn't serious. In the confusion that followed the blackout, he accidentally cut himself. The wound was relatively minor, and he's recovering well. I got an update from the officer who accompanied him to the hospital. He's been seen by a doctor and is waiting for a surgeon to put in a few stitches. He'll be back tomorrow."

While my fellow dancers processed this information, I answered texts from Barbara and Rachel. When my mother and aunt realized I was standing behind them, they jumped up and headed in my direction. Barbara carefully picked her way past the people sitting next to her, but Rachel was too excited to slow down. She must have squashed quite a few feet, judging from the pained reactions she elicited.

I met them halfway. "The two of you need to go home. There's nothing further you can accomplish here. I'll call later."

Barbara managed a wan smile. "Good thinking."

Rachel pointed an accusatory finger at Barbara. "Your mother wants to leave because she needs a cigarette. I think we should stay and do some real investigating."

A hint of color reddened Barbara's pale face. "By all means, Rachel. Let me know how it goes. But if the police arrest you for trespassing, or for interfering with a crime scene, I'm not posting bail."

Patience isn't always a virtue, especially when it came to my aunt. "Rachel, go home. Immediately. If you won't listen to me, I'll get Officer Morelli to escort you to the door."

Rachel looked over her shoulder and pulled me close. "Why aren't you leaving?"

My pricey tutu lost a few more crystals when I extricated myself from my aunt's clutches. Bobbie would surely have a fit when she saw the damage. "I work here, which is the only reason you were allowed in at all. And because I'm still at work, I don't have time to argue with you."

She sighed. "This is most ungrateful of you, Leah. But fine. Let it be on your head."

"Consider it done."

With a great show of dignity, she pulled on her coat and hat. With excruciating slowness, she snugly inserted each finger in her gloves.

Barbara murmured, "Well done, Leah." The two women walked away, whispering and gesticulating. They were almost at the exit when my mother hurried back. She had one glove in her hand. "It's freezing outside. Can you help me find my missing glove?"

"Nice try. I'll buy you a new pair."

She gave a quick look to Rachel, who stood in the doorway, tapping her foot, and blocking the exit.

My mother pretended to find the glove, which was in her pocket. "I wanted to ditch Rachel and join you. But if you're determined not to include me, you have to find Olga."

I pointed to the exit. "On it."

I climbed the side stairs to the stage to rejoin my fellow dancers. The curtain was closed, which made the large space feel intimate.

Madame greeted me warmly. "Lelotchka, we wait for you. I have few words to say and then all dancers must go to studio to finish rehearsal. We must make up for this time we lost."

Standing with her head high, her legs turned out, and her arms gracefully curved, Madame showed no sign of fatigue. "Today was scary time. But no harm done. My dear dancers, please not to worry. Your concern must be for performance. Leave all else to me." She looked in the wings, and after a moment of hesitation said, "Is better to continue talk at studio, *n'est ce pas?*"

There was general agreement and a sense of relief. The theater, which was our home, felt menacing. The stage itself, which represented the pinnacle of all we hoped to achieve, was filled with shadows, both real and imagined.

Olga peeked her head out from behind one of the backstage curtains. As inconspicuously as I could, I made my way to where she was waiting in the wings.

She picked me up in a bear hug so strong the bones in my back cracked. From someone else, the embrace could have been painful, but from Olga, it felt good. She was better than a chiropractor.

When I was safely back on my feet, she filled me in on the details of how she ended up in a broom closet with Madison and Ethan. "The stage go dark. I not know what happened. I grab kids and take to safety. Where no one can find."

My deep affection for this good-natured woman made me patient. "I don't understand why you didn't answer my texts. I was terrified something awful had happened to you. And I was frantic about Madison and Ethan. No one knew where they were."

Olga spoke softly. "Was whole point. That no one know where kids are. Too many accidents, Lelotchka. Cannot risk little ones. I see you onstage when lights go out. So I know you not have phone. What if killer is using your phone? Is easy to break into dressing room and get phone."

"My phone is locked. Facial recognition. You don't have to worry about someone taking it and pretending to be me."

"Killer could threaten you. Make you unlock phone. Or tie you up and hold phone to face. Then killer send message. Technology can be tricky, Lelotchka. Too dangerous to trust when children in danger. I answer only to Detective Sobol. He come to rescue."

I remembered how Tex had been fooled by a message purporting to be from me. Once again, I'd underestimated my friend's quick thinking and technical knowhow. "You're right, Olga. I shouldn't have second-guessed you."

She tapped a finger against her head. "I think always how to keep children safe. Now I must take care of Madame. She act fine, but I can tell she feeling not good. Will take her to studio in taxi."

We found Madame locked into a conversation with Evelyn Brill. When Madison's irate mother saw us, she stopped talking to Madame M and regarded Olga with a hostile glare.

Evelyn didn't address Olga, and instead directed her remarks to Madame. "Who takes kids into an enclosed room filled with poisonous chemicals? What kind of person holds kids hostage during a blackout? I'm registering a formal complaint with Mr. Cameron. And then, I'm calling my lawyer. I want that woman," she pointed to Olga, "out of here."

Madame labored to frame her answer in English. "Mrs. Brill, you not understand. Olga, she protect children. Not want to cause harm. Is opposite. Please to not speak so hard against my good friend. I trust her with my life. You must thank her. Not make trouble with Brett or lawyer."

Evelyn was unmoved by Madame's plea. "You may be right about Olga's good intentions, Madame Maksimova. But the children were never in any danger, other than from her. Honestly, the woman strikes me as more than a little unstable. I hope Madison recovers from her trauma without serious emotional damage."

I itched to tell Evelyn she was the one who was overexcited, not the mild and peaceable Olga. As for Madison, the young dancer showed far more resiliency and good sense than her mother.

Madame struck a conciliatory note. "You are upset. This, I understand. You are mother. But please to consider what I tell you." She patted Olga's massive forearm. "Olga better than anyone. She is trained bodyguard. You not."

Froufrou, the gentlest of dogs, growled at Evelyn. Madame picked up her pooch and gracefully dismissed the angry parent.

With the affectionate tone she reserved for us, she said, "My dear dancers, we must go now to studio. Police will talk to you, yes? But not to worry. Simple mistake that make lights to go out. I will give you notes for performance there." She paused. "But good idea for you to not be alone."

Chapter Nineteen

Ambivalence is a wonderful tune to dance to...
—Erica Jong

T he dancers left the theater in three large groups and trudged to the studio, accompanied by a chill wind and freezing rain mixed with sleet. The air grew icier the longer we walked, and a barrage of tiny hailstones stung our cheeks. We hurried to escape the bitter weather, racing to make each green light and rushing past brilliantly decorated windows celebrating the holiday season. The sidewalks were treacherous, and I nearly wiped out on a patch of black ice.

Horace grabbed my waist and held me steady. "Take it easy, girlfriend. We can't afford to lose our beautiful Sugar Plum Fairy."

Kerry whipped her head over her shoulder, but her fair hair was still in a ballerina bun, and thus the gesture lost some of its usual ponytail-flicking scorn. "Pay no attention to his flattery, Leah. He'd buy you a diamond ring if he thought you'd help him take Tex's place as Cavalier. Or Romeo."

Horace said, loudly enough for people up and down Broadway to hear, "On the topic of jealousy, Kerry, I bow to your greater experience." This got a big laugh.

Although I was grateful for Horace's sudden kindness, I remained wary. Kerry's meanspirited assessment of his motives was probably accurate, but even without her acid comments, I wouldn't have trusted him. Was there anyone in the company, other than Madame, Olivia, and Tex, whose friendship I could depend upon?

Madame ordered coffee, cold drinks, sandwiches, and cookies delivered to the studio. Food isn't allowed inside the classrooms, so we ate in the large waiting area, spreading our coats on the floor and making ourselves as comfortable as we could. Despite the persistent cloud of fear that hung over us, the impromptu picnic felt almost festive.

When we finished our meal, Madame gave us detailed notes on our performance. She was gentle but unsparing in her comments. With a mountain of work ahead, we marked through the sections she'd critiqued. Muscle memory, honed over many years of training, enabled us to internalize the improvements we needed to make, in spite of weary bodies and frayed nerves.

A team of NYPD officers interrupted at irregular intervals to interrogate us, which fueled rumors regarding the cause of the recent blackout. Judging from the whispered conversations on the sidelines, I wasn't alone in harboring doubts about the official account the police had given to explain why the lights went out. When it was my turn to be questioned, Kerry leaped into the place I vacated. My rival wouldn't literally murder anyone to achieve stardom, but I didn't put it past her to metaphorically stab me in the back.

Francie brought me to a remote cubicle in the main office. Although we didn't know each other well, I liked and trusted her.

"Francie, you've probably figured out I've taken a personal interest in this case. Is there anything you can tell me that you didn't want to say publicly?"

She didn't hesitate. "Can't do it, Leah. But you can help me. Where were you when the lights went out? What did you see?"

I stared at a blank wall, trying to visualize the stage. "I was at the foot of the escalator, which limited my view of the rest of the stage. I assume the usual lineup of corps dancers were in position, since if they weren't, Brett would have said something. Dewdrop and the Flowers were in the wings, stage left." In response to her blank look, I explained, "Kerry Blair was the Dewdrop Fairy. The Flowers were the ones in long pink tutus. They were almost certainly still in the wings, since they had to make another entrance for the finale."

She frowned and said, "Where was your dance partner?"

"I assume Tex also was in the wings, waiting for his cue, when the lights went out. He was trying to get away from the chaos onstage when he found me. He was more scared than I was, and we climbed up to the platform to avoid getting trampled."

Francie's impassive response gave no indication of what she was thinking. "How long after the lights went out did he find you?"

I was too anxious to sit still and gave into the urge to pace. "Not more than five minutes. The first thing I did was check up on Madison and Ethan. When I realized they were missing, I climbed back down. I heard someone cry out, which I now know was Nelson. That's when I ran into Tex. Or, to be precise, when he ran into me."

Francie made me go over each moment in chronological order. When the interview ended, she refused to tell me anything, other than the sanitized version she'd given us at the theater. I was halfway down the hall when she called me back.

Her words fell far short of enlightening. "Think about the two people who are likely to be of interest to us. I know you're on a mission, but you might want to reconsider who you can trust. Be smart, Leah. Ballet is not real life."

I knew what she was thinking. And I knew she was wrong. Ballet isn't real life, but, like all art, it's more psychologically real than mere facts.

"Tex is innocent. He knows he's being set up, but he doesn't know who's doing it. I admit he behaved irrationally today, but who could blame him? He needs protection, not suspicion."

Francie, always so stolid and sure, asked me to wait while she weighed a response. "I'm here to protect you and the other dancers. But I can't promise that I'll be able to save you if you fall."

I hoped that was a metaphor.

Burning with the need to talk to Jonah, I texted him. His one-word response: **Later** didn't do much to quell my impatience.

By the time we finished, the sky was dark, and the streets sparkled with holiday lights. I approached Olivia with some wariness. She'd been understandably disappointed in my vague promise to include her in future investigations. I lingered outside the main classroom and resisted the urge to eavesdrop on her whispered conversation with Tex. By the time they finished talking, the studio was nearly empty.

Tex tossed a flannel shirt and sweatpants over his leotard and tights and left. Olivia beamed with a look of pure happiness. The reason for her good cheer, despite the upheaval caused by the blackout, was obvious. "I don't know what you told Tex, but we're, well, we're back together. How can I ever thank you?"

I headed to the dressing room. "I'd be happy to take credit for the uptick in your love life, but this time around, I can't. Honestly, Olivia, I didn't think he heard anything I told him."

She smiled. "You must have done something. Because we're going out tonight. Dinner at his place." She took out a protein bar. "But you know me. I can't wait that long to eat."

I blocked the seductive smell of chocolate by slathering my back with an ointment that reeked of camphor and menthol. "Don't gloat. I, too, am going out to dinner, but I've blown most of my calorie count for the day."

Olivia, who'd eaten one sandwich and had stowed two more in her dance bag, said, "I don't know how you do it. If I have to miss a single meal, I get hangry. And I don't understand why you're on a diet. How much skinnier do you want to be?"

I pulled down the corners of my mouth and mimed excessive pain. "This waistline is the result of intense suffering in pursuit of my art."

Talking about my weight was a lot easier than talking about the Choreographers of Crime and our plans to investigate the murders of Maurice and Eddie. Olivia was sensitive, and I didn't want her to feel left out.

I decided not to stick too closely to the truth. "Listen, Olivia, I, uh, I talked to Madame, Gabi, and Melissa, and they'd love you to be part of our group." I left out any mention of Barbara or Rachel.

She was enthusiastic. "That's amazing! I'll tell Tex all about it tonight."

I took out a towel and rubbed down my legs, hiding my face in the process. "It might be better to keep him out of the loop for now. Let's wait until we have something concrete. I'll keep you posted."

Her smile lost a few watts of brightness, but she assented without hesitation. "No problem. Though it's too bad, I can't tell him anything yet." She walked around the partition that blocked a line of sinks and checked to make sure no one was there. Gossip is as central to our world as fad diets and medically inadvisable doses of over-the-counter painkillers.

She returned and reported, "The coast is clear. So spill. Is Jonah the one you're meeting for dinner? Talk to him, Leah. I'd feel a lot better if I knew Tex was definitively off his radar. I promise not to say anything to anyone. Even Tex."

I applied another layer of ointment to my sore muscles. The problems Tex and I experienced when he lifted me over his head hadn't caused serious injury, but repeated misfires had left a line of angry bruises. "I don't think the police consider Tex a prime suspect. But he's not in the clear yet."

Olivia frowned. "Who are you seeing tonight, if it's not Jonah?"

"Zach. He's taking me to that new Indian restaurant by the High Line. Masala Magic."

Olivia was impressed. "That place costs a fortune. He must be really rich. Or," she teased, "really in love."

I shrugged. "Or none of the above. It's a meal, Olivia, not a proposal."

Before we parted, she said, "I hope you talk to Jonah soon. I know today's blackout was a technical glitch, but it made me realize how scared I am. How scared I've been."

A false sense of security would do her no good. "I'm scared too. Please, Olivia, don't do anything reckless. Don't go anywhere or do anything unless you're around other people."

Another one-hundred-watt smile. "Tex said the same thing. He promised to stay by my side and keep me safe."

Chapter Twenty

The higher up you go, the more mistakes you are allowed...
—Fred Astaire

My favorite Indian restaurants line a seedy stretch of the East Village. They were utterly unlike the elegant dining establishment Zach had chosen, which was located on a red-hot block in Chelsea. I was accustomed to eating in dimly lit basement dives with soft music and hot food. Masala Magic was brightly lit, and the hard surfaces gleamed with glass, steel, or stone. It was also extremely loud.

I gestured to the lamp above us. "You could perform surgery under those lights."

Zach spoke loudly over the pounding music. "I assure you, the food is better than the atmosphere."

The waitress brushed against Zach as she delivered our meal. She was excessively attentive to him and kept her back to me. Her preference was understandable. Even without "doctor" before his name, Zach's bright blue eyes, dark hair, and ringless left hand exerted a magnetic pull.

The food was so good, I needed the self-restraint of a Buddhist monk to refrain from eating an entire portion of saag paneer. Zach took a forkful from my plate and said, "It's spinach. Would it kill you to eat the whole thing?"

I spooned some of the spicy mixture onto his plate. "It wouldn't kill me, but it might put tomorrow's rehearsal on life support. The day after our last performance, I'm going to celebrate with a bagel breakfast, a pizza lunch, and an ice cream soda dinner."

"If you're willing to go on the record, I promise to have all three items waiting for you, plus a magnum of champagne." He reached across the table, took my chin in his hand, and examined the side of my head. "It looks as though you're healing nicely. Any problems from that bruise?"

"No, no problems with my head. My feet are another story. Brett's choreography is complicated, and, as if that weren't nerve-wracking enough, we have the added pressure of being stalked by a camera crew that records every whisper and misstep."

Satisfied with his examination of my injury, he resumed eating. "I forgot about the movie. How can it go forward without Maurice?"

"Nelson has plenty of footage. I don't know how it was supposed to end, but he now has a tragic conclusion no one saw coming." I told Zach about the power outage and said, "It's a good thing for Nelson he's a documentary filmmaker. What's happening at ABC is stranger than fiction."

He looked up. "Nelson Merrill was in the emergency room today."

I was eager for information. "How badly hurt is he? The police told us almost nothing."

Zach hesitated. "It would be a violation of privacy for me to give you any details. What did the police say?"

"Not much. They claim Nelson's injury occurred when someone bumped into him. They said an electrical problem caused the blackout."

He leaned across the table. "I can't discuss his medical condition, but I can tell you that the way Nelson described how he got hurt strongly suggested his fall was no accident."

I felt each muscle tense, although Zach's assessment didn't surprise me. "Things did get pretty wild when the lights went out." Ignoring annoyed looks from the people seated next to us, I stood in the space between our tables to relieve the pressure on my knees. "I've been thinking a lot about the night Eddie died. My latest theory is the killer approached him from behind, thinking he was Nelson, and ended up murdering the wrong guy. Nelson's so-called accident today could have been an attempt to correct that earlier mistake."

I stepped behind Zach and waited until the waitress finished refilling out wine glasses before continuing. "What we know, with a fair degree of certainty, is that the killer was strong enough to hurl Maurice off the platform, force Eddie over a balcony, and shove Nelson hard enough so that he ended up in the emergency room."

Zach pushed his plate aside. "Do you think one of the dancers could be guilty?"

I shifted my weight from one foot to the other. "Not a chance. My money's on Brett. He's strong, and he had both motive and opportunity."

Zach persisted. "What's going on with your friend Tex?"

"Obviously, Tex was set up as the fall guy, which leaves open the possibility the killer could be a dancer, because the rumors about him having an affair with Brett are likely to have come from inside the company. However, if I think about the dancers on a personal level, as opposed to an abstract one, no one seems remotely likely to have committed murder. Some people, like Kerry and Horace, are extremely unpleasant. But not ever violent."

He polished off the rest of the food. "Has the NYPD made any progress?"

I checked my phone for the tenth time that evening. "I don't know. I was hoping to hear from Jonah, but so far, he's not talking."

Zach took my hand. "You were with Eddie less than an hour before he was killed. Same for Maurice. I hope the police are providing some level of protection, since they seem incapable of making an arrest."

Melissa had objected, on moral grounds, to using Zach to get information. Although I'd argued against her, now that the time had come, I was nervous about following through.

"I want you to help the investigation. Sloane would never confide in me, or the police, but she would to you. She's good friends with Charlotte, who was good friends with Maurice. The two of them might have information that would shed light on a possible motive."

He coughed briefly, the way people do when they don't want to say what's on their mind. "I'll ask her anything you want. And as long as we're on the topic of my ex-wife, I guess this is as good a time as any to let you know I'm taking Sloane to the gala."

I opened my mouth, but he didn't let me answer. "Before you jump to conclusions, I want you to understand it means nothing. One of her friends bailed on her, and she doesn't want to go alone. I couldn't refuse."

"Don't worry about it." I wanted to say more but decided the ensuing discussion wasn't worth it. I was, after all, using him to question Sloane. I couldn't reasonably complain about when and how he did so.

He seemed relieved. "Thanks for taking it so well. I honestly couldn't get out of it. And speaking of honesty, what's the deal with you and Jonah? Is he the reason you've been so distant?"

I wasn't ready to admit, even to myself, how much real estate Jonah had come to occupy in the formerly vacant chambers of my heart.

"Jonah has nothing to do with our relationship. Sloane is the one who's come between us. You're taking her to my gala performance. I think that says it all."

"Sloane and I are divorced. You can't get much more separated than that. Or are you using her as an excuse? Maybe this isn't about Sobol. Maybe you're not ready for a committed relationship."

I left unexamined his remark concerning commitment. "I'm not accusing you, and I'm not making excuses. I've never asked you about the details of your marriage or your breakup, but it's clear Sloane still cares deeply for you. Over time, I realized those feelings are mutual. You have a child, although that's not all that binds you to her. And let's be honest. You haven't exactly been banging down my door."

He tossed his napkin on the table. "I'm a doctor. Surely you can understand how demanding my work is. You're the same way with your career."

"Yes, I am." I appreciated Zach's respect for my profession. He never trivialized it.

"Don't tell me you want to be friends. I want more than that."

I didn't want to hurt his feelings, but I also didn't want to string him along. "I know. That's why we should stop seeing each other."

He got up from his chair to sit next to me on the banquette. "I admit I haven't, as you say, been banging down your door. But don't lock me out." He put his arm around me. "I'll take what I can get. For now."

Chapter Twenty-One

Some men can't talk and dance at the same time...
—Ginger Rogers

The morning after my date with Zach, my jeans felt uncomfortably tight. Unlike some ballerinas, I never forced myself to throw up after a big meal, although I was sympathetic to those who did. This was not a topic I discussed with outsiders. People who don't live in our world have a hard time understanding how dance normalizes this kind of behavior. In lieu of more extreme measures to lose weight, I started my day with Barbara, who believed breakfast was the most unimportant meal of the day.

My mother had a pot of coffee waiting. She poured me a cup but held back from putting it on the table. "I'm holding this coffee hostage until you tell me what happened after Rachel and I left the theater."

I took off one shoe and put my stockinged foot on the counter, testing the limits of my sore hips and tight jeans. "Nice try, but I'm not in the mood for blackmail. You'll get nothing from me until you tell me about your field trip to Charlotte Dankworth's studio. As quickly as you can, please. I have to be at work soon."

For once, she didn't argue. "If you sit down like a normal person, I'll let you win, since I have an early appointment with my dermatologist and don't have time for a lengthy debate. It's been ages since my last visit."

I peered into the hallway before sitting at the table. "Have you told Rachel? She disapproves of Botox more than cigarettes."

Barbara took out a compact and examined her face in the mirror. "She doesn't know it yet, but she's in for a big surprise. I'm taking her with me. I've arranged for a complimentary consultation and scheduled her appointment after mine. Chatting with those lovely people about the sorry state of her aging skin will take at least an hour. My plan is to ditch her and go to the theater alone. Rachel has been seriously cramping my style."

This didn't sound promising. "I wouldn't get my hopes up if I were you. Be prepared to have Rachel ditch you first. She's perfectly capable of heading for the theater while you're getting lifted and injected."

Barbara was slightly rattled at this possibility. "I didn't think of that. What should I do?"

"That's easy. Go to a museum. Eat lunch. Take her shopping. Or check out the Christmas tree at Rockefeller Center and go ice skating. Anything is preferable to watching a long and boring rehearsal. It's a waste of time trying to get information from the kids' parents. They know nothing."

I omitted the real reason I didn't want her at the theater, which was my serious concern about her safety. The killer was either an insider or was intimately involved with one. If he or she learned of my investigation, the easiest way to hurt me was through her. I wasn't as much worried about my mother's prudence as I was about my aunt's. Discretion was not Rachel's strong suit.

Again, Barbara didn't argue. This time, however, her placid acceptance made me suspicious. My mother doesn't bother arguing when she's made up her mind.

With continued good humor, she said, "I'll think about your suggestion and take it under advisement. As for your aunt, don't be so sure she won't agree to a few hits of Botox. I've been a good influence on her. Thanks to me, she purchased a beautiful gown for the gala. The one she wanted to wear looked like a prom dress, circa 1985. All she needed was big hair and purple eyeshadow to qualify for a role in *Back to the Future*."

Barbara can be brutal. Funny, but brutal. "This is indeed excellent news. What about her plans to find a permanent place in the city?"

"She contacted a real estate broker and has made a few appointments to

150

look at apartments. I can hardly wait for her to move."

She put the back of one hand to her forehead, mimicking extreme pain. "Don't get me wrong. I love her dearly. But it will be a relief to have the place to myself. I have to finish the first draft of *As You Kill It* by next month, and I have no idea who the murderer is. I thought I knew, but he turned out to be innocent."

She reached for a pad and scribbled a few notes. "You won't believe what Professor Romanova is up to this time. Changing her area of expertise from Chaucer to Shakespeare has given me, my character, and the series, a new lease on life."

I respected her devotion to writing. Let others judge my mother for prioritizing her relationship with fictional characters over her sister or for placing two real-life murders in the same category as her highly improbable plots.

"I'm happy for you and for the success of Professor Romanova's latest adventure. As for Rachel, don't be so hard on her. She looked lovely at Charlotte's reception."

Barbara tossed the notebook aside and said, "That was thanks to me. After we left the theater yesterday, we went to the hair salon. Although I had to practically handcuff her to the chair, she let my stylist cut her hair and prune the Amazon forest she calls eyebrows."

Rachel entered the kitchen, dressed in jeans, a tie-dyed tee shirt, and two neatly groomed eyebrows. "Did I hear my name?"

My mother set a place for her at the table. "Rachel, dear, you're too young for clothes that need carbon dating."

She jingled her brassy peace sign earrings. "I can't help being so much younger than you."

Rachel's reminder of the difference in their ages prompted Barbara to rub non-existent lines from her forehead. "Truer words were never spoken." She snapped shut the compact. "But as charming as those Woodstock era clothes are, this is no time to channel Janis Joplin. Didn't you see the outfit I hung on the closet door?"

"Not really my style. And the pants were way too tight. I need room to breathe." She brightened. "Although living with you has done wonders for my waistline."

I interrupted my mother before she could begin a lecture on the merits of strategic fasting. "I'd love to discuss fashion and makeup, but I'm here to find out what happened at Charlotte's gallery yesterday. So spill, ladies. I don't have much time."

Barbara took out a vape pen, her newest way of dealing with nicotine withdrawal. "It was an interesting morning. I was anticipating the kind of reception she gave us when we first met, but Charlotte was like a different person, perhaps because Victor was with us."

Rachel said, "A few years ago, Victor's law firm represented her in a big lawsuit. If you want to know more about Victor, ask me. I know him a lot better than your mother."

Barbara shut her eyes, as if to blot out Rachel's contribution to the conversation. "At the reception, Charlotte wasn't willing to admit I was a functioning member of the human race. But at the gallery, it was a whole different story. She had my latest book with her, the hardcover edition, and asked me to autograph it."

Rachel drilled Barbara with a fierce gaze. "Charlotte was more impressed with me. When I told her about my ballet school, she said I should get a job at American Ballet Company. Leah, I want you to put in a good word for me."

I tried to be diplomatic without raising Rachel's hopes of employment at ABC. "This is all fascinating, and I'm delighted to hear you had such a good time. But did you find out anything relevant to Maurice's murder? Or any clues about who could have killed Eddie?"

Barbara rapped my knuckles with the morning newspaper. "Of course. Your aunt may believe Charlotte was fascinated with her tales of running a ballet school in Duluth. But I wasn't fooled." She sniffed, "Nor was I taken in by her sudden interest in my writing. As if her purchase of my book, which is now selling at a deep discount, would somehow make me feel obligated to spend six figures at her gallery. I played along, of course."

I was ready to shake her. "Fewer words and more information would be most welcome."

My mother, when pressed, is capable of brevity. "Charlotte thinks the clue to Maurice's murder lies in a cold case Nelson investigated years ago. She said Nelson took the job at ABC so he could get evidence to nail that killer. Maybe Maurice was Nelson's source, and that's why he was murdered."

I swallowed the wrong way and started choking. Rachel, with extreme force, slapped me on the back. When I recovered from her assault to my vertebrae, I said, "If Charlotte's right, then we've been looking at this all wrong. I thought Maurice was the central figure. Not Nelson. But that does lend credence to the possibility that the killer attacked Eddie, thinking he was Nelson. Tell me more about this cold case."

Barbara, the plotter of improbable mysteries, was no slouch when it came to analyzing real-life situations. "Charlotte said Nelson got his start by investigating a case of arson that happened when he was still in college. He and Maurice were friends with someone who died in the fire. And now Maurice is dead, Eddie is dead, and Nelson may also be in danger."

I buttoned my coat and wrapped a scarf around my head and neck. "That fits in with what Eddie told me, which means I have good news and bad news. The good news is this might be the break we were looking for. The bad news is the two of you will have to cancel today's plans and spend the day watching Nelson's movies. Take notes and make a list of names. Start with the most recent and work your way back. I'll join you as soon as I can."

Barbara called her dermatologist. Over the sound of recorded music, she said, "Tell Madame, Gabi, and Melissa to meet here after rehearsal. We need to plot our next moves."

Rachel said, "It was my idea to talk to talk to Charlotte."

Barbara forgot about her call and shot back at Rachel, "What's your point?"

Rachel poured cream and sugar into her coffee. She must have gone food shopping, for Barbara would never allow either item to sully her sparely stocked refrigerator. "My point is that when we crack the case, it will be thanks to me."

Chapter Twenty-Two

The only weapon I had was my dancing.
—Maya Plisetskaya

My sister was waiting at the stage entrance. She wore a large backpack and a look of intense concentration. We signed in, and I brought her to my dressing room. Pointing to her heavy bag, I said, "I see you've come prepared. What's inside?"

She opened the zipper. "Laptop, bagels, and a book by Hannah Arendt."

I examined the cover of the book. "Is this research for one of your classes? Or are you writing a new book?" Melissa, like our father, was a professor of philosophy and was the author of two best-selling, Aristotelian-inspired books on childrearing. Aunt Rachel had good reason to refer to my sister as the smart one.

She put two bagels on the table. "Yes and no. I'm using it in my classroom, but I also thought it might help refine, or redefine, our approach to the murder investigation. Hannah Arendt wrote about something she called the banality of evil. Even though Arendt was writing about the Nazis, I think there's something in there for us. Reminding us that seemingly good and nice people are capable of committing horrific crimes. True evil doesn't appear with horns and an ugly face. It's attractive and tempting, which is part of the danger. Someone at ABC is hiding behind a friendly façade."

Her words unnerved me, and I put the book down. "Barbara and Rachel also have a theory about the crime, although it's not as intellectual as yours. I don't have time to go into it now, but we'll meet here after class, and I'll clue you in then."

I skinned out of my street clothes and into a leotard, tights, leg warmers, and sweater. While Madame got us ready for the dress rehearsal with a rigorous barre and center, Melissa sat in the audience. At the close of the class, Madame dismissed us for a brief break to allow us time to get into costume. Melissa followed me to my dressing room.

I told her about Charlotte's theory. She was more puzzled than excited. "If Charlotte is right, I'm terribly wrong. I'd been thinking a dancer was the most likely suspect."

"I know the dancers better than you do, Melissa. Trust me, you can cross all of them off your list, especially in light of this possible theory."

She remained doubtful. "I hope you're right. Let's remember, though, the source of this information. We're hearing secondhand something Charlotte said, which doesn't qualify as a smoking gun. If we assume, however, that the clue to the murders is in Nelson's past, the killer would have to be roughly his age. Who is old enough to qualify as a suspect?"

I cut a length of dental floss, and rummaged through a sewing box for a suitable needle. "Bobbie York, our costume mistress, is about Nelson's age. Charlotte also fits the bill, although she's not a likely candidate. She wouldn't have told Barbara she thought the killer was connected to someone in Nelson's past if she was guilty. And neither Charlotte nor Bobbie is strong enough to have committed the murders."

Melissa picked up the floss, holding it with two fingers. "Are you going to clean your teeth with something that's sitting on top of your grimy makeup case?"

I took back the white string. "Of course not. Dental floss is a lot stronger than regular thread. I use it to sew the ribbons to my pointe shoes. Much more secure." I squeezed three drops of glue inside each shoe, slipped my sore feet inside, and secured the knot with a few stitches.

A discreet knock interrupted us, and a male voice said, "Leah, are you in there? Can you make some time for us to talk?"

I cracked open the door. "I wish I could, Nelson. I have to be on stage in fifteen minutes."

He leaned against the door jamb. "You have more time than you think. That moving staircase is acting up again and giving Brett fits."

I looked at Melissa. "Okay with you?"

She nodded, and I invited him in. "We might as well get it over with, as long as you don't mind the tight quarters."

Nelson shifted the camera to his right hand and winced. "It was bad luck to have cut my right arm. But we'll make it work. I can prop it up on this shelf." He dragged a chair to one side of the room and positioned me with my back to the table. "I suggest we have your friend wait outside. This won't take long."

I introduced Melissa. She was cordial but firm. "I'd be happy to wait outside, as long as you keep the door open."

Nelson shook his head. "Too noisy. We have to keep the door closed."

My sister smiled to take the sting out of her refusal. "Then I fear you're going to have to wait until after the dress rehearsal, when you can find a space big enough, and quiet enough, to include me. I'm sure you understand why I don't want to leave my sister alone."

He took off his glasses, which made him look oddly vulnerable. "I know these aren't ideal circumstances. But I don't pose any danger to Leah. Far from it."

Melissa did an excellent job of pretending to be shocked. "Of course not, Mr. Merrill. I wasn't suggesting any such thing. But I'm not taking any chances, however remote."

I unhooked my tutu from the hanger. "Don't take my sister's words personally. She's very protective."

Nelson said, "Understandable. But unnecessary. I wouldn't hurt a fly."

"Until the police identify the killer, the dancers are at risk." With less detachment and more warmth, Melissa said, "Please forgive me for not offering you condolences on the loss of your cameraman."

Nelson's voice grew hoarse with emotion. "Thank you. Eddie was more than my right-hand guy. He was a close friend. It's been a tough couple of days. The only thing keeping me going is my work."

My sister picked up the book by Hannah Arendt, the one on the banality of evil. "Nelson, I'm more scared for you than I am of you. You have to be careful. Don't you have another cameraman you can trust?"

He gingerly repositioned his injured arm. "I'm looking for a replacement, although no one can truly replace Eddie. We were together for many years, and this injury isn't helping matters. It isn't healing as fast as I'd hoped."

If I had any doubts about the severity of the wound on his arm, they were put to rest by his evident pain. "I hope you feel better soon. How did it happen?"

He scratched his head. "Don't really know. I was backstage when the lights went out. I was trying to get to an exit when someone pushed me with enough force to send me flying. I dropped my camera and fell. I guess I got cut on a jagged piece of metal, something that's part of the scenery. People were rushing around." He rubbed his arm. "I think it was an accident, but I'm not sure. Whoever knocked into me hit me pretty hard."

Melissa took out her notebook and started writing. "How long after the lights went out did it happen? Could you tell if the person was male or female? Tall or short?"

He chewed the inside of his lip. "The police asked the same questions. It happened a few minutes after the stage went dark. I think it was a guy. Hard to tell how tall he was."

Most of the company had been onstage for the finale when the lights went out. "Nelson, do you have any enemies? I'm concerned your accident was no accident."

He rested the camera on his lap. "Are you kidding me? I get death threats all the time. You saw how Jonathan Franklin treated me at Charlotte's party. He hates me because I called him out for the slumlord he is. You can't do what I do without making enemies. On the other hand, no one in the company has any reason to resent me or wish me ill. Brett and Bobbie are the only ones I knew before coming here, and they're both friends."

Nelson's words gave credence to Charlotte's theory regarding the murders. Something in the filmmaker's past had connections to the present. The warning bell sounded, which put an end to our conversation.

For many days, I'd dreaded being interviewed by him. Now, I couldn't wait. "How about we meet immediately after the run-through? I'd be happy to talk then."

He headed to the auditorium, and Melissa followed me backstage. I whispered to my sister, "Add Jonathan Llewelyn Franklin III to the list of people old enough, and mean enough, to qualify as our murderer."

Chapter Twenty-Three

Dance is an everyday job...
—Gene Kelly

I n the days leading up to opening night, the escalator repeatedly hiccupped on its uphill journey, and the gears remained prone to alarming creaks and groans. Despite the technical glitches, I mastered my fear of heights and learned to dance as effortlessly on the platform as I did on solid ground.

The stagehands worked overtime to fix each problem, and the final dress rehearsal was remarkable for what didn't happen. No one got hurt. No one went missing. We danced the entire ballet without interruption. The tempo of the music was neither too fast nor too slow, and the redesigned lighting was exquisite. Warm colors suffused the party scene in the first act. Ghostly blue and purple hues illuminated the wintery Snow scene. Act II, the Kingdom of Sweets, glittered with crystalline purity.

All the moving parts of the complicated scenery worked in sync with the dancers. The Christmas tree magically grew from six feet to forty without a hitch or stutter. The escalator glided smoothly to the platform above, and the kids' places on the cloud-like structure at the back of the stage made them look as if they were floating on air. It was a perfect dress rehearsal.

Tex was still tentative during our most technically challenging lift, but he managed to get me aloft without dropping me. After the run through, I wanted to practice a few more times, but Bobbie needed him for a costume fitting. With our time in the theater so limited, Horace took his place and showily muscled me high above his head.

My antipathy toward Horace vanished with the opening music to our duet. He dropped his narcissistic and careless attitude, and an elegant Cavalier emerged. I sought, as I always do, the magical connection that comes to life during a pas de deux.

René Vernier, the legendary choreographer and founder of American Ballet Company, described the moment when the man extends his outstretched palm as a declaration of love.

According to Mr. V, each gesture had to be as legible to the audience as spoken language. When the Cavalier opens his hand, he is saying, *Will you love me forever?* When the woman places her hand in his, she is saying *Yes*. And when the man lifts her, the ballerina must declare, with every muscle in her body, *I trust you with my heart and my life.*

When the rehearsal ended, Horace said, "Leah, it's always a pleasure to dance with you. I know Tex is Brett's first choice, and yours. But I'm happy to step in any chance I get. We haven't always seen eye to eye offstage. But onstage, I think we're an unbeatable team."

I took his outstretched hand. He pulled me close and hugged me. I couldn't have been more astonished if a passel of pigs had taken flight. Horace was infamous for his callous treatment of women, including Kerry and Olivia. I never considered him an enemy, but I never trusted him, either. This was a side of him I hadn't seen before.

Nelson had the cameras rolling all day and didn't stop, even after the curtain came down. He and his crew continued to film us until Brett and Madame finished giving us their final notes on our performance.

Madame began by bringing Gabi forward. Kerry whispered, "What's *she* doing here?" With an accusatory finger, she pointed to my best friend and then at Olga, who stood protectively behind the children. "Don't we have enough outsiders crowding the place?"

Horace immediately defended Gabi. "Kerry, for once in your life, will you please shut up? Before she retired, Gabi Acevedo was ten times the ballerina you'll ever be. We're lucky to have her." A chorus of quiet approval from the dancers silenced Kerry, at least temporarily.

Madame ignored the whispering and said, "My dear dancers, most of you know the wonderful Gabriela Acevedo. Many of you have danced with her before she retire. Or if too young, have seen her dance, yes? She so kindly joining me to help today. Is extra eyes and ears. Gabi dance every part in *Nutcracker*. She know it as well as I do."

Gabi was dressed in a leotard and stretchy pants that emphasized her long thin legs. She looked as stage-ready as she did before giving birth to Lucie. My friend stretched her arms wide, as if to include all of us in a group hug, and said, "I'm so happy to be back. I've missed you. If you need anything, anything at all, don't hesitate to let me know."

She stayed onstage to chat with old friends and to offer guidance to the Dewdrop Fairies. Gabi had been a killer Dewdrop, and her YouTube videos were a master class in how to execute every step of that role. Kerry, despite her previous objection to Gabi's presence, fixed her large blue eyes on my friend and stayed to hear her advice.

Madame and Brett left the stage, and Bobbie York took over. She forced several dancers to stand and wait on weary legs while she made tiny alterations to their costumes. I was one of the unlucky ones on her hit list. I stood without moving, as she examined me from multiple angles. She poked at the back of my tutu. "What happened to your costume? Have you put it through the spin cycle of the washing machine?"

She tugged at the hem, which was missing a row of pink crystals. A seamstress stood ready with a box full of sharp pins. I jumped back, unwilling to give Bobbie the chance to pierce me. Tex stood a few feet away. I put my finger to my lips to stop him from taking the blame for the damage he'd unwittingly caused. Bobbie detested me, so giving her another item for her list of grudges wouldn't change how she felt. Tex, however, had enough problems without incurring her undying ire.

I blocked Tex and said, "Not so fast, Bobbie. I'll leave the costume in my dressing room or deliver it personally. You don't need to use me as a pin cushion for this kind of repair."

Bobbie's assistant, unaware of any subtext, was more accommodating than her petulant boss. "No problem, Leah. I can have this fixed in two minutes. You go rest up before tomorrow night."

Thwarted in her desire to cause me pain, Bobbie corralled three quaking, teenaged ballerinas.

I lingered onstage and waited for Bobbie to finish. The costume mistress was not pleased with my scrutiny. "Why are you still here? Don't you have someplace to be?"

I held my ground. "Bobbie, how well did you know Maurice?"

Startled by my question, she poked the unsuspecting young dancer in her midsection. "My personal life is none of your business."

I swallowed my irritation. "I heard you and he were tight. I'm really sorry for your loss."

Distracted, she poked the ballerina a second time. "We were acquaintances. Never good friends. And don't ask me about the murder. I was in the costume room when the poor guy died."

Too bad. Bobbie had an eye for detail and sucked up visual information with the energy of a high-end vacuum cleaner. "What about Nelson? Are you friends with him?"

She tugged at the costume, this time without stabbing the quivering dancer. "The same. I knew him, and his girlfriend, but not well. Those guys were all alike. All on the make." She said, with more tenderness than I'd ever heard from her before, "Not like my Peter."

This was dangerous territory. If I agreed that her husband was a wonderful guy, she'd be jealous. If I disagreed, she'd be offended. "Thanks anyway. I didn't expect you'd know anything. I'm a wreck over Maurice's and Eddie's murder, but that's not your problem."

Bobbie removed three pins from her smock and placed them in her sewing box. "Who said I didn't know anything?"

She shoved the ballerina in her back to dismiss her, toppling the skinny kid into the scenery. "Brett made Maurice's life a living hell. And vice versa. Their marriage was on life support."

This was disappointing. "Yeah. I heard. Thanks, anyway."

My lack of interest worked more effectively than a direct plea. Bobbie liked to be on top. At her winking invitation, I followed her upstage. I hoped for insight, but all I got was a repetition of familiar gossip.

"Maurice found out Brett was cheating on him." Her eyebrows wiggled up and down. "With a much younger person."

An older man cheating on his spouse with a young rival reminded her of why she hated me, and she stalked back to center stage, where a group of corps dancers waited.

I stayed beside her. Maybe she wasn't talking about Tex. "Who? Was it a dancer? Male or female?"

She thought for one long minute, enjoying the power of having me at her mercy. "Sex was the least of their problems. That whole shtick they had going, about having a marriage of heart and art? The art part of that wasn't what it seemed, any more than the rest. If you ask me, what kept those two together was secrets and lies."

"Thanks, Bobbie. I owe you one."

Bobbie recoiled, as if shocked at her own failure to maintain a frosty distance, and she left without another word. I remained onstage and waited for Nelson to finish talking to his camera crew. He was apologetic. "Leah, I know we said we'd meet after rehearsal, but Malcolm here screwed up the schedule and double-booked me."

He brushed off Malcolm's apology with a friendly look. "No worries, my man. Happens to the best of us." Turning back to me, he said, "I don't want to keep you waiting. I can come to your place later if that works better for you. Say, in an hour or two? I won't stay long. The at-home interviews with the dancers I've done so far turned out really well. I'm looking forward to doing more of them."

He took off his glasses and wiped his eyes. "Obviously, things have changed from when we started. I didn't expect the documentary about Maurice to turn into a murder investigation, but I follow where the story leads me, even if it's to places I don't want to go."

My heart ached for him. "I understand the pressure you've been under. You don't have to explain anything to me. Eddie told me all about it."

I was distracted by a text from Barbara, reminding me of our planned meeting at her apartment. I regretted not being able to talk to Nelson. "I wish I could see you later, but I've got an appointment. We'll talk tomorrow."

The footlights dimmed, leaving a small circle of light centered on the two chairs. I didn't see anyone waiting, other than Melissa. "Who are you meeting now?"

Nelson stared into the wings, breathing heavily. Malcolm answered for him. "Horace. He should be here any minute. Tex is scheduled first thing in the morning. And Madame Maksimova two hours before curtain."

Nelson fingered his bandage. "Right. I'll call you tomorrow when I finish with Tex."

Melissa waved at me from the first row of seats and signaled her impatience by drawing a finger across her throat.

I said, "Sounds good. I'm an early bird on performance days and will be here with plenty of time before Madame's class."

"Then tomorrow it is."

I hurried to join my sister. Nelson walked with us. "You're right to be so cautious. We'll hook up tomorrow. In the meantime, be careful what you say."

A chill breeze blew past us as a group of stagehands exited, and Horace entered. "Right back at you, Nelson."

Chapter Twenty-Four

Nearly everything in life goes in threes and fours…
—Ninette de Valois

Melissa and I returned to the dressing room. I took off my costume and pointe shoes and used a tennis ball to iron out the knotted muscles in my back. It was a painful but necessary procedure.

My sister put her hand on my forehead, as if to check my temperature. "Are you well? Madame, Gabi, and Olga are at Barbara's, and they're waiting for us. Can't you exercise later?"

I flinched as the tennis ball hit an especially painful spot. "You have to give me a few minutes before we go outside, or my muscles will freeze. Madame, Gabi, and Olga can wait. None of you is going to be dancing in front of thousands of people tomorrow."

"I don't know how you do it. I'd rather listen to one of Barbara's lectures about dieting than dance onstage." She held out my jeans and sweater. "I'll give you a massage if you get dressed and get going. If I don't get some sunlight, I'm going to shrivel up and die. I don't know how you spend your days inside a theater, without a window or a breath of fresh air from morning to night."

I stopped rolling and stowed the tennis ball in my bag. "I've never thought much about it. Fresh air and sunshine aren't a priority for me."

"That's probably why you look like a vampire drained you."

I yielded to her entreaties and dressed in three layers of clothing and two pairs of socks. She slung her backpack over one shoulder, and we left.

We were almost at the large dressing room for the corps de ballet when I stopped. "Should we invite Olivia to come with us? I promised to include her."

Melissa kept walking. "No. We can't talk freely in front of her, and we have no time to waste." My sister is rarely wrong about anything, one of many talents she inherited from Barbara. Still, I hesitated.

She tugged at my sleeve. "You can meet with Olivia tomorrow. I'll come with you. Invite her to breakfast."

My feet stayed rooted to the floor. "What if she's in danger?"

Despite her anxiety to leave, my sister remained patient. This was one trait she did not inherit from our mother. "Unless you have a specific threat in mind, seeing her can wait until tomorrow. Will delaying twelve hours make a difference?"

"It might. What if the specific threat Olivia needs protection from is someone everyone likes and whom she adores? You're the one who thinks it could be someone we consider a friend. You and that author, Hannah Arendt, made me think more about evil having an attractive face."

She rested her heavy bag on the floor. "You suspect Tex."

"I'm far from ready to pin the murders on him. But his behavior on the day of the blackout worries me."

I tried to visualize what occurred in those chaotic minutes. "Tex could have attacked Nelson and then got me up onto the platform so he could push me off and make it seem as if I also had an accident. I'm not saying that's what happened, only that it's possible. I don't seriously suspect him. In fact, forget it. I'm probably wrong, but—"

She finished my thought. "But you might be right. What possible motive could Tex have had to hurt you? Without you, he loses his role as Cavalier."

"If he wanted to hurt me, it's because he had a motive that outweighed his professional ambitions. Bobbie thinks the rumors about him having an affair with Brett are true, although she didn't mention Tex by name. If he thinks I have evidence against him, he'll kill me too. The same goes for Olivia. He knows how close we are."

166

She pulled me past the closed door. "You win. Text Olivia, and tell her to meet us in about an hour."

When we were safely out of the theater, and away from possible eavesdroppers, I had second thoughts. "Do you think I'm being paranoid? I hope so much I'm wrong."

She jumped back as a bus screeched to a stop and threw up a spray of dirty, slushy water. "Right or wrong, we can't take any chances. Check your messages. Did Olivia get back to you?"

I fished my phone from my pocket. "She'll be there. We'll have to figure out a tactful way to warn her. That's not going to go well, especially since Tex has renewed his relationship with her, which now looks like a big, red flag."

Melissa forced me to wait until the light turned green, although we had plenty of time to sprint ahead of oncoming traffic. "Don't say anything about Tex until we find out what Olivia knows."

"I made the mistake once of not trusting Olivia. I'm not going to do it again. We owe her the truth."

My sister was compassionate but unyielding. "That's why we need to be careful. Everything you've said about Olivia rings true to me. But her loyalty may prove to be a liability, not an asset. If she believes, even in the face of evidence against him, that Tex is innocent, she could compromise and complicate our investigation. We're far from understanding the circumstances that led to two murders, and one possible attempted murder."

I didn't answer. Once again, Melissa was right.

Barbara's apartment building hadn't changed much since Melissa and I lived there. Even the doorman was the same. Gerald showed us the latest pictures of his grandchildren and then announced our visit via the house intercom system. We rode the elevator to the eleventh floor. Melissa put her arm around me in wordless support.

Barbara stood by the open door. "What took so long? I thought I was going to have to come to the theater and pull you free with the Jaws of Life."

Madame and Gabi were on the sofa. Olga towered behind them. All three were looking intently at Barbara's computer screen when Melissa and I walked in. The usual chatter was absent.

Their silence unnerved me. "What did I miss?"

My aunt entered, bearing a plate of sandwiches from Zabar's. "It's about time you two arrived. While you were busy dancing the day away, I cracked the case."

Barbara ignored Rachel. "Watch this. It's the last five minutes of Nelson's most recent movie."

A photograph of a young woman with long hair and a mischievous smile filled the screen. The haunting notes of a Bach cello suite floated under Nelson's voiceover. "Thirty years ago, on April 18th, the woman I loved was murdered, a victim of arson. The police are still looking for Heather Ford's killer or killers. So am I. If you have any information, please contact this number." A picture of Heather's gravestone took the place of the pretty woman, the contact number and a website scrawled in red across it.

Barbara stopped the video. "Rachel and I have watched five of Nelson's cold case episodes. They all end the same way."

Rachel chewed on a pastrami sandwich. "You know what this means? It means Charlotte was right when she said the clue for the murders lies in the past. We got that important information thanks to my interrogation technique." She wiped a smear of mustard from her mouth. "I've always been highly perceptive. It's like my gift."

My sister broke in before Barbara could debate Rachel on the extent of her intuitive powers. "No one knows yet what this means. Except, perhaps, the killer. But it does raise some interesting questions. The first is Nelson's motivation to do the documentary on American Ballet Company. It's so different from his other work."

In the comfort of Barbara's apartment, I regained my appetite and devoured the inside of a corned beef sandwich. "This fits in with what Melissa and I were talking about earlier. Let's start with a review of what we know so far. Nelson and Maurice knew each other in college. They both knew Heather Ford, the girl who died in the fire, and whose killer Nelson seems to have been pursuing for the last thirty years. At first, we assumed

Nelson agreed to do the project as a favor, because Maurice's career was stalled, and the movie would have given him new relevance."

Rachel interrupted. "That's not what Charlotte said. She said Maurice's work is more popular than ever."

My aunt was going to need more proof than that to convince me. "Charlotte Dankworth is an art dealer. What did you expect her to say? She can't be impartial."

I ditched the sandwich and paced back and forth across the room. "It now seems possible Maurice was doing Nelson a favor, rather than the other way around. According to Eddie, Nelson was supposed to be in California, filming an investigation about a serial killer. Instead, he came to New York, the scene of this earlier murder. Maybe Maurice was helping him, and they uncovered new information about the fire that killed Heather. What we need now is a clear line from one event to the next."

Barbara said, "Leah is right. Nelson didn't simply report on cold cases. He investigated them as well. The movie about ABC gave him cover and was a convenient excuse to question people connected to Maurice, who, by extension, might have known Heather."

Melissa rewound the video. "Who else is the right age to either know about, or be guilty of, the murder of Nelson's girlfriend?"

Rachel was triumphant. "Jonathan Llewelyn Franklin III, that's who. Mr. Bigshot Real Estate Guy. You saw the last five minutes of this movie. The rest of it was an exposé on the Franklin family's real estate holdings. A lot of it reported on how badly the buildings were managed. Faulty wiring and other problems resulted in multiple fires. In one of them, two kids and a firefighter died." She looked at each of us in turn. "That makes two cases of arson."

Olga, who had been listening intently, objected. "Not exactly the same thing. The fire that kill Nelson's pretty friend was arson. Fire at Mr. Franklin's building was not deliberate."

Rachel ignored Olga's logical response and wagged her index finger at me. "Leah, stop pacing and give me the number of that nice detective, so he can arrest Jonathan. It's best if I do the explaining."

I didn't follow Rachel's command to sit still. Nor did I give her Jonah's phone number. "I regret having to disappoint you, but your theory doesn't add up. Jonathan wasn't in the theater when Maurice died. This case is far from over."

Barbara withdrew a volume from the floor-to-ceiling bookshelf and flipped through the pages. "Professor Romanova also would disagree with Rachel. If we follow the line of reasoning my character uses, we're missing motive in addition to opportunity. Jonathan is odious, but why would he murder Nelson after the fact? The movie was released last year. Nothing would be gained by killing Nelson now. As for opportunity, as Leah pointed out, Jonathan wasn't in the theater when Maurice was killed."

Madame cleared her throat. "We did not notice him, but that not mean he not there. No one would question if they saw Jonathan. He is ex-director of company. And still member of board of directors. He know theater well from when he was director. He also was at Charlotte's party."

Barbara lost a bit of her certainty. "If he was there, which none of us can prove, that still leaves him with no motive." She put the book down and picked up her wine glass.

Rachel examined Barbara's book and held it up for the rest of us to see. Although it was a murder mystery, the cover was bright and cheerful. "With all due respect to your powers of observation, I don't think we should be taking advice from a fictional sleuth whose latest investigation is titled *The Merry Knives of Windsor.*"

My aunt's opposition restored Barbara's earlier confidence. "You can mock me all you want. Professor Romanova is never wrong. If we follow her methods—"

Rachel spoke over Barbara's protests. "Professor Romanova isn't a real person! You created her! I don't understand how you can talk about her as if she was sitting in this room with us. We can't follow her methods because they're not hers. They're yours. And, if you don't mind me saying, you're a writer, not a detective."

Melissa positioned herself between Barbara and Rachel. "Let's put discussions about Professor Romanova aside for the moment. We have to find out what happened, in between Maurice's death and Charlotte's party, that could have motivated the killer to attack Eddie."

A gust of wind rattled the windowpanes and gave me goosebumps. "I agree with Melissa, although I think we should include the possibility that the intended victim was Nelson."

Gabi crossed and recrossed her legs. Like me, she found it difficult to sit still. "The clock is ticking. We need to warn him."

I sat on the radiator to ward off the chills coursing through my body. "Nelson is smart. So are the police. They surely know he may be in danger. I'm meeting with Nelson tomorrow, after some epic delays. I'll question him about the arson case that killed his girlfriend."

In her eagerness to speak, Rachel knocked her plate to the floor. While Barbara rubbed brown mustard from the pale carpet, my aunt said, "Why is everyone ignoring my opinion? You're all going to feel quite silly when I end up nailing the killer."

Melissa soothed her. "Rachel, you're absolutely right. It's far too soon to say definitively the case is closed."

My sister's statement bore no clear connection to what our aunt said, but because Melissa signaled agreement, Rachel didn't argue.

Restless, I left my seat on the hissing radiator and stretched out on the carpet, as far from Rachel as I could get and still be in the same room. "If the killer was motivated by some earlier connection between Maurice and Nelson, Eddie's death might have been part of the killer's original intention all along."

Rachel eyed Olga, who was reviewing the end of Nelson's movie, frame by frame, with Madame. She gnawed at a sour pickle and said, "What's your day job?"

Olga said, "I am cleaning lady. And I phish with spear. Am good with computers."

Madame said, "Olga is smart with computers. You know about this phishing business? Can make much money."

Rachel remained suspicious. "Isn't that illegal?"

"I mostly work for good guys. But must pay bills!" Her friendly pat on

Rachel's back nearly knocked my aunt off her feet.

The Choreographers of Crime needed a unified plan. "If the killer is going to strike again, there will be no better time than opening night." I checked the time. "We've got less than twenty-four hours to figure one out."

Chapter Twenty-Five

Ballet: Something pure in this crazy world...
—Misty Copeland

The intercom buzzed, startling us all. Barbara pressed a button and said, "Yes, Gerald, send her up." She replaced the receiver and turned to me. "Why is Olivia here?"

I looked at the circle of disapproving faces. "Olivia may be able to help us, and we may be able to help her."

In contrast to our glum group, Olivia was positively glowing with good cheer. She accepted Rachel's offer of a sandwich and said, "I have good news!"

Madame patted the sofa. "Sit, my dear, and tell us all what you know."

Olivia sat but couldn't squelch her bubbling energy and almost immediately sprang up again. "Tex is in the clear. I can't give you too many details right now, but that part of this nightmare is over."

Rachel said, "That's the first sensible thing I've heard today. I've already cleared him of all charges."

Olivia stared at her. "How did you find out? I didn't learn about it until this evening."

Barbara repositioned the sandwich platter so that it was farther from my aunt's waving arms. "Pay no attention to Rachel, my dear. Tell us what you've learned."

"Okay, Ms. Siderova. You got it. After rehearsal today, a certain person showed up and said they had evidence he was innocent. This person swore us to silence, but we can all relax now. Tex and I are celebrating later tonight."

Melissa led the chorus of negative yelps. "Bad idea. Don't meet with Tex tonight. I'm happy you're happy. But we're going to need a lot more information than that to share your optimism."

Olivia appealed to me. "I don't understand. Don't you believe me?"

Her hurt expression pained me, but not enough to spare her feelings at the expense of her safety. "Of course, I believe you. It's Tex I don't trust."

She blinked back tears. "What will it take to convince you?"

This was no time for misplaced pity. "The apprehension of the murderer. I'm sorry to say this, but I can't discount the possibility that Tex is using you to influence me."

Olivia's voice trembled. "It wasn't Tex who told me. It was someone else, someone who had no reason to lie or to cover for him."

"You think this mystery man, or woman, has no reason to lie to you. That doesn't make it true. If this person is conspiring with Tex or has been duped by him, you could be in danger. Do not, under any circumstances, meet with him tonight."

Madame said, "You must listen to Leah and to Melissa, who know about all things. Tell Tex I need you to come early to theater, and you cannot meet tonight because you must go home to rest. Not to stay up too late." She patted Olivia's arm. "Do not feel bad. Is close to truth."

My sister got to the heart of the problem with a logic that put the rest of us amateur investigators to shame. "What reason did your secret source give you for keeping the information secret? Has your informant contacted the police?"

Olivia lost her uncertainty. "The police know. She told them before she told us."

I silently noted Olivia's choice of pronoun. The person who approached her was female. Who could this mysterious woman be?

Barbara said, "This is a classic distraction from the truth. I used the same tactic in *Blades, Bodies, and Beowulf*. In that book, Professor Romanova uses her skill with literary analysis to nail the killer." She frowned. "Although not until three more people were killed."

Rachel looked at the ceiling, her hands held wide, as if speaking to a higher power only she could access. "Again, with the books." She returned her gaze to us and said, "There must someone here besides me who thinks we shouldn't take advice from a fictional Russian professor."

I stopped my aunt before Barbara could brain her with *The Merry Knives of Windsor*. "We all have our areas of expertise. Let's put them to use. Before anyone else gets hurt. Or dies."

Lost in thought, the argument between Rachel and Barbara barely registered. I ticked off each suspect. "Charlotte, Brett, Nelson, and Bobbie either have information about the killer or themselves are guilty."

Rachel corrected me. "You left out my suspect. Jonathan Llewelyn Franklin III. Maybe Maurice had evidence that the fire in Jonathan's building was arson, not negligence. Or, maybe Jonathan was also guilty of the fire that killed Nelson's girlfriend. I call that a great motive."

Rachel's sensible hypothesis surprised all of us. Barbara stopped cleaning the carpet and hugged her sister, who was well-pleased with our praise.

Olivia, calmed by my list of suspects which left out Tex, said, "What should I do?"

I was annoyed with myself for not thinking earlier of the simplest way out of Olivia's, and our, problem. "You said the person who confided in you and Tex has the ability to clear him publicly, but for some reason, has elected to do so privately. You also said she gave the police this information. You have to confirm the truth of her claim. Call Jonah and tell him exactly what you know."

She jumped up. "I'll do it right now."

I shared Jonah's contact with her, and she went into the kitchen. I didn't question her need for privacy, since I wanted her out of the room.

I spoke quickly. "Before she comes back, let's review the other suspects. The most pressing question involves Tex. I'm no longer willing to assume the rumors about an affair with Brett aren't true."

Barbara lightly smacked me on the shoulder. "Why didn't you bring this up earlier?"

"Since Kerry and Horace were the ones gossiping about him, I figured they were trashing him to help their chances of replacing us. But when I got the same info from Bobbie, I couldn't ignore it any longer."

I doodled in my notebook to avoid looking at the circle of faces. "This is hard for me. Tex is my dance partner and my friend, which made me as prejudiced as Olivia. I didn't want him to be guilty. I still don't."

Madame's voice cracked. "I not want that either. Cannot believe it could be true."

Olivia's return silenced us. She looked nearly as cheerful as when she first walked in. "Detective Sobol was really nice. I feel a lot better now."

I was relieved. "Did he confirm your mystery woman contacted him?"

She hesitated. "Um, not exactly. Not in so many words. But he didn't sound surprised. He thanked me for telling him and said he'd be at the theater tomorrow."

I fished a bottle of Excedrin from my bag and swallowed two tablets with a gulp of coffee. Melissa held out the remains of my sandwich. "You're going to burn a hole in your stomach if you don't eat something with that."

I took a small bite and forced it down my throat. "Tell me something I don't know."

Chapter Twenty-Six

Why waltz with a guy for ten rounds if you can knock him out in one?
—Rocky Marciano

The meeting at Barbara's apartment became a battlefield of competing theories. Rachel remained convinced Jonathan Franklin was the killer, and his motive was revenge for Nelson's scathing documentary on his family's role in a series of deadly fires. Olivia was less confrontational, but equally positive whoever the killer was, it wasn't Tex.

Barbara believed Brett was guilty. She made the most compelling case. "The husband is always the prime suspect. Brett had motive, means, and opportunity. His relationship with Maurice was on the rocks, and he stood to gain financially by his death. He was at the scene of both murders. If Nelson unwittingly filmed something incriminating, both he and Eddie would have posed a threat. Brett also has insider knowledge about the technical workings inside the theater and could have orchestrated the blackout in order to attack Nelson." With an apologetic look at Olivia, she said, "If more than one person is involved, it makes sense that Tex was part of the plot."

The rest of us remained uncertain. Although we were much further along in understanding what was possible, even probable, we still had no concrete proof.

Melissa took charge. "We've gathered some interesting information tonight. The next step is to act on what we've learned. I'm worried about opening night. Anything can happen. We have to be ready."

I rubbed my aching head, willing the pain to go away. "I'm going to need a rain check on taking any action tonight, other than getting some rest. As for tomorrow, I'm a nervous wreck. I'll be dancing on a set that's held together with chicken wire and a prayer. And what would I do if I unmasked the killer during the performance? There isn't any room for a cell phone, let alone a weapon, inside a tutu. Believe me, I've tried. Let's wait until the gala to do anything. All of our suspects will be there, and for better or worse, the performance will be over."

My sister was quick to reassure me. "Your job will be to dance like an angel. Or a Sugar Plum. Either one works for me. Let us do the rest." She put one hand on my shoulder and pointed to Olivia and Gabi. "You backstage ladies will take no chances. No heroics, please. If you see anything suspicious, text Jonah and then text me."

Olga looked up from her screen. "Or me. Olga will come with running."

"I'm sorry, Olga. I forgot you'll also be backstage. Your job, of course, is to keep the kids safe and to be on call if things go south." Melissa turned to Madame. "Will you be backstage or in the audience?"

Madame, with an unsteady hand, put down her cup. "Usually, I am in audience for most of performance. But I think not tomorrow. Better I should be where I can look after my dancers."

Gabi, like me, was too restless to stay seated. My friend walked from the window to the door and back again. "We're overlooking some important details. What if we're wrong about our prime suspects? If the killer is someone else who belongs backstage, it's not enough to caution Leah and Olivia to be careful. Especially Leah. In addition to the dancers, half of New York City knows she's the one who nabbed the ABC Killer. That alone makes her a target."

Melissa cut through Rachel's loud objections to consider Gabi's theory. "Did you have someone in mind we haven't considered?"

Gabi stopped pacing. "Yes. We haven't fully considered Horace. Maybe he executed a classic misdirection. Horace might have been the one who was romantically, or at least sexually, involved with Brett. Or Maurice. Did Bobbie specifically name Tex?"

Thinking of Horace's recent kindness made me less willing to credit him with murder than I would have been at any point in the last two years. "Bobbie didn't say it was Tex, but she implied it. Listen, I know Horace is no saint. He gossips, his treatment of women is loathsome, and he's ruthlessly competitive. That doesn't make him a killer. And, as far as I know, he's never been sexually involved with a guy."

She didn't give up. "He's also the person who has the most to gain by getting Tex out of the way. If Barbara is right, and the killer wasn't working alone, maybe it was Horace, and not Tex, who was an accomplice."

I appealed to Olivia. "We trust you. Do you trust us?"

She didn't hesitate. "You know I do."

"And we've shown you how much faith we have in you. But you have to tell us who your source is. Anything less is beyond unfair. It's dangerous."

She hugged her arms across her chest. "You're not going to like this. It was Savannah Collier."

There was a sharp intake of breath from everyone except my aunt. Rachel's use of social media was limited, otherwise, she couldn't have missed Savannah's relentless attacks against me.

Barbara updated Rachel on a few of Savannah's crimes against humanity, and I reminded Olivia of the same. "You know Savannah as well as I do. Her whole career as a pseudo-journalist and would-be influencer is based on lies. What did you tell her?"

Olivia put a hand on her heart. "I swear, I said nothing about you."

My young friend was so innocent. "Savannah has an inside source at the company. Someone is feeding her pictures of closed rehearsals. If it's Tex, then anything you told him she now knows."

I hated what I had to say next. "Tex's sudden change of heart where you're concerned now looks like a calculated move to earn back your trust. Savannah knows we're friends. She's not getting an invitation to join Mensa anytime soon, but she's smart enough to know I'm likely to be investigating. What did you tell her? And more importantly, what did she tell you?"

Barbara and Rachel stopped talking to listen to Olivia. She ignored them and looked directly at me. "I swear, I didn't mention you at all, even though she asked me a few times if you were on the case. She also wanted to know

179

if you were working with Jonah."

Ah yes, Jonah. I couldn't wait to get my hands on that good-looking and charmingly evasive homicide detective. He and Savannah deserved each other. I mentally wished the two of them a relationship that would make the marriage between Macbeth and his wife look like the apex of happy domesticity.

"What evidence did Savannah have to prove Tex's innocence? Did she offer concrete facts? Are you sure she wasn't making things up in an attempt to get you to confide in her?"

Olivia was on the verge of tears. "Savannah said Horace could confirm Tex wasn't at the scene of Maurice's murder, but he hasn't gone public, since Tex hasn't been charged. Don't think too badly of Horace. He wasn't going to let Tex take the blame for the murder. In the excitement that followed the discovery of Maurice's body, he forgot about it."

Melissa shut her eyes, putting her Ivy-League-educated brain cells to work on the problem. After a few moments, she shivered and returned to the land of the fully conscious. "Gabi's concerns about Horace are quite a bit more credible now. I don't think Horace would commit murder and implicate a fellow dancer in the crime in order to get a role on opening night. But he could be working with someone else who's using him."

Madame needed both hands to help her get out of her seat. Fatigue worsens her arthritis, and I suspected stress did as well. She said, with a firmness that brooked no argument, "Leah and Olivia must go home to rest. Same for rest of us. Is big day tomorrow. Our plan until after the performance is to stay safe and to help others stay safe. We know who to be careful of. Who to fear." She uttered a few words in Russian and paused, perhaps waiting for our agreement.

Olga translated. "We will not be left with the nose."

This made no sense to me, although Madame seemed satisfied with Olga's explanation of her arcane bit of wisdom.

Melissa translated the translation. "We will not be fooled by anyone."

Madame was pleased. "*Dah.* No fools here."

I wasn't as sure of either statement as my two Slavic friends. We still had no clear path to finding the killer, other than to question each of our suspects and hope the killer didn't catch on.

I refused Melissa's offer to spend the night at my place. As much as I appreciated my sister's loving attendance, I was weary of our circular debate. There was only one person I wanted to see, but I struggled with the decision to contact him. I never humiliated myself by pursuing a man uninterested in me.

When Jonah responded, I made it clear that our meeting, like the one he had with Savannah, was business. Not pleasure.

Chapter Twenty-Seven

You need chaos in your soul to give birth to a dancing star...
—F. Scott Fitzgerald

Jonah arrived less than an hour after I called him. He brought a bottle of wine and placed it on the kitchen table. "What can I do for you, Leah?"

I pointedly didn't open the wine. "You can tell me what Savannah told you. Then you can tell me about all the other stuff you've kept hidden."

He rummaged in a kitchen drawer and took out a corkscrew. Thanks to Melissa's obsessive clean gene, it was in better order than at any time since I moved in.

He opened the wine and said, "Savannah is good friends with Kerry."

"Neither Savannah nor Kerry knows the meaning of friendship. They're both self-serving liars."

He poured the wine into two glasses. "I understand your feelings toward Savannah, but what's the problem with Kerry? She's ambitious, sure, but so are you."

This conversation was not going according to the script I'd prepared in advance of his arrival. "Answer the question, Jonah. It's late, and I'm tired. Tired of many things, including your evasiveness."

"I'll answer your questions as best I can." He corrected himself. "As best I can, given the fact that I'm a cop and you're not."

"The suspense is killing me."

Jonah laughed, although I meant the words to sound mean, not funny. He said, "Kerry gives Savannah inside info about the company, and in return, Savannah posts about what a talented dancer Kerry is. I've met with Savannah twice. She told me she thinks Bobbie York is the killer based on some complicated reason having to do with the company's finances. I couldn't figure out what gripe Savannah has against the costume mistress, but I know you also don't get along with Bobbie."

I crossed my arms. "You left out the part about Horace. Did Savannah tell you he could provide an alibi for Tex?"

He added more wine to both glasses, although I hadn't touched mine. "Yes, but Savannah's deductions are not the gold standard for detection. Forget her, and let's talk about you. What have you and your buddies come up with?"

A woman with less to lose would have withheld information. But lives were on the line. I told him about all our theories, including the ones I thought unlikely.

He didn't dismiss anything. "These are all good ideas. We've covered a lot of the same ground."

"And what's your conclusion? Do you know who did it? And do you know why?"

He leaned back in his chair. "I'm close. Can't make any moves until I get concrete proof. The DA won't proceed unless I can provide him with evidence that'll stand up in court."

Thinking of my mother's detective novels, I said, "The smoking gun."

"Exactly. Forensics couldn't do much with the crime scene, which had more fingerprints than the bathroom at Penn Station. No eyewitnesses. Plenty of possible motives, but, as you say, no smoking gun."

"Why won't you name your prime suspect? Or suspects."

"They're similar to yours. Beyond that, I don't want to go."

He was so irritating. "What about our agreement to share information? Was that a ploy to use me?

"It was a stupid idea for a lot of reasons. Mostly because I love you. In the end, I couldn't bring myself to put you in danger."

He spoke so casually, I wasn't sure if he meant he loved me or was using the term as a figure of speech. The latter seemed more likely. "You need to catch the killer. I can help."

"No. That's why I'm here. To tell you to back off. When we began, I did want you to be part of the investigation. And yes, part of my motivation was to have an excuse to spend time with you. But there were practical reasons as well. You had no known ties to Maurice. I figured you were far enough from his world to be safe. At the same time, you're close enough to all the suspects to learn things they wouldn't necessarily tell me."

Jonah's phone buzzed with a text. He glanced at it and turned the phone face down. "Eddie's death changed all that. There you were, at the scene of another crime, after spending half the night talking to the victim. And the box of chocolates that had Tex's ballet slippers inside? I still don't know if you were the specific target or if the killer simply chose a handy receptacle in a random room. It's not worth the risk. How do you think I'd feel if something happened to you?"

Under the warmth of his gaze, I unbent enough to take a sip of wine. "You're at an impasse. So are we, but we're not giving up."

His look was amused. "I suppose Madame Maksimova and her bodyguard are on the case as well? What about your mother? And, um, her professor?"

I pressed my lips together to iron out an answering smile. "What do you think? Barbara is depending on Professor Romanova to solve the case, my aunt Rachel is convinced Jonathan Franklin is the killer, and Olivia doesn't care about anything except making sure Tex isn't charged. There's only one way to get the evidence we need. If I can rattle enough cages, the killer will come out to play. And then we'll have him. Or her."

He jerked forward so forcefully he nearly upended the table. "No. Too dangerous."

"Not if we're prepared. Think about it. You can't stop me, but you can help me. The pressure is…it's making me…."

I went to the sink to rinse out my wine glass because it afforded me an excuse to hide my face. I don't cry in public, as I'm quite unattractive when I weep. In the movies, actresses look radiant when tears drip down their faces. My skin gets blotchy, my eyes swell up, and my nose turns red.

He stood behind me and put his hands on my shoulders. "Don't cry, ballerina girl."

I turned and pushed him away. "I'm not your girl. I'm an adult."

With great gentleness, he brushed a strand of hair away from my wet and blotchy face. "I know. Sit down, my—sit down, Leah. Let's talk about your plan. When all this all over, we'll celebrate."

I eyed him. "What did you have in mind?"

He drew me close. "I'll think of something."

The doorbell rang, shattering the tender moment. I pressed the intercom, and Savannah's throaty voice answered.

I said, "Go away, Savannah. I'm busy."

She screeched, "Let me in. I promise, I'll make it worth your while."

Jonah said, "Let me take care of this." He met her in the lobby. They went off together, and he didn't return.

The next morning, I awoke with stiff limbs and an aching back. Jonah texted to tell me he would be at the theater. I didn't respond, although I burned to know what happened during his impromptu rendezvous with my arch nemesis. On the long list of succeeding texts, Barbara's took precedence.

My mother didn't bother with pleasantries. "Leah! What are you wearing to the gala?"

I was torn between relief she was safe and irritation at her obsession with clothing. "Does that information qualify as an emergency?"

My mother was stunned into a brief silence by my question. When she recovered, she said, "Of course, it's an emergency. Maybe not life and death, but serious nonetheless."

"I'm wearing the pink dress. Floor length, tulle overskirt."

Her emotional response was more appropriate for a steerage passenger on the *Titanic*, who had just received news about the shortage of available lifeboats. "Are you serious? You wore it to the Met Gala. Unacceptable, Leah."

In quick succession, Barbara sent pictures of gowns she deemed more appropriate. Scrolling through them, I reconsidered my decision to wear pink. Not because I shared Barbara's horror at wearing a dress others had seen multiple times, but because a dark color would be better for the inconspicuous role I hoped to play.

I interrupted the barrage of texted photos. "You choose. Make it anything black or dark blue. Nothing bright."

She sounded disappointed. "Are you sure? That scarlet silk gown would make a stunning statement."

"I want to fade into the background. Not wave a flag."

Barbara relented. "Fine. Call if you need me. I'll drop the dress off at the stage door."

"Sounds good. Stay with Rachel. I'll see you—"

She cut my goodbye off mid-sentence. "Do you have a date?"

I shouldn't have been surprised by the real reason for her concern over my appearance. "No."

"Isn't Zach going to be there?"

"Yes. With his ex-wife."

Barbara exhaled loudly as she digested this news. "He may be arriving with Sloane. That doesn't mean he's going home with her."

"Let's reschedule that conversation. I can work you in sometime next year." I exited my apartment building and headed to the subway. The wind was as unrelenting as my mother.

Barbara, as usual, had the last word. "As long as next year means I'm toasting you as the mother of the bride, I'm in."

On my way to the theater, I bought an armful of small gifts and stowed them in a corner of my dressing room. It was a *Nutcracker* tradition for the Sugar Plum Fairy to give the kids treats on opening night, and I wanted them to have the same magical experience I'd had at their age.

I arrived so early, the only people I met were stagehands. In the peace of my private space, with its comforting odor of perfume and makeup and the indefinable smell of all theaters, I felt calmer than at any time in the previous few weeks. It was as much my home as my apartment, perhaps more so.

Bobbie slammed the door open, interrupting my pre-performance rituals. Startled, the costume mistress dropped a pair of fierce-looking scissors with a loud clatter. "What the hell are you doing here?"

"This is my dressing room, and I'd appreciate more courtesy. Knocking before entering would be a good start."

She recovered her usual air of confident irritability. "Obviously, I didn't know you were here."

I pointed to the scissors. "Whom were you expecting?"

She snatched the scissors from the floor. "No one. I'm here to check your costume."

Although I hadn't planned on questioning anyone before the gala, Bobbie's unexpected appearance was too tempting to pass up. I didn't bother with diplomacy, which never worked with the perpetually irate Bobbie.

"As long as you're here, you might as well know I heard you had a powerful motive to kill Maurice, which you conveniently didn't mention yesterday."

I had no idea if Bobbie had a motive. My assertion was an attempt to pry information from her.

Her skin paled, and her confident, contemptuous façade vanished. "Don't believe Brett's lies. I don't know how he can live with himself, slandering his dead husband while pretending to be overcome with grief. A person like that has no morals and no shame."

I couldn't imagine what Bobbie was talking about. Did she think Brett killed Maurice? Or had Brett falsely accused her of the deed?

Hoping for insight without revealing the full extent of my ignorance, I said, "We're in agreement about Brett. Does anyone else know about, er, about it?"

She stabbed the air with her scissors. "I don't know how you found out. Was it Nelson who told you? I'm sick of him and his constant questions. Heather's death was a tragedy, but Nelson is as bad as the rest, using her death as an excuse to poke his nose where it doesn't belong."

Her fierce motions unnerved me, and I reached behind for the doorknob. "If Brett is threatening you, or lying about you, you're going to need all the help you can get."

She shoved me aside and bolted. I texted Francie. **Need you asap. In my dressing room.**

The police officer arrived, red-faced and breathing heavily. "What's going on, Leah?"

"We need someone to keep close watch on Brett and on Bobbie York, the costume mistress. I think she may be in danger."

Her brow furrowed. "Brett's covered. As for Ms. York, it's a little late to make changes, but I'll let Detectives Sobol and Farrow know. They should be able to move someone. Why the sudden worry about her?"

"I think Bobbie might be in possession of the same information that got Maurice killed. Don't let her out of your sight."

Chapter Twenty-Eight

The dance goes on forever. So shall I. So shall we.
—Gelsey Kirkland

S hortly before the first call, I brought my gifts of candy and flowers to the kids' dressing rooms. Thankfully, the parents weren't allowed backstage access. The adults had their own waiting area, apart from the performers. Most of them were probably in the audience.

The gong sounded for the kids to line up backstage. They took their prearranged places without direction, lining up in pairs. The rehearsal mistress, who'd trained them for months, stood at the front of the line. Officer Alvarez brought up the rear. Flanked by their sober presence, silence took the place of the dressing room chatter.

I waited with them. "Are you nervous?"

The kids answered me with muffled giggles and moans. A tiny girl tugged at my sweater. "We're all so nervous, we can hardly breathe!"

"That's a good sign. You should be nervous. I know I am!"

They weren't sure if I was kidding them. I wasn't. Unlike murder investigations, stage fright was something I knew a lot about. "You're going to be scared right up until the moment you step onstage. Those nerves will give your performance extra energy. Once you begin dancing, I promise you won't be nervous."

Madison and Ethan were at the front of the line. She whispered, "What if something bad happens?"

I wasn't sure if Madison was referring to her performance as Clara or the possibility of something more dire. For all the kids' resilience, the murders affected them deeply, none more than this talented young dancer.

"You have my solemn promise. Nothing bad will happen. When you get on stage, your body will take over. And you'll be great."

Melissa was waiting for me in my dressing room, despite my text telling her I was well-protected and didn't need additional hovering. She rarely betrayed inner turmoil with the kind of nervous energy that kept me in constant motion. That night, however, she couldn't stop fidgeting.

When we learned the curtain would be delayed beyond the usual five-minute grace period, she became increasingly agitated. "I hope everything is okay. I hope everyone is okay." She grabbed her phone. "I'm going to text Barbara. See if she knows what's going on."

I tried to calm her. "This is opening night. Maybe management decided to cash in on the high-class crowd ordering pricey drinks at the bar. You have to relax. You're driving me crazy."

Melissa's eyes were glued to her phone. "Barbara said the mayor arrived, along with a bunch of other celebrities."

"See? It's like I told you. Tonight's performance, or to be more precise, tonight's gala, is a hot ticket on the social calendar. It wouldn't look good, for Brett or for the company, to start the performance and force the mayor to cool his heels in the lobby."

My sister was indignant. "They should make him follow the same rules as ordinary people."

I was more pragmatic and less emotional. "This is no time to alienate our donors. They're the ones who keep us afloat. As for our political friends, let's look on the bright side. The mayor has probably got plenty of security with him, especially in light of recent events. Jonah has a dozen or more cops supplementing the usual number, not just for the bigwigs, but for us."

She looked up from her phone. "When did you talk to Jonah? After you left Barbara's apartment, you said you were going straight home."

I put my foot on a chair and tied the ribbons on my pointe shoes. "I called him when I got home."

"Is he going to be at the gala as well as the performance?"

I sewed extra stitches in each knotted ribbon. "Of course. He's conducting a murder investigation. All of the suspects will be there." I didn't tell her about Savannah's surprise visit, or about Jonah's abrupt departure.

She played nervously with a tray of bobby pins. "Where's Officer Morelli? You said she was assigned to keep you safe."

I removed the tray from her twitchy fingers. "Please, Melissa. Stop fiddling with my stuff and go check on Barbara and Rachel. I love you, but you're getting in the way of my preparations."

She was suspicious. "What more could you possibly do to yourself? Your face has so much makeup on it I can barely recognize you. That bossy dresser glued your hair into place with enough spray to blow a Jupiter-sized hole in the ozone layer. I don't trust you. You might do something stupid."

I held out her coat. "Your confidence in me is genuinely heartwarming. As for the rest of my preparation, that bossy dresser is on her way to get me into my costume. In between then and now, I have to mentally prepare for the performance. Alone."

She opened the door. "Have it your way. Before I go, however, I'll check that Morelli is on duty. As for our mother and aunt, they don't need me. Their favorite lawyer, art collector, and man about town is with them." She checked her watch for the tenth time. "I suppose I could protect them from coming to blows over their competition for Victor's affections."

I pretended to be struck by a sudden thought. "Don't let either of them go off alone with Victor."

Her jaw dropped as dramatically as a cartoon character's. "We've never discussed Victor as a suspect. Do you think he's guilty?"

I didn't suspect Victor of anything more deadly than social climbing. I merely wanted Melissa to leave, and Victor Roth was a convenient way to convince my sister to do so. Scrambling for something plausible, I said, "Victor is the same age as Nelson. At Charlotte's party, he said something about there not being more than three degrees of separation between everyone there. That applies to him as well. Now get out there and do what you do best. Engage him in conversation and dig up whatever dirt you can."

She left. Three seconds later, I ran down the hall after her. "Ask Victor about Bobbie York. Find out if he knows her. Or knows anything about her that could help us out."

She bit her lip. "If you think there's the slightest chance Bobbie is involved, I'm not leaving. She's the costume mistress. She could disguise herself in one of these ridiculous getups, and no one would recognize her."

"Bobbie is guilty of a deeply unpleasant personality, which isn't against the law, although perhaps it should be. We'll question her at the gala. Not before."

I returned to the dressing room, but my solitude didn't last long. Although I expected Tex to stop by, Horace was my next visitor. He was dressed in a long dark cape for his role as Drosselmeyer, the mysterious man who gives young Clara the gift of a magical nutcracker. His beautiful face was hidden under heavy stage makeup, and his golden hair was tucked into a black wig and topped by a large hat.

Horace had a bouquet of red roses half hidden behind his back. He presented them with a flourish. With a bashful look, he said, "I know we haven't been as close as we once were. And maybe that's my fault. Let's start over. *Merde*, Leah."

I couldn't have been more surprised if it had been Bobbie bearing gifts and offering apologies. We were both too heavily made up to embrace. I blew him a kiss instead. "I'm really touched, Horace. And *merde*."

He tipped his large hat. "Anytime."

The shadowy world behind the curtain was as familiar to me as the iconic fountain in front of Lincoln Center. I knew the location of the tissue boxes, the section of flooring with a frayed edge, and where the electrical cables were coiled like snakes. If only people could be as predictable as those inanimate objects.

During the intermission, the dancers in Act II swarmed the stage for a last-minute warmup, dodging the stagehands who were setting the scene and laying out the props. Madame, of course, was there to provide advice and encouragement. She was dressed in an elegant black lace gown. Diamond hairpins held her chignon in place, and she moved with queenly grace, but her clenched hands belied her calm exterior.

I drew her aside. "Madame, what's wrong? Are you ill?"

She fluttered her fingers. "I am fine and perfect, Lelotchka. Was wanting to tell Brett about nothing important." She turned and spoke in Russian to Olga before hurrying off.

I grabbed Olga. "What did she say?"

Olga kept her eyes on Madame. "She say he doesn't have a tsar in his head."

I didn't have time to parse one of Madame's obscure Russian references. "Olga! Please pay attention to me. A star? Who doesn't have a star?"

My friend patted the top of her head. "*Tsar.* Not star. Lelotchka, you understand?"

"No, I don't understand. Who doesn't have a tsar in his head? And why does that worry Madame?"

Olga frowned. "Mr. Brett Cameron. He has no tsar in head. Madame want to talk to him, but he not here. Stagehands not see him. Madame, she say it not make sense for choreographer to be talking with guests when performance happening. Dance is most important. Mayor and people with money not important." She blinked. "But mayor of New York City, maybe he important, and Brett have tsar in head after all."

I was relieved Madame's distress sprang from her concern about the performance and wasn't connected to anyone's health and safety. With that worry assuaged, I refocused on my preparations.

As usual, I was sick with stage fright. I gave myself the same sage advice I'd dispensed to the kids, but it didn't help. Knowing the nervousness would abate once I started dancing didn't make me feel better. Some obscure and exceedingly unhealthy part of my psyche refused to allow me to believe the performance wouldn't end in disaster.

Tex didn't look any steadier than I felt.

I took both of his clammy hands in mine. "*Merde.*"

He seemed distracted. "Yeah, uh, sure. *Merde.*"

I took a deep breath. *Showtime.*

The sound of applause filtered through the closed curtain. It was part of our performance tradition for the conductor to take a solo bow before the second act began and to allow the audience to acknowledge the musicians as well. I focused on my breath. As always, I paid a silent tribute to René Vernier, who coached me when I first joined the company. He would remain in the wings until the last second, before rushing to his reserved seat in the audience.

He always said the same thing to us. The same thing I told the kids. "Be great."

All around, my fellow dancers conducted their individual magic rituals. Olivia tugged on her tutu three times. Madame, who hovered in the wings, muttered to herself in Russian. The music began, and the curtain rose on Maurice's set. There were audible gasps from the audience as the glittering, ethereal scenery was revealed to them.

The pas de deux for the Sugar Plum Fairy and her Cavalier was the culmination of the ballet. The music swelled, and I stepped onto the slowly moving escalator. My arabesque stayed steady as I gestured toward the stars that twinkled overhead. The lights around the perimeter of the stage dimmed. One spotlight followed me. The other followed Tex. When I reached the top, I stepped, with one pointed foot, onto the platform. It shuddered, swayed, and collapsed.

Chapter Twenty-Nine

A ballerina's life can be glorious. But it does not get any easier.
—Alicia Markova

Seconds passed like hours as I teetered over the broken platform, with one foot on the stairway and the other stretched toward a landing that no longer existed. One inch, one breath forward, and I would fall. I pulled my shoulders back and tensed my stomach muscles to keep my body anchored to the vibrating stair. Arching my back, I used the weight and strength of my torso to keep from plunging to the floor below.

Through the roaring in my ears, I heard gasps and screams. Somehow, I managed to tumble backward, avoiding the gaping chasm. The moment I was safe, the curtain dropped. I allowed myself a peek below. The stagehands, most of the male dancers, and several police officers were frozen in space, ready to catch me if I fell.

After experiencing in real life the nightmare that haunts people who fear heights, I couldn't move. It wasn't a rational response, but my body refused to listen to what my brain was telling it. Jonah ran onto the stage and climbed the stairs three at a time. He put his arm around me. I tried to stand, but my legs buckled. With infinite care, he helped me remain upright.

I struggled out of his embrace, afraid of revealing how weak I felt. "No! Give me a minute. I'm scared. Not hurt. I don't want people to see me like this."

He kept one arm around my shoulder. "The curtain is closed. Quit being such a drama queen."

His teasing words helped me, more than sympathetic ones would have, to regain my equilibrium. We slowly made our way down the stairs to the crowd below. Brett brought me a chair. "We've got EMTs on the way."

Zach charged onto the stage and made straight for Brett. "Mr. Cameron. I'm an emergency room physician. He extended his hand. "Dr. Zach Mitchell."

Brett stared at Zach's hand, as if unsure what to do with it. Zach left him and rushed to my side. He cupped my face in his hands. "Are you hurt?"

I pressed one hand against my chest to slow my breathing. I'd had enough shocks to last me a lifetime. "Thank you, Zach, but I'm fine."

He didn't leave. "I'm here if you need me. I can wait backstage."

Brett walked with stiff steps toward us. He looked worse than I felt. "Thank you, Dr. Mitchell, for your swift response." The stricken choreographer pushed back his dark hair, which had escaped its neat ponytail. "I appreciate your offer. I suggest you take a look at a few of the girls in the corps de ballet. Though they're mostly shaken up. It's a miracle none of them were badly hurt." He flicked a piece of plaster from Olivia's head.

Brett turned to face the rest of the dancers. Some were weeping. Others were rigid with shock. He clasped his hands to keep them from trembling. "You have twenty minutes to compose yourself. The show will resume at that time. The stagehands will clear this mess." He dabbed his wet eyes. "Do it for Maurice. And Eddie. And Leah."

Brett beckoned to Kerry. Heedless of onlookers, she stripped off her Dewdrop costume and grabbed a Sugar Plum Fairy tutu from a dresser. Horace pulled off his hat, cloak, black shirt, and pants. Underneath, he was wearing white tights and a thin tank top. Bobbie rushed onstage, holding up a white and silver tunic. With graceful fingers, Horace buttoned up his costume and assured Brett, "I'm ready. You can count on us." With unusual demonstrativeness, he gave Kerry's shoulder an affectionate squeeze.

My legs were still wobbly, but my voice was firm. "Not so fast. If the show goes on, it will go on with me."

I didn't look to my fellow dancers for support. It wasn't fair to put them in that risky position. They knew Brett was going to be the new director of

ABC. With the performance of a lifetime on the line, it would be foolhardy for any of them to challenge him.

The kids, however, were too young to calculate company politics. They pushed aside the grownups and formed a protective circle around me. Madison pressed her tear-stained cheek against mine, and Ethan said, "Who thinks Leah should be our Sugar Plum?" A chorus of high-pitched cheers reverberated across the stage.

Tex and Olivia, as rising stars with the company, had the most to lose, but they were the first to add their voices to the kids'. Olivia said softly, "Please, Brett. Let her dance."

Tex was more defiant. "You can do what you want with me. But when that curtain opens, it's going to be Leah onstage. Or no one."

The adult dancers joined them and began clapping in a slow, steady rhythm that grew in intensity.

Too choked with emotion to speak, I responded to my colleagues in our shared language. Using the ancient art of ballet pantomime, I pressed my hands to my heart and to my lips, and then, palms up, stretched my arms to them. You didn't have to be trained in dance to get the message, but the gestures had exceptional emotional resonance for us. The dancers echoed back to me that silent expression of love.

Brett's face purpled in response, but he didn't fight back. "As you wish." He leaned over to whisper in my ear. "Don't screw this up. If you fail, we all go down."

Jonah and one of the dressers followed me into the wings. While she fussed over my costume, he fussed over me. "You can't do this. Five minutes ago, you couldn't walk. And now you're going to dance? You'll hurt yourself."

I thanked the dresser, who ended up not having much to do. The stiff tulle of my costume was undamaged. My hair was still in place, thanks to the shellacking it got earlier. My makeup, however, needed work. I didn't remember crying, but at some point, my eyeliner had migrated to my cheekbones. The dresser held up a mirror, and Olivia rushed in, bearing makeup. With swift, short dabs, I repaired the damage. The prosaic task of getting ready for a performance calmed me.

I looked up from the mirror at Jonah. "Thank you for rescuing me tonight."

He blew an exasperated breath through closed lips. "Some rescue. I didn't do anything."

I clenched a cotton ball. "We can debate the issue later."

Jonah pulled me deeper into the wings. "I don't want you or your friends to take any chances tonight. Don't be stupid, Leah. Brett should end the performance."

I flexed my feet to make sure they were still working. "Brett is the choreographer, and his future depends on the success of this production. The killer would have to take out the entire company before he'd agree to stop the performance." I wiped cold sweat from my forehead. "Do you think the collapse of the platform was deliberate? It might have been a random accident. Maurice's set design, while beautiful, has always had problems."

"We won't know if it was sabotaged until after forensics examines the pieces. For now, we assume the worst. What have you said, or done, to make the killer think you're a threat?"

With grim efficiency, the stagehands removed the last remnants of Maurice's cursed stage set. "It looks as if we're ready to resume the performance. Let's continue this conversation later."

His voice was cold. "Answer the question, Leah."

"I may have mentioned something to Bobbie about her past history with Maurice. You know this already. Francie said she was going to tell you."

"Morelli told me you thought Bobbie was in danger."

"I may have miscalculated. If she's not in danger, she might very well be a danger."

After a hurried discussion about how we would adjust the choreography, the lights dimmed. Freed from the tension of having to perform on the platform, I danced with a joy and lightness I'd struggled to hold onto amid the shadow of the previous weeks.

Tex took the stage with reckless, exciting abandon. He jumped with airy grace and landed each pirouette with confident poise. When it came time for the one-armed lift over his head, he swept me into the air with a flourish that brought cheers and spontaneous applause.

The final notes of Tchaikovsky's brilliant music were lost in the roar of the crowd. They didn't wait for us to finish before standing, cheering, and clapping.

We bowed and curtseyed. Four kids brought bouquets of flowers for me, for Tex, for Madame, and for Brett. The audience showered us with even more applause, as the apron of the stage filled with fragrant blooms.

The curtain came down, but the clapping continued. I looked at Tex. We weren't prepared for this outpouring of support. Brett emerged from the wings and signaled for the curtain to reopen. One of the stagehands handed him a microphone.

Our suffering but jubilant choreographer waited for complete silence. "Ladies and gentlemen. We have dedicated this performance, and this production, to the memory of Maurice Kaminsky, my loving partner in life and in art. I know if he were here with us, he would be as moved as I am by your support. I want to thank everyone at American Ballet Company for making this night possible. We always planned on giving you an exciting evening." He paused. "Maybe not quite *this* exciting."

A ripple of laughter rose from the audience. When it died down, he said, "Most of all, I want to thank you, the people of New York City, for being the best audience in the world. My heart is, always and forever, with you."

Deafening cheers, stomping feet, and shouts of *Bravo!* rocked the theater. The stagehands stood in respectful attention. Many dancers were tearful. When Brett came backstage, we gave our final bow of the evening to him and added our applause to the thunderous roar of the crowd.

Brett trembled with emotion. "It has been the greatest privilege of my life to have worked with you all. I've choreographed for many ballet companies. None came close to ABC." He drew a deep breath. "The last few weeks have been challenging in ways we couldn't have imagined when we began this journey." He clasped his hands, as if in prayer. "For the next few hours, though, I want you to put all that aside and celebrate with me. Tonight, we look to the future. Not the past."

He cut short our applause and returned to his habitual brusqueness.

"Please check your email for directions on how to answer questions regarding tonight's unfortunate accident. This is no time for improvisation. Follow the script. It's designed for your protection, as well as the company's."

We remained in place until he exited the stage. The moment felt too solemn for words. Post-performance relief helped mitigate our sober mood, as did the well-wishers waiting backstage.

Barbara pushed past the crowd to embrace me. "I have a surprise."

Behind her, my father stood with open arms. He embraced me, and said, "Well done, Leah. Well done."

I hadn't realized how much I'd missed him until I saw him. I held his hands and said, "I'm so happy you're here. When did you get into town?"

Rachel waved her arms like an irate traffic cop at a busy intersection. "Are we going to stand here all day talking? Or are we going to the party?"

Barbara handed me a garment bag. "I hope you like it." Inside was a strapless, blue velvet gown embellished with tiny silver butterflies. It was perfect.

Melissa followed me to my dressing room, and the rest of my family headed to the gala. "Leah, what really happened? Did someone tamper with the set? I thought I was going to pass out, watching you up there."

I wiped the makeup off my face. "No one knows how it happened. Jonah said he'd let me know as soon as he hears back from forensics."

"I don't have a good feeling about this party. We might be better off skipping it."

I eased my feet into silver sandals, which had convenient openings for my bunions. "We can't miss the party. The Choreographers of Crime have work to do. And I'm counting on you to help."

She closed her eyes and drew her brows together. "Maurice was the first victim. Eddie was the second. Nelson was an attempted third. And you were the killer's fourth target. Let's assume Maurice's death was the primary objective. Eddie and Nelson must have had some connection to Maurice that put them in danger. Think, Leah. What could it be?"

I copied Melissa and closed my eyes, although my brain cells are not in her class. "Nelson and Eddie filmed us nonstop for over a week. They must have recorded proof of the killer's guilt. Something they innocently told me."

I opened my eyes to find her staring at me. "Correct. What did you say or do to make the killer think you are also in possession of that incriminating evidence?"

Goosebumps popped on my arms. The uneasy feeling I'd had, in the aftermath of Eddie's death, returned. Of all the chance and random things Nelson and Eddie had told me, which piece of information was the key?

Melissa picked bobby pins from my hair. "Who wants you out of the way?"

"This is a ballet company, Melissa. One of the greatest ballet companies in the world. My departure would ensure another dancer's rise." In response to her disapproving look, I added, "Don't tell me it's not the same in academia."

Melissa thought she had the last word. "College professors don't kill each other to get tenure."

I brushed the gunk out of my hair. "Don't tell that to Barbara. It's the plotline in all of her books."

Chapter Thirty

In order to be a good soldier it is necessary to know how to dance...
—Plato

Four security guards stood behind Olivia and three other young dancers at the entrance to the ballroom. The guards wore blue uniforms and stoic expressions. The dancers wore floor-length gowns and bright smiles. Their job was to direct guests to their assigned tables and to check each person's name against the list of attendees. When I walked in, however, the women abandoned their posts and swarmed around me like teenaged kids reuniting after summer break, although less than an hour had elapsed since we were onstage together.

Olivia had tears in her eyes. "You did it!"

Her three companions vied to embrace me. "You killed it!"

I returned their compliments with sincere gratitude and admiration. They were the most vulnerable of the group that supported me, and when the performance resumed, they'd been brilliant.

Melissa and I skirted the dance floor, past the choice tables where the biggest donors were seated. My family occupied a table at the outer perimeter of the room, also known as No Man's Land. It was not a favorable placement for social climbing but excellent for making a quick getaway.

My mother inspected me with a critical eye. "That dress is perfect, if I do say so myself." She pushed the breadbasket across the table, as if worried the carbohydrates would magically transport themselves to either her or me.

Rachel picked out a roll and dropped it on my plate. "She's too skinny if

202

you ask me. She could disappear behind a pole."

I'm used to having people judge me for how I look and to discuss my body as if didn't belong to me. In one sense, it didn't. This was not some abstract idea. It's written into our contract. If we show signs of "noticeable weight gain" we could be terminated. Aside from that potent deterrent, the humiliation from peers provided a powerful incentive. ABC's dreaded "fat talk" was legendary, and when I returned to the company following knee surgery, I came perilously close to being called into the office to discuss my weight.

In an effort to redirect the conversation, I asked my father if his wife had made the trip from California with him.

My mother jumped in before he could answer. "Ann couldn't get away. I believe her chakras posed an insuperable barrier to flying. What happened, Jeremy? Did the moon fail to make it to the seventh house?"

My father was amused and not offended. "Barbara, your concern for Ann is commendable. She wanted to come, but she recently started a new job and couldn't get away."

The lines on his forehead and dark circles under his eyes worried me. "Thanks so much for making the trip, Dad. But as long as we're talking about appearances, you look like you could use some rest. Please don't feel obligated to sit through dinner. I'm off tomorrow, and we can catch up then."

He patted my hand. "I'm fine. I caught the redeye last night and wanted to surprise you. But you're the one who provided most of the night's surprises. What happened?"

"We don't know yet. The platform could have collapsed of its own weight. Or it could have fallen thanks to shoddy workmanship."

My sister was unsparing in her judgment. "I suspect sabotage."

Dad closed his eyes, a habit my sister had either inherited or unconsciously imitated. "What do the stagehand do with the fake snow? Do they keep it or throw it away?"

"They keep it in big bags and reuse it. Why do you ask?"

He opened his eyes. "Tell your detective friend to check the bags. During the snow scene, I noticed pieces of plaster falling from the underside of the platform. I notified the staff, but they may not have had sufficient time to inspect the scenery or report my concerns. It's possible a forensics team can get fingerprints from the fragments."

Zach approached the table, interrupting the sudden, anxious silence my father's words inspired. The server who followed him brought a bottle of champagne. My parents welcomed him warmly. In deference to their feelings, I didn't ask Zach where he and Sloane were seated. There was plenty of time to explain why he was there as his ex-wife's date and not mine.

The waiter popped the cork on the champagne bottle. Under other circumstances, I would have gladly downed an entire glass, but I wanted to stay sharp. I pushed back my chair. "I need to stretch my legs. Zach, why don't you come with me?"

He offered me his arm and, when we were out of earshot, said, "What's on your mind, Leah? I find it hard to believe that after all you've been through tonight, you're in dire need of more exercise."

I guided him toward the bar. "Have you spoken to Sloane?"

He stiffened. "I did. She didn't have much information, although she did say Brett and Maurice were happily married. She's certain they were in love and equally positive Brett isn't guilty of murder."

"That's what Charlotte said, too." I jiggled his arm to get him to relax. "Do you need to get back to Sloane? It's fine if you do."

"There's no rush. I would prefer to be your date." His eyes scanned the room and rested on Jonah. "Speaking of dates, who's Detective Sobol with? She looks familiar."

"That's Francie. Officer Morelli, to be precise. As for pairing up, whatever the reason, you're here with your ex-wife."

He stopped. "Forget about Sloane. I want to talk about Sobol. I hold him responsible for what happened to you tonight."

"I won't discuss Sloane if you promise not to discuss Jonah." I prodded Zach toward the bar. "First stop is Jonathan Llewelyn Franklin III."

"The real estate guy?"

"Exactly."

Although I'd met Jonathan's wife for the first time at Charlotte's reception, Leonora acted as if we were old friends. "What a wonderful performance! I danced in *The Nutcracker* when I was a kid, but I don't think I've seen it since then. And you were such a trouper. I was in awe."

Jonathan was less enchanted. "Doesn't look good for ABC to have half the scenery crash onto the stage. This is a public relations nightmare. Believe you me, heads are going to roll come Monday. We pay those stagehands a fortune, and they screwed it up."

I sat on an empty barstool and said, "I believe the collapse was deliberate and not the result of anything the stagehands did or didn't do. Jonathan, as a member of the board, I presume you'll be briefed in full. Not many people have your access."

Like many weak men with jobs bigger than they are, any reminder of his importance pleased him. "That's true. I'll keep an open mind until I get a full report."

Leonora gasped. "That's awful! But why? What possible motive could anyone have to do such a terrible thing? You could have been killed." She leaned closer. "Leah, I think you know a lot more than you're telling us. Spill! I swear not to tell anyone."

I silently thanked her for giving me the perfect opening. Pretending to hesitate, I said, "I could get into all sorts of trouble if you blabbed."

She mimicked locking her lips and throwing away the key. "Wild horses couldn't drag it from me."

With a cautionary look over my shoulder, I said, "A reliable source told me Maurice's killer engineered tonight's disaster." I inclined my head closer to hers. "The killer is someone who's known Maurice for a long time. We're talking almost thirty years."

She turned down the corners of her lovely mouth. "I wasn't born thirty years ago. I can't begin to guess who it is." She turned to her husband. "But Jonathan might. He and his whole family were close with Maurice."

Jonathan elbowed her. "Nah. My genius wife is wrong, as usual. Didn't know the guy."

Nice try. "You were at Charlotte's reception following Maurice's funeral. Why were you there if you had no connection to him?"

His tight smile looked forced. "Leonora doesn't know what she's talking about. For me, it was a social event."

Zach said, "I'm surprised to hear you don't know him, given the fact that your family is so involved in the art world."

Jonathan gulped his drink and wiped his mouth with the back of his hand. "I knew Maurice socially. Which is the same as not knowing him at all. Sorry I can't help."

I stayed pleasant. "You did know Nelson, though."

Jonathan slammed his drink on the bar hard enough to break the glass. "Nelson Merrill is no friend of mine. He's a worthless con man."

Zach tightened his grip on my shoulder. "Great talking to you." He placed his glass on the bar and said, "You'll have to excuse us. Leah's family is waiting."

I was annoyed with him. When we were a safe distance away, I said, "Why did you make us leave? I still had questions for him and for Leonora."

"I'm sure you did. Before you upend any more wasp nests, we need to talk. Come with me."

He led me to the doors that opened onto the balcony, where a few hardy people smoked and vaped.

I pulled away. "I'm not going outside. I'll freeze to death."

"We need a few minutes away from possible eavesdroppers."

"Watching those people shiver is enough to give me hypothermia. Say what you have to say here. No one's listening."

"That's what you think." He handed me his suit jacket. "Take this."

Without further argument, I let him drape his jacket around my shoulders. The blast of Arctic air when he opened the door took my breath away. "Make it quick. Getting pneumonia is not on my to-do list for the evening."

His attitude rivaled the weather in bitterness. "Toss the to-do list. It's not your responsibility to find the killer. It's a crazy and dangerous plan."

My teeth were chattering so violently I could barely get the words out. "I'm an adult, Zach. I make my own choices. No one is forcing me to act.

But if you want to continue this conversation, it's going to have to take place someplace a whole lot warmer. My body is about to shut down."

We abandoned the smokers and squeezed through the growing crowd. He said, "Is there any place we can talk privately? Other than the balcony?"

I knew every inch of the theater. "Follow me."

Zach and I ducked under a red velvet rope and walked two flights up to the cheap seats. Less than an hour earlier, the Family Circle section had been mobbed. It was now deserted except for a cleaner, who swiped a duster up the banister of the opposite staircase. He didn't appear to notice us.

I rubbed goosebumps from my cold arms. "What were you going to tell me while we were talking to Jonathan and Leonora? I wasn't finished grilling him."

Zach sat on the top step. "Two people were watching you. Stalking you. Savannah Collier was one. She was taking pictures the whole time. Brett Cameron was the other."

"I can't do anything about Savannah, who's been a thorn in my side for months. As for Brett, I wish I'd seen him. I want to talk to him before he gets caught up in the whole social frenzy he's so fond of. Maybe he wanted to tell me why the set collapsed, and he didn't want to do so in front of Jonathan, who's still an influential board member."

Zach resisted my effort to get him to stand up. "Not so fast. I don't want you to be alone with Brett. Not tonight. Not ever."

"Don't be ridiculous. He isn't going to talk frankly if you're with me. I'll let you know later what he says."

He pulled me down next to him. "You're not getting rid of me so easily. How do you know he's not the killer? He could have been the one who set you up tonight."

His opposition frustrated me. "I understand why you suspect Brett. Before the performance, I did too. But not anymore. If you saw him after the curtain came down, you'd understand. He's genuinely mourning Maurice's death. He couldn't possibly have killed him. No one is that good an actor."

He stretched out his legs. "Maybe. Or maybe he's suffering the pangs of guilt."

"I don't think so. Logically, Brett is a likely suspect. It's common knowledge his marriage to Maurice was troubled. But you can say that about plenty of marriages. Divorce would have been a much saner and safer solution than murder. After all, Brett wasn't dependent on Maurice. He's a successful choreographer. He'll probably be named ABC's new artistic director."

Zach remained skeptical. "I'm not saying the murder was premeditated. They could have had a fight, and things got out of hand."

I hoped that by conceding his point, we could end the conversation. "I suppose that's possible. Brett does have a temper. But not a murderous temper. He's ruthless about his choreography but not ruthless enough to kill someone over it."

"I'll have to take your word for that, although I wasn't taken in by his humble speech to the audience. It seemed calculated to me."

"Agreed. I think there are more credible suspects, but I won't take unnecessary risks with him or anyone else." I stood up. "It's time we got back to the party."

The custodian got into the elevator, and we took the stairs, which was a mistake. My knees ached worse than usual, and I regretted not taking the elevator with the cleaner.

I paused on the landing to stretch. "The other objection I have to tagging Brett as the murderer is his friendship with Nelson. I suspect the wound Nelson got on the day of the blackout was a bungled attempt on his life."

Zach took my arm. "You know Brett better than I do. However, a man who kills his husband isn't going to let friendship stop him from a second murder, if his life and freedom are on the line."

I pulled away. "You can't attach yourself to me."

"I think I can. Stop fighting me."

"I'm not fighting you. If I promise not to go into any dark, underground mazes, will that satisfy you?"

"Do I have the choice?"

"No."

With Zach trailing behind me, I circled the crowded room, looking for

Brett. I couldn't find him, and no one knew where he went.

Peter York, looking lost, waylaid me. "Leah, have you seen Bobbie? She should be here by now."

"Sorry, Peter. I haven't seen her since before the performance. She's probably overseeing the costumes. Why don't you check backstage?"

He tugged at his tight collar. "She would kill me if I went backstage. You know how she gets when she's working. A one-track mind."

That got my attention. "Did you call her?"

He patted his pocket. "Of course. She texted she was on her way. But that was a half-hour ago. I suppose I'm overreacting. But after what happened onstage tonight, I can't help but worry."

Brett was missing. Bobbie was missing. I had an uneasy feeling that someone else, someone who should have been at the party, was also absent.

"Don't worry, Peter. I'll find her."

Chapter Thirty-One

We are the dancers, we create the dreams.
—Albert Einstein

When I returned to the bar, Jonathan was without his wife and had Olivia cornered between two high-backed chairs. I tapped his shoulder, and he whirled around, annoyed at the interruption.

"This is a private conversation, Leah."

"I apologize for interrupting you, but Olivia is going to be in serious trouble if she doesn't get back to the reception table." I turned to my friend. "It's not my place to tell you what to do, but you should go before anyone notices you're gone."

My friend mouthed a *thank you* and slipped away. Jonathan watched her go. When she was lost in the crowd, he surveyed the room for fresh prey.

I had one last mission for Zach. "Tell my family I'll join them shortly. Then you should get back to Sloane. I'm sure she's wondering where you are."

He tensed. "Why? Where are you going?"

"I'm going to look for Bobbie. I'll notify you if I leave the party." I didn't put a time frame, however, on when I would inform him. Technically, I was telling the truth.

A woman with a press pass approached. I whispered to Zach, "Leave now. Unless you want your name in the papers tomorrow."

The reporter lifted her glass. "Ms. Siderova. That was an amazing performance."

I knew most of the dance critics, but her face was unfamiliar. "Isn't Karl here tonight?"

"He was here earlier. He's probably filing his review of the performance. I'm on the news beat. Several dancers have spoken off the record about tonight's onstage crash. Can you comment as well?"

"No."

She continued to press me. "Is that 'no' you can't comment, or 'no' you won't comment?"

I smiled to take any possible sting from my response. "Either one works."

I thought the conversation was over, but Ms. News Reporter didn't share my view. "Ms. Siderova, what is the company trying to hide?"

Good question. Unfortunately, I wasn't any better informed than she was. "I suggest you contact our public relations department. They handle requests from the press. If you'll excuse me, I'd like to get back to my family."

She kept talking. "Don't you think the dancers should have a voice?"

Horace joined us. He dropped gracefully to one knee and kissed my hand, which set off a flurry of picture-taking. His modeling career made him more recognizable than most dancers, and when the reporter caught sight of his golden hair and classic profile, she abandoned me and chased after him.

No sooner was I relieved of one distraction than another, more deadly one, intervened.

"Why if it isn't the woman of the hour!"

Savannah blocked my exit and clicked a rapid series of pictures as part of her ceaseless effort to post unflattering photos of me.

My social media troll didn't rate the kind of polite demurrals I offered the news reporter. "Get out of my way."

She wore a hot pink dress and an ice-cold glare. "My, my. Aren't we testy today? I don't blame you. I'd be upset too, if Kerry Blair was named as lead ballerina in *Romeo and Juliet*."

I caught my breath. Ten minutes after the platform broke down, Kerry was ready to take my place. Could she have been the one to engineer its collapse? Or was she simply capitalizing on my misfortune?

Savannah purred with enjoyment. "I see you don't yet know. Kerry is going to be promoted to principal dancer. Which means there isn't much room at the top for ballerinas who are past their prime. So sorry to be the one to break it to you!" She batted her lashes with deliberate, insulting pleasure.

I lifted my chin. "I'm delighted to hear Kerry's getting the promotion. She deserves it. She's not like some people, who quit after one year."

Savannah lost her complacent expression, and her lip quivered. I immediately regretted my cruelty. No one knew better than I the pain of rejection and the emotional toll of constant, critical judgments.

She curled her fingers. "I hate you. I've always hated you."

I dropped the combative and defensive pose I always wore with her. "I don't understand why. I never did anything to you."

She blinked away tears. "You treated me like dirt."

I searched my memory but came up with nothing. "I honestly don't know what you're talking about. I can barely remember dancing with you."

Her fury returned. "That's my point. You didn't know I existed."

This, sadly, had a germ of truth to it. "I never meant to hurt you."

She bared her teeth as if about to bite. "But I did mean to hurt you. And I'm not done."

I didn't quail. At least, not on the outside. "Don't threaten me. I don't scare easily."

"I have friends in high places. How else could I have gotten dirt on you and everyone else in the company?" She brought her face so close to mine I could see the sheen of sweat on her nose. "I know who my friends are. Do you?"

Although we were surrounded by hundreds of people, I felt the cold chill of fear. Unequal to the task of dealing with Savannah's malice, I conjured up the Wicked Fairy in the ballet *Sleeping Beauty* to help me out. For the second time that night, I used ballet pantomime to convey my emotion. She got the message. To a dancer, the gestures were as legible as spoken language.

Her complexion burned hotter than her dress. "That's not as funny as you think, although the role of an old witch suits you perfectly. It's your career, not mine, that's going to be cursed and fall into a dead sleep."

The electronic squawk of a microphone blurred her next words. The head of fundraising stood at a raised podium in front of the room. After a few welcoming remarks, she announced dinner was served. A chamber music quartet took possession of an improvised stage.

Emotion and exertion robbed me of strength and energy. I turned my back on Savannah, as I should have done from the start. As I wound my way back to our table, I mentally checked off who was there and who should have been there but was not. Peter York sat next to an empty seat, which meant Bobbie was still missing. Jonah and Francie, if they were still in the ballroom, were well hidden. And Brett Cameron, our choreographer and guest of honor, was not on the dais. Sloane Mitchell sat next to an empty seat, but Zach was not missing. He had relocated to my table, in a chair wedged next to mine.

With great reluctance, I heeded my family's call to join them for dinner. The server placed an elegantly composed plate in front of each of us. The glistening salmon, artfully stacked string beans, and golden potatoes didn't tempt me. Nor did the prime rib Zach ordered. I wanted a peanut butter and jelly sandwich. Or a black and white cookie. Something comforting. Under Barbara's censorious gaze, I regained possession of the breadbasket and silently applauded the culinary genius who included raisin pumpernickel bread. Those chewy slices tasted like heaven.

As if by accident, I knocked my fork off the table. Zach bent over to pick it up, and I slipped his steak knife into my evening bag. I nudged Melissa with my knee and inclined my head toward the exit.

My beloved sister got the message. She rose and said, "I'm off to the ladies' room. Hopefully, the line isn't too long."

Without apparent hurry, I said, "I'll join you."

Zach was suspicious. "I'll go too."

I put a reassuring hand on his shoulder. "It would be extremely unfair for you to use the ladies' room when there's no line at the men's room."

As intended, my comment ignited a hot discussion. In most theaters, the bathroom wait time for women during intermission can extend beyond the intermission itself, whereas men never have to stand in line. With the opening I'd given her, Barbara could be counted upon to keep the conversation lively while Melissa and I were gone.

My sister and I walked fifteen feet toward the bathroom, at which point I took a sharp right. She hung back. "I'm guessing we're not headed to the bathroom."

"Correct. We have two missing people. Brett and Bobbie. We need to find them."

My sister scrunched up her face. "Maybe they're backstage. They might not have finished whatever it is choreographers and costume people do after a performance."

"No. Brett would leave his cat in a burning building before missing this gala. As for Bobbie, she texted her husband that she was on her way, but she's still MIA."

Melissa said, "Whatever you have planned, we have to stick together. And not do anything overly stupid."

"Of course. Otherwise, we'll end up like the victims of a cheap horror movie, who walk by themselves down dark paths after a crazed killer starts picking them off one by one."

Melissa wavered. "Call Jonah. This is his territory, not ours."

I tapped a message and waited. "No answer. And no response from Francie Morelli either."

My sister continued to hold back. "Have you tried calling Brett and Bobbie?"

"I don't have Brett's cell number. I'll try Bobbie again, although if she doesn't pick up, it doesn't mean she's in trouble. I'm not on her A list." I put the phone on speaker, and Bobbie's ringtone sang out a brief musical phrase from Mozart's opera, *The Magic Flute*.

Melissa flinched. "What kind of message does Bobbie think she's sending by using that song as her ringtone? The Queen of the Night had one of the worst breakups in history, other than Aunt Rachel and ex-uncle Mark."

I put my finger to my lips as Bobbie's gravelly voice recording took the place of the music. I left her a voicemail. "Bobbie, this is Leah Siderova. Please call me back and let me know you're okay. Peter is worried about you, and so am I."

I nearly dropped the phone when a text from Bobbie popped up. **Tell Peter I'm ok.**

Melissa was relieved. "She's alive and unharmed. Let's go back."

Thinking of Olga's warning about cell phones, I said, "How do we know she's the one who sent the text? What if she's being held hostage? Or worse? We need to do something. Now. It might already be too late."

My sister took out her phone. "We're not doing anything without backup. I'm calling Olga. If we get caught up in a situation we can't handle, at least there will be three of us who can call nine-one-one for help. Plus, Olga is, well, Olga."

Melissa didn't bother with the speaker. Olga's booming voice was audible without it. "Wait for me, dear friend. Am taking Madame home. Will be back soon."

I couldn't stand still any longer. Melissa trailed after me. She was as nervous and as uncertain as I was. "What should we do, Leah? We can't file a missing person report for two people who've been gone for less than an hour. Should we call nine-one-one?"

I pressed my palms against my forehead. "You're the genius. You tell me. Does this qualify as an emergency? Or have the events of the night made me so paranoid I see threats where none exist?"

Melissa reverted to her precise and logical self. "There are three possible scenarios. One is that the killer has Bobbie and Brett. If that's the case, your phone call may have put them in even more peril. The second possibility is either Bobbie or Brett is the killer. The third is that they're working together and are both guilty."

My head was throbbing. "You left out the fourth option, which is that they're fine and are having torrid sex in the costume room. What if we called in an emergency that doesn't exist? And police cars and an ambulance show up in front of dozens of reporters and bloggers, asking what happened? This would entail extreme embarrassment for me, as well as for Brett, who's in line to become my future boss."

She looked at her watch. "Although it feels as if ten years have passed since the curtain went down, the gala began forty-five minutes ago."

I consciously controlled my breath, slowing it down from frantic panting to moderate panic. "It's not too late to save them. If they need saving."

Her feet stayed rooted to the floor. "What if we walk into a situation we can't handle? What if Bobbie and Brett deserve a prison sentence instead of a rescue?"

Guilt overtook fear. "Melissa, you're a mother. I shouldn't have asked you to come with me. Go back. I'll figure this out on my own and keep you posted."

"Abandoning you now would be highly unethical. I'm sure you know what moral philosophers since the beginning of time would have to say about that. How can I look my children in the eye if I let you down when you were most in need of help?"

Arguments with my father and Melissa took place on a rarified plane of rhetorical analysis that tended to give rise to more questions without delivering direct answers. This was not an occasion that was conducive to methodical deliberation.

"If I were as smart as you, I'm sure I could find a philosopher to back me up. We're running out of time. Go back. I'll text if I need you."

"You're not going anywhere without me."

I was scared, but not as scared as I would have been without her. "I'm not going to argue with you. I'll message Jonah and Francie and let them know if they don't hear from one of us in thirty minutes, it means we're in trouble. Take out your phone, so we can enable them to track our location."

The cleaner was still at his post. I made sure his back was to us before proceeding. Armed in stiletto heels, with cell phones and a single steak knife, we went into battle.

Chapter Thirty-Two

All false art...destroys itself.
—Immanuel Kant

Our first rescue mission was one we hadn't planned. A strangled scream sent us rushing to the reception area, where Jonathan had Olivia pinned against the wall.

I took off my shoe and slammed him on the back of his head. Melissa followed with a sharp punch to his ear. Jonathan dropped his grip on Olivia and spun around. In the split second before his fist could make contact with my face, I ducked, and he stumbled to his knees. With great restraint, I didn't kick him when he was down. As insurance against further violence, I withdrew the steak knife I'd swiped from Zach's place setting.

He scrambled to his feet. An angry flush reddened his face. "What the hell do you think you're doing?"

Melissa had her small fists cocked. "We could ask the same question of you."

Olivia tucked a torn strap into the bodice of her dress. "Leave him alone. I'm fine."

My sister took out her phone. "Stay where you are, Olivia. We'll get one of the police officers here so you can press charges."

Jonathan stood up and straightened his jacket. "You two are way out of line. The little tease lured me here. I did nothing."

I concentrated on Olivia. "What were you doing here by yourself?"

Olivia hugged herself with skinny arms. "It was my turn to cover the desk.

217

We were taking turns, so all of us could spend some time at the party. But I'm fine. Let him go. I'm okay."

Melissa, who understood enough of our world to sympathize with her reluctance, said, "Times are different now. Dancers don't have to put up with this kind of intimidation anymore."

Olivia and I knew better, and when Jonathan strolled off, we didn't stop him.

A pulse throbbed in Melissa's throat. "I don't believe this. Are you going to let him get away with attacking you?" Olivia stared at her feet and didn't answer.

I gave my trembling friend a gentle hug. "Go back to the party. Find Olga and have her escort you to a cab. She'll protect you."

I waited for Olivia to leave before tending to my enraged sister. "The Franklin Family Trust is one of our biggest donors. A fundraising gala is neither the time nor the place to press charges, although I had other reasons for letting him go. We can't risk diverting the police when a killer is on the loose. And if the killer is Jonathan, we have to leave him enough rope to hang himself."

She was not pacified. "Your logic is flawed. If we can get him locked up for attacking Olivia, the police will have plenty of time to book him for murder."

It would be nice if the world worked the way Melissa thought it should. But it didn't.

I offered my sister a compromise. "Let's finish what we started and find Bobbie and Brett. Then we'll deal with Jonathan."

She bit her lip but offered no further argument as we headed into a shadowy backstage corridor. The stagehands and custodians were gone. I knew, without checking, the guard at the stage door was also gone. His job was over when the dancers left for the night.

The dim night lights, which replaced the bright working lights, made passage down the crowded corridors perilous. Racks of costumes impeded our progress, and I flinched each time a gauzy piece of fabric grazed my arm. The sound of sobbing drew us to the farthest reaches of the hallway. We stopped outside the costume room. The door was closed.

"What now?" Melissa whispered.

"We need the element of surprise. Wait here, and don't move."

I retraced my steps and, using my phone as a flashlight, located one of the stagehand's toolboxes. I picked a wrench so heavy I needed two hands to carry it.

Thick carpet muffled my steps. I handed Melissa the steak knife I'd swiped from Zach's plate and put my mouth to her ear. "You stay outside and out of sight. I'm going in. And if anything happens, stab first. Ask questions later."

She immediately dropped the knife, which came close to piercing one of my favorite toes. "That's crazy! We need a better plan."

"It's too late for that. If the killer is inside and I get trapped, call nine-one-one and run back to the party yelling at the top of your voice. That should buy me some time."

Our indecision ended with the sound of broken glass and a loud thud. I slammed the door open in a move I learned from watching tv cop shows. Holding the wrench in front of me, I was ready to swing to kill. Bobbie and Brett jumped to their feet, too stunned to cry out.

I had a completely irrational urge to laugh at myself. There I stood, like a character from the game *Clue*. Leah Siderova, with a wrench, in the costume room. Bobbie's eyes were red and her face blotchy. She looked worse than I do when I cry.

I waved the wrench at Brett. "On the floor. Keep your hands where I can see them."

Melissa yelled from the hallway, "I'm calling the police!"

Bobbie pulled a fistful of tissues from the supply box. "Why are you here? Go away."

This was not the reception I anticipated. "I, um, I'm rescuing you."

Brett didn't drop to the floor or reach for a weapon. Instead, he tilted his head to one side. The choreographer was irritated. Impatient, even. But guilty? No.

He stepped over a pile of shattered glass. "That demented woman attacked me. She threw a cup at my head. I had to barricade myself behind the table to avoid getting anything else thrown at me." He adjusted his bow tie and brushed back his thick, dark hair. "If you need further assistance, I'll be at the gala. As the guest of honor."

I didn't attempt to stop him. What would I charge him with? Making people cry was not a crime. And if it were a crime, there wasn't a jury in the world who would convict him, given the ample provocation our antagonistic costume mistress regularly dished out.

Bobbie was nearly incoherent with rage. "If you don't get out of here, I'm going to be the one calling the police."

I took a seat. "Show some gratitude. I thought you were in danger. Your husband was looking for you. Fool that I am, I came to help you."

She sniffled into a bunch of tissues. "I told you to stay away from him."

I shouldn't have mentioned Peter. The Egyptian pyramids would crumble before Bobbie's jealousy did. But given her devotion to him, her failure to respond to his calls was curious. "Why didn't you call him? He's waiting for you."

She threw the tissues into a wastebasket. "It's more likely you were the one he wanted to be with. Every time he comes to see ABC, he can't shut up about you. He doesn't notice anyone else. As for this stunt, all I have to say is your behavior is borderline harassment. I should report you to the police."

Melissa was compassionate. "There's no need to threaten us. We mean you no harm. Why are you crying? Maybe we can help."

Bobbie's mouth twitched. "Brett wants to bring in a new person to take my place. This is the second time in less than a year I've had to fight to keep my job." Her voice rose. "I may not be the most likable person on staff, but I am the best."

I didn't mention her habit of spitefully sticking dancers with pins, although that was the sort of behavior an employer might reasonably censure. "Is that what all this was about? Your job? We thought the killer cornered you, and your life was in danger."

"That's because you have the IQ of a tutu." She inspected her face in the mirror and groaned. I didn't blame her. She did look rather awful. Sisterhood, paired with an intense desire to get back to the party, won out

220

over our petty quarrel, and I brought her some makeup from my dressing room. She accepted it without thanks.

While Bobbie repaired her face, Melissa prodded her. "Tell us more about what Brett said."

Bobbie wiped black streaks from her cheeks. "He said we needed more young people who would promote the ABC brand. He claimed it was Maurice who wanted to fire me. That was a lie, of course."

Her explanation made me realize how badly I'd misinterpreted her earlier claim about Brett. I looked over her head at Melissa. Bobbie seemed to be a victim. But in life, as in dance, appearances can be deceptive. "Did Brett say anything else about Maurice?"

"What difference does it make? Brett is a coward and a liar. Maurice would never betray me. Brett is using a dead man to justify firing me. You can't argue with a corpse."

She closed her eyes halfway to apply fresh eyeliner and mascara. I itched to give her a few tips, but Bobbie would go to her grave before accepting my advice. She gave her reflection one last look. Satisfied with the mask of makeup, she marched past us.

I hurried to keep up with her. "Tell me about the cold case Nelson was following, the one involving Heather Ford. The person who set the fire that killed her is still at large, and now we have two more murders that appear to be connected to that investigation."

Bobbie shivered. "I-I don't know anything about it."

"Yes, you do. Why else would you have mentioned Heather's name to me? I think you, and not Brett, is the one who's a liar and a coward. Did Brett try to blackmail you? Threaten you with the loss of your job if you didn't cover for him?"

Bobbie bolted through the door and down the hallway. I grabbed her skirt, and she stumbled. I stepped on her gown to pin her to the floor. One move and the sharp heel in my shoe would rip her dress.

"Time to come clean, Bobbie."

She gave us a twisted smile and gestured to the stairway behind us. "Too late, ladies. My dance card is full."

Jonah, Francie, and three plain clothes police officers, their guns drawn, charged toward us. Bobbie used this distraction to get out from under my shoe, nearly toppling me in the process.

Jonah said, "Leah and Melissa. Step away. Ms. York, lie down with your hands over your head."

Bobbie tried to brave it out. "You're making a big mistake, Detective."

He didn't budge. "Do it. Now."

Weeping tears of rage, she complied. Francie searched her and her evening bag. "She's clean, Detective."

Jonah flicked a quick glance at me. "Did she threaten you?"

I couldn't rid myself of the feeling that there was something wrong about the scene. "No, she didn't threaten us. Do you think we could have a minute to talk privately?"

"Not now, Leah. I'll be in touch later."

"Two minutes. That's all I need."

Leaving Bobbie under the watchful eyes and weapons of the other officers, Jonah let me lead him far enough away to ensure secrecy.

I leaned against the wall to steady my suddenly weak legs. "I don't think Bobbie is guilty."

"I don't think she's guilty of murder, but I suspect she knows a lot more than what she's told us so far. Withholding evidence is also a crime. Go home, Leah. Leave the rest to me."

I was furious. "If you weren't armed, I'd punch you. Or worse. Don't leave me out, Jonah. I can help."

He spoke as coolly as if we were distant acquaintances. "Your work here tonight is over. I can't stop you from returning to the party, but I strongly suggest you go home. I will be advising Ms. York to do the same."

I looked into his dark eyes, which gave no indication of what he was thinking. "You said we'd work together."

"Those plans are no longer relevant."

"Are you—do you want to come to my place later?" The words stuck in my throat.

He stepped back. "You're here with Dr. Mitchell. He'll take you home. I'm sure he's worried about you. I won't be finished until late."

I was careful not to seem too eager in the face of his indifference. "I doubt I'll be asleep, no matter how late you are. And I'm off tomorrow. Call me. I'll be waiting."

Melissa and I returned to the gala. Peter was still sitting in front of an untouched drink at the bar. He leaped to his feet when he saw me. "Did you find her?"

I was at a loss. What was my obligation to Bobbie, to her anxious husband, and to the murder investigation? I sent a mute appeal to Melissa. Ethics was her area of expertise. Not mine.

My diplomatic sister executed a classic non-answer. "Bobbie is so dedicated. I don't know what ABC would do without her."

Peter was so eager to agree, he nearly spilled his drink. "I tell her all the time they don't appreciate her enough. Brett's been giving her a really hard time, but she's a trouper." He gestured toward the bar. "Can I buy the two of you a free drink?"

"Thanks, Peter, but I'm on my way out. Tonight's performance took a lot out of me."

He kicked bashfully at the stool next to him. "You were wonderful, Leah. I don't know how you did it, but you're really special. I, well, I think you're beautiful. That is, you're a beautiful dancer." He broke off to check his phone. "Whew! That was Bobbie. Good talking to you." He bustled away.

I was miserable. "We should have told him what happened."

Melissa watched Peter until he disappeared into the crowd. "It wasn't our place to do so, and even if it was, we don't yet understand what happened. Are you really ready to leave? Or was that a ploy to escape talking to Peter?"

"All of the above. I'm too tired to stand, let alone run around in circles trying to figure out which of our suspects is guilty of murder."

With that perception peculiar to sisters, she said, "What did you and Jonah talk about?"

"Not much. I told him I didn't think Bobbie was guilty, and he agreed with me."

She shut her eyes for a brief moment and then widened them to fix me with her stare. "I guessed as much. I think any presumption of innocence is premature, but that wasn't what I was driving at. Did you talk to Jonah about anything else?"

I pretended not to know what she was asking. "What else is there?"

"I realize the situation wasn't conducive to romance, but I think you need to sort out this on-again, off-again relationship you have with him."

I was miserable, but not miserable enough to make my sister unhappy as well. "He's in the middle of a double homicide investigation. He doesn't have time for anything else. As for this relationship you think I have with him, it hasn't changed. Jonah and I are friends."

She held back as we approached our table. "I'm not sure if you're lying to me or you're lying to yourself. When you're ready to talk, I'm ready to listen."

"If we ever did have something more than friendship, it's over. Too many things got in the way, I guess. His job. My job. The murder investigation. Savannah Collier."

"You should tell him how you feel."

"I don't know how I feel."

She was gentle. "Yes, you do. And so does he. If he's putting you off, I can think of only one six-foot-tall reason why." She broke off to greet Zach.

With a big smile, she said, "The line at the bathroom really long. I hope we didn't miss dessert."

Chapter Thirty-Three

Of all the wonders that the world had to offer, only art promised immortality.
—Sergei Diaghilev

Barbara was disappointed with my decision to leave the gala. "You've been gadding about all night. We haven't had a minute to talk, and I've made some interesting observations." She raised her eyebrows and pulled me close. "Tell me where you've been."

In matters of clothing and style, my mother's advice was unerring. I was less inclined to rely on her for romantic, professional, or investigative assistance, although her insights were always entertaining and often apt. With Zach by my side, however, I couldn't discuss my trifecta of misery: Jonah's indifference, Kerry's ascension to the role of lead ballerina, and my growing certainty about the identity of the murderer.

"You'll have to carry on without me. We'll catch up tomorrow."

Zach brought my coat, and we headed toward the exit. Jonah was at the door. He nodded without making eye contact. "Good evening, Dr. Mitchell. Make sure Leah gets home safely."

Zach put a protective arm around me. "You don't have to worry about that. I'll take care of her."

I itched with the urge to kick the shins of both men. "Why are you talking about me as if I wasn't here? I'm not helpless." I yanked the door open and stomped past the brightly lit fountain in the center of the plaza and down the illuminated staircase to the street. Zach easily kept up with me. High-heeled shoes aren't well suited for impromptu fifty-yard dashes.

A sudden wind whipped open my coat. The hem caught the sharp edge of a metal garbage can, which resulted in a sickening scratch of torn fabric. I was seized by a grief not warranted by the damage to my clothing.

"It's a sign. The perfect symbol of my disintegrating life."

Zach pushed aside my clumsy fingers and unhooked the coat. "What are you talking about?"

"This whole night has been a disaster."

"You had a great performance. Why can't you be happy with that?"

It was a question worth considering. For most of my life, a great performance, even a great class, was a source of unalloyed happiness. I tried to regain the feeling of euphoria I had onstage. It didn't work. "I don't know what's wrong with me."

He took my arm. "Maybe dancing isn't enough for you anymore."

I stepped away from him. "That's not it. That's never going to be it."

"Maybe the stress of a double murder has made you rethink your career. It's time you realized there's more to life than being onstage. Whatever it is, Leah, I want to help."

I scanned the street for a cab. "You're a good man, Zach. Too good to waste your time with me. I'm not in the market for a long-term relationship."

He drew me back from the curb and kissed me lightly on the mouth. Zach was more than a friend. But less than a partner.

He stroked my hair. "I can take care of myself. And I will drop anything and everything to take care of you."

His words were heartfelt, and, at the same time, not true. We both knew it. I stepped back into the street, and a passing cab screeched to a stop. I got inside but didn't slide over to make room for him. "Go back to the party. Sloane is waiting for you."

He didn't argue. I spent the next two hours waiting for Jonah to call. He never did.

I woke up with a sore back. This was an extremely unfair development. The Fates had decreed I would suffer a lifetime of sore knees. Developing back problems was overkill. I made coffee and allowed myself ten minutes of peace before connecting with the world. When I did, I was shocked to find myself on the front page of the *New York Times*. Not the Arts section. The front page.

The picture scared me almost as much as the event itself. The photographer caught me in the split second before I pulled myself back to safety. My arms were outstretched, my back arched. The pointed foot of one leg stretched over empty space. The other leg, the one that anchored me, was less than six inches from the edge. The picture hammered home how close I'd been to the end of my career. And possibly, my life. I tried to look on the bright side. The photographer's angle and perspective prevented a closeup of my contorted face but provided a graceful outline of my body.

In the third paragraph of the story, the reporter quoted an unnamed source at the company, who said I would be starring in *Romeo and Juliet*. Was Savannah misinformed when she told me Kerry would dance Juliet? Or had she lied to me because she wanted me to suffer? The reason didn't matter. The opportunity to dance in the iconic role did. Margot Fonteyn was forty-five when she danced the part with Nureyev. Compared to her, I was still a baby. Practically a teenager myself.

I enlarged the photograph, this time examining the platform and not how I looked. The break wasn't clean. The edge was splintered, and the glittery paint on the underside had bare patches, confirming my father's suspicions and mine. The structure had been deliberately damaged before the performance. The time frame for doing so was narrow, as the platform had been rock-solid during the dress rehearsal.

Despite aching legs and back, I did some warmup exercises, too restless to sit still. I kept my phone silenced and facedown. Texts, emails, and social media could wait. Paralyzed by indecision, it became clear to me my real self was not up to the job. I discarded Leah Siderova and became Juliet Capulet. There was a heroine for the ages. She takes charge, takes chances, and is resolute in her determination to achieve her goal. I ignored the sad fact that I had no Romeo and that Juliet's story didn't end well. Her inspiration helped me get on with my day. And my life.

With the sound of Prokofiev's music thrumming in my ears, I got to work and faced the flood of texts and emails that had poured in overnight. At the top of the list was a text from Olivia. **Pressing charges against Jonathan. Found out he attacked 2 other dancers!**

One problem solved. My friend's path forward wouldn't be easy, but with the weight of multiple voices, perhaps Jonathan Llewellyn Franklin's predatory reign would end. I wondered how his wife would handle the news. If Leonora wanted to escape an unhappy marriage, she'd have plenty of ammunition.

I sent a group text to my family and another to friends saying I was spending the day in bed and was turning off my phone. I hesitated before returning Nelson's call and decided he, too, could wait. I needed a plan before talking to him.

My stomach was so empty it hurt. Thanks to Melissa, the inside of my refrigerator was clean, but thanks to my indolence, it was empty. The laundry bag, however, was stuffed. I dragged a week's worth of dirty clothes to the laundromat, shoved them into two unoccupied washing machines, and headed to Mr. Kim's bodega for some breakfast.

He was excited to see me. "You famous!" He held up a copy of *The New York Times* and pointed to my picture. "You want to buy? I save you three."

I averted my face as two customers turned away from a rack of potato chips to inspect me. Dressed in a pair of worn jeans, clunky boots, and a puffy coat that made me look like an ambulatory sleeping bag, I was not anyone's idea of a celebrity.

"That's really thoughtful of you, Mr. Kim." I paid for the coffee, a muffin, and three newspapers and returned to the laundromat. For the next hour, I ate, drank coffee, and read through my notes on the murder investigation. I got nowhere until, hypnotized by the sight of clothes spinning in the dryer, something clicked.

Jonah picked up my call before the end of the first ring. I didn't mention his failure to return my messages. "I know who the murderer is."

He sounded out of breath. "I'm kind of busy right now. I'll get back to you later."

"Unless you're talking to Nelson Merrill, you're wasting your time. He wants to meet with me. And I believe he's the killer."

He was sharp. "Do not contact him. Meet me at the precinct in thirty minutes."

"I'm at the laundromat. I can't leave. Someone will steal my clothes."

In the background, I heard the sound of traffic and the screech of a siren. "I'll meet you there. Give me the address."

Jonah arrived shortly after I finished folding my last shirt. He hauled the laundry bag over his shoulder. "I guess this means we'll have to talk at your place."

His cool tone irked me. "Not if you don't want to. I'll take the clothes upstairs and meet you at the precinct. Sorry you wasted your time coming here."

He resisted. "Leave the bag to me. Let's get this over with."

We climbed all five flights to my apartment without talking. Thankfully, I didn't have to further strain my back with the heavy laundry bag.

He dropped the clothes as soon as we arrived and said, "How did you fix upon Nelson as the murderer?"

I sat on the sofa and opened my notebook. "I didn't at first. Brett was on top of a long list of other suspects, but when I reviewed the evidence against him, I realized Nelson checked off most of the same boxes. The problem was motive. Nelson didn't seem to benefit from either Maurice's murder or Eddie's. If anything, he appeared to have been damaged by their deaths."

Although I was sitting, Jonah remained standing. "What changed your mind?"

"The collapse of the platform. It wasn't an accident." I showed him the newspaper photograph that revealed the damaged underside of the platform. "No one, except for Sugar Plum, dances on it. If the killer thought he had to get me out of the way, it meant I knew something important. But why wait until opening night? Something I said, in between the last dress rehearsal and the performance, scared the killer. And the only person I talked to, other than Bobbie, was Nelson."

Jonah unbent enough to sit down but not enough to drop his aloof manner. "What did you say to tip him off?"

I wished there was some way to avoid telling him how thoughtless I'd been, but no plausible excuse came to mind. "It was a casual conversation. We were talking about setting up an interview, and I could see how sad and stressed he was. I told him he didn't have to explain how he felt, because Eddie had told me his backstory. I was trying to express my sympathy for his loss, but he thought I knew more than I did. He told me not to talk to anyone else. Is that enough to convince you?"

"You don't have to convince me. I think you're right, although I came to that conclusion from a different angle. Unfortunately, we still don't have enough to arrest him."

"My father suggested you comb through the bags of fake snow. A few pieces of plaster from the platform fell during the Snow scene, and they might have Nelson's fingerprints on them. The large pieces that fell when the platform collapsed were handled by stagehands and dancers, who had to move them out of the way. Those smaller pieces were swept into bags and weren't touched by anyone else."

Jonah stood up. "Anything else before I leave?"

"Yes. We should get a copy of the video tribute from Maurice's funeral and comb through it. He and Nelson's girlfriend studied at the same school, and there might be something in one of the photos that links him with her and with Nelson. I still don't know what Nelson's motive was, but if I had to guess, it's tied to that arson case. He's obsessed with it."

"Good thinking, Leah. I'll have Francie get in touch if we need you. Don't let Nelson inside under any circumstances. You shouldn't be alone." He was brisk and businesslike. "Call Dr. Mitchell. I'm sure he'd be delighted to spend the night with you. I'm surprised he's not still here."

I'd had my heart broken many times, starting with Alan Lipschitz in the sixth grade. None of those disappointments came close to how I felt at that moment, listening to Jonah palm me off on another man. For the first time, I understood where the term heartbreak came from. It literally hurt me to breathe.

There's no point in telling a guy you care about him when he's stopped caring about you. It's like pistachio ice cream. You can't persuade someone to choose pistachio instead of chocolate by explaining how great it is. Or how great you are.

Jonah drew closer. "Are you okay? I know you've been through a lot. If Zach can't come, and you're scared to stay alone, pack a bag, and stay with your mother. Better yet, head to Jersey and stay with Melissa. I don't know why I didn't think of that before. Call your sister. I'll drop you off at Penn Station."

I stared through the window to avoid his gaze. "I'm not going anywhere. Your best chance to pin the murder on Nelson is to use me, because I'm his next target. He'll be on his guard when he talks to you, but I pose no such threat. I'll invite him here and get him talking. You wait in the bedroom. I'll tell him my suspicions. If he's guilty, I'll know it. We'll know it."

He slammed his fist against the wall. "No. You are not to contact him."

"Do you have a better idea? When I told you I thought Nelson was guilty, you said you thought so too. Why?"

Unlike me, Jonah didn't need his notes. "We're examining CC footage from last night. Looks like Nelson was at the theater, disguised as a custodian. Unfortunately, we can't get a definitive ID. He's a filmmaker and probably knew the location and angle of the cameras. Even if we manage to identify him, it won't be conclusive enough for the DA. But it helps. The rest of what I've got is similarly circumstantial. Nelson had the same opportunity and means as everyone else in connection with Maurice's and Eddie's murders. He also had the technical know-how to kill the lights on the day of the blackout and arrange for himself to get injured badly enough to make himself look like a victim."

I sat on my hands to keep them from trembling. Nelson had shadowed me throughout the gala. "I saw him last night. But didn't recognize him. He was on the top level, the Family Circle, when I was talking with Zach. And he was in the lobby when you and I were talking. I knew there was something wrong, but I couldn't figure out what it was. Nelson knows all about disguise and misdirection. He's spent his whole career figuring out how killers get away with murder."

"Right. What got me from the start was his strong personal connection to the victims that predated the murders. I don't know if he took this job for the sole purpose of murdering Maurice, or if something happened after the fact to provoke him, but that's not of immediate importance. Later, when we have to establish premeditation, it will be."

The missing pieces of the puzzle slowly clicked into place. "Eddie told me Nelson planned to do a documentary on a serial killer in California. Nelson's excuse was that wanted to do Maurice a favor, because his friend's career was stalled. But Nelson was the only one who said Maurice's career was in decline. Eddie was repeating what his boss told him. Maurice won a Tony last year for his set design for *Hamlet*. His star was far from fading. Charlotte and Jonathan said Maurice's work was gaining in popularity. I should have realized that discrepancy earlier. Nelson is a practiced and plausible liar."

I picked up my phone. "If you don't want to help, I have plenty of people who do."

"Is there anything I can say to stop you, short of arresting you?"

Since a repetition of the words "I love you" didn't appear to be in the cards, I shook my head. "I have to get back onstage tomorrow. Not doing anything means waiting for Nelson to strike at me again. Or hope he makes a tactical error that provides evidence of his guilt. The stress is killing me."

"I don't want a civilian involved. Too risky."

The urge to strangle him overtook the urge to undress him. "Since when? You promised me we'd work together."

"Back off, Leah. If you hadn't called, I'd be questioning him instead of talking to you. Last night was different. Half the department was there to guard you."

"That didn't stop Nelson from sabotaging the platform or trailing me all night long. How can I dance, knowing he's stalking me?"

He spoke without discernible affection. "You win. Make the call. I'll arrange for backup. And if you ever want to make a career change, I suggest law school." He instructed me to stay in the living room, and he went into the bedroom to test the acoustics.

I spoke no louder than I would if he was in the same room. "Can you hear me?"

He called out, "I can hear you, but not well. Make sure you speak a little louder when Nelson gets here."

We returned to the kitchen to wait. If all went according to plan, Nelson would end the day behind bars. As for me, the possibility of a happy ending felt farther away than ever.

Chapter Thirty-Four

We are what we repeatedly do.
—Aristotle

I tried to sound casual during my phone call with Nelson. "Sorry I missed you last night. I'm off today if you'd like to come over, but tomorrow also works." I attempted a laugh, which came out sounding like a croak. "You have to promise not to tell my sister we're meeting without her. You know how protective Melissa can be."

He was brief. "I'm twenty minutes away."

I texted him my address and apartment number. Although Jonah was on high alert in the bedroom, I was terrified. My apartment is a railroad flat. The front door opens into the living room. The kitchen is on one side, and the bedroom on the other, down a narrow hall with built-in closets. No room was large enough for me to position myself more than a few feet from the man I suspected of killing two people. The man who planned to make me his third victim.

Nelson showed up five minutes early, which rattled me. I buzzed him in and undid the locks and safety latch. He refused my offer to hang up his coat and placed a large backpack against the wall. To my dismay, he relocked the door, which would prevent easy access to the police officers stationed outside the building.

His eyes darted around the apartment. "Are you expecting anyone else? I'd like to get this over without interruption. It's taken long enough, although given what's happened since I arrived, we now have a lot more material to work with."

I didn't look toward the bedroom. "I'm alone. Everyone is exhausted after the gala." I stopped, as if struck by something that hadn't occurred to me earlier. "Where were you last night? I didn't see you at the party."

He pulled down the window shade and unhooked the curtain. "I was there. Got some excellent footage of you during the performance."

I kept fishing. "Did you film the gala as well? I don't remember seeing you."

"A filmmaker's job is to be invisible. Let's get down to business."

He positioned one chair in front of a portable barre, which is not most people's idea of fashionable décor, but was essential to me. He moved a second chair from its usual place and wedged it in front of the hallway to the bedroom. With unexpected quickness, Nelson reached for my phone. I snatched it away from him.

He was adamant. "You have to turn it off. I've had any number of interviews end up on the cutting room floor because a phone started ringing."

As if to prove his point, my phone buzzed with a text from Olga. One quick glance was all I needed to intuit the rest. My Ukrainian friend, whose tech skills were as formidable as her physical strength, had hacked her way into Maurice's files. I pressed the buttons until the screen went dark.

Nelson took the phone and placed it out of reach. "Let's start with last night. Tell me about your decision to continue the performance after the accident with the scenery. What was going through your mind?"

The stage fright I felt before every performance was nothing compared to the terror this seemingly genial man inspired. My body jerked with tremors of pure fear. Using the breathing techniques I depended upon before the curtain goes up, I subdued instinct into self-control.

My voice wasn't as obedient as the rest of my body. For good reason, no one had ever asked me to speak onstage. I hoped Nelson would attribute my quavering voice to nervousness about being on camera. I began with a summary of the prepared answers ABC sent after the performance.

He put down his camera. "I was hoping for a more personal response. How did you feel? What were you thinking?"

I looked directly at Nelson, trying to gauge his mood, but the light glinted off his glasses, and I couldn't see his eyes. "I think the same person who killed Maurice and Eddie was after me."

Nelson didn't pick up the camera. "Tell me about your relationship with Maurice Kaminsky."

Worried about my dwindling supply of courage, I said, "That's not really what you want to know, is it? As you've probably guessed, Eddie told me all about you, and Maurice, and Heather. I know what happened, Nelson. I know it was you."

He lunged at me, reaching for my neck. I ducked to avoid him, but he caught me in a stranglehold. My feet left the ground, and I struggled to breathe. It was like one of those nightmares when you try to scream but can't utter a sound.

Jonah charged into the room and pointed a gun at Nelson. "Let her go. Hands up."

Nelson let my feet return to the ground but continued to hold me in a suffocating grip with one arm. He pulled a switchblade from his pocket and pointed the cold steel against my throat. "One move, Detective, and you can kiss your ballerina friend goodbye."

Jonah's edged closer. "She's of no use to you. Drop the knife."

Nelson's voice rose. "Back off! I'm taking her with me. It'll make for one hell of a movie, don't you think? Ditch the gun, Detective. Or there will be no happy ending for her."

He snaked his leg around mine and pressed his heavy boot on my foot. He didn't stop until we heard a loud crack. "I'll break every bone in her body, one by one, if you don't drop that gun."

I was too scared to feel any pain, but Jonah flinched when he heard the sound of my fractured toe. Inch by inch, keeping his eyes on Nelson, Jonah bent his knees and put his gun on the floor.

Nelson was shaking. "Kick it here. Don't make any false moves. I have nothing left to lose."

Jonah held out his arms, palms upturned. "Then why not let her go? We don't need her. Talk to me."

"Nice try. But we both know she's my ticket out. Did you really think I didn't have an exit plan? I thought you were smarter than that."

I kept very still. "You don't have to threaten me, Nelson." I could feel my foot beginning to swell. "And you didn't have to hurt me. Why do you think I invited you here? I hated Maurice." I stared at Jonah, willing him to shift his gaze from Nelson to me. "Listen carefully. I'm like Juliet. I know how to *let go.*"

Would Jonah understand what I was about to do? He tensed his shoulders and flicked one eye closed an eighth of an inch. He got it.

I immediately went limp. Surprised by the deadweight of my body, and, perhaps, weakened by his recent injury, Nelson lost his grip and dropped me on the floor. From a nearly prone position, I swiped at the base of the barre, and it crashed between us, knocking the knife out of his hand.

Jonah jumped over me and onto him. They rolled over each other, reaching for the gun. I grabbed it and slammed it against Nelson's foot, the only part of his body where I could be sure of hitting only him. He howled with pain. Jonah pinned him face down to the floor and cuffed him. I wondered if I'd broken any of his toes. If so, the punishment didn't equal his crime, but it did provide some poetic justice.

Nelson squirmed and cursed.

Jonah kept his knee on Nelson's back and recited his Miranda rights. The filmmaker turned his head and gave Jonah a twisted smile. "Don't bother. I know the drill by heart." He looked at me and shrugged. "It wasn't personal."

My throat was dry, and my voice hoarse. "You tried to kill me." With the pain in my foot finally making itself known, I added, "And you broke my toe. That's personal, Nelson."

"No. I wanted to scare you. Not kill you. You don't understand."

Jonah's voice was icy. "Then explain it to us."

Nelson yanked at the handcuffs. "I wasn't going to go through with it. I don't kill innocent people."

More lies. "What about Eddie?"

Nelson gave me a contemptuous look. "Eddie wasn't innocent. He threatened me. Said if I didn't step aside and make him the director, he was going to turn me in."

At the sound of heavy footsteps, Jonah had me unlock the door but kept his team waiting on the landing. "Why did you kill Maurice?"

Nelson blinked slowly. "Because he was guilty. For years I searched for Heather's killer. Turned out, the guy I was looking for was right in front of me the whole time. You don't believe me? Check it out for yourself."

I retrieved my phone and opened the file Olga sent me. "Is this what you're talking about?" I didn't understand their import, but Nelson did.

Tears poured down his face. "I don't know how you got those pictures, but they prove I'm right."

Jonah motioned to the waiting cops. They pulled Nelson to his feet and escorted him down the stairs.

I hobbled to the sofa and removed my shoe. Jonah bent down to examine my foot but didn't touch me. "How bad is it?"

"Not bad. I've broken this toe a few times."

He looked sick, but he spoke with clinical detachment. "I'll take you to the emergency room. When you're done, we're going to need your statement. And those images on your phone."

"I don't need a doctor. I know what to do." I limped into the bathroom and taped the injured toe to the two surrounding digits. "Don't look so stricken. A cracked toenail is much worse. I'll be back on pointe tomorrow."

I changed into elastic shoes, and we left the apartment. Mrs. Pargeter was on hand, as she so often is, to monitor the comings and goings in the building. "Are you under arrest?"

I held onto the banister for support. "Not this time, Mrs. Pargeter."

She peered over her spectacles to get a better look at Jonah. "You should keep an eye on her. She keeps very irregular hours."

With a straight face, Jonah told her, "Ms. Siderova is already a person of interest."

Satisfied, she retreated to her apartment.

Jonah stood two feet away from me. The emotional distance between us could be measured in miles. "You did great, Leah. We'll try not to keep you too long."

The streets of New York City were bright with holiday lights and cheerful Christmas wreaths. A light blanket of early snow frosted the sidewalks, and the snowplows were out, spreading sand and salt. Traffic was slow. I should have been happy. Mission accomplished, and I was alive to tell the story. Jonah was mostly silent as we drove to the police station. He asked me twice if I was okay. I said yes.

Despite the snowfall, the steps in front of the police station were jammed with reporters. Jonah drove to the back of the building. There was a palpable sense of excitement inside. Jonah left me in a waiting area, where I fidgeted on a plastic chair bolted to the floor. I texted Melissa the bare outline of what happened, explained where I was, and instructed her to pass on the news to the rest of the family.

She answered immediately. **Call when you're done.**

Detective Farrow escorted me to an interview room. The walls were painted a hideous shade of green, and the table that stood between us was marred with unidentifiable stains. I kept my hands in my lap and didn't ask where Jonah was.

Farrow took my statement. I was nervous, and although I kept my coat on, I couldn't get warm. "Can you keep my name out of the papers?"

He used his pen to gouge dirt out of the creases in the table. "I don't talk to the press. If there's a trial, you'll have to testify, although it's doubtful Mr. Merrill will contest the charges. You and Detective Sobol witnessed his confession to the murders. But you never know. The guy's got powerful friends."

I hugged myself to keep from shivering. "I want to get back to my life. The way it was before Maurice died."

Farrow was sympathetic. "It's still a mob scene out there. Officer Morelli volunteered to see you home."

I was touched. "Thank Francie for me. But I can manage."

"If you don't want to go with Morelli, call someone else. You shouldn't be alone."

The irony in his words stabbed me. Being alone was the one part of my life that was unlikely to change. "Thanks, Detective Farrow. I appreciate

239

that, but I can take care of myself."

Jonah caught up with me by the back exit to the precinct. I didn't know what to say, other than goodbye.

His tone was kind, his manner distant. "Thanks for your help today." I tried to pass, but he blocked my way. "Why are you upset? It's all over now."

I knew only one way to handle emotion, and that was through burying my real self in a fictional character. The tough Cowgirl in the ballet *Rodeo* came to mind. I squared my shoulders and rocked on the balls of my feet, as if ready for a fight. And then, somehow, I lost my appetite for pretense. It was time to be honest, not for Jonah, but for myself. Leah Siderova, however weak and flawed she was, would have to handle the situation on her own.

"I'm upset because you keep pushing me to be with Zach. I get it, Jonah. If you want me to be with another man, it's because you want to be with another woman." I swallowed my tears. "Or you just don't want me. And that's okay. I wouldn't wait around for me either if I were you." I stepped out into the snow.

He pulled me back. "You're the only woman I want, ballerina girl."

"Then why did you—"

"Stop talking."

And I did.

The snow was six inches deep by the time Jonah and I arrived at my building. In what can be described as a miracle on par with the one on Thirty-fourth Street, a car pulled out from a parking spot in front of my building, and Jonah backed into the bare rectangle it left. When we got to the top of the stairs, I swung open the apartment door, and he scooped me up in his arms.

I struggled against his grasp. "I don't need a man to carry me across a threshold. I'm not a trophy."

He understood, as no other man ever did. "I love you. Not as a trophy. As a treasure."

He kissed me, softly at first. Then harder.

Chapter Thirty-Five

Leave the stage before the stage leaves you.
—Tamara Karsavina

The morning after Nelson's arrest, I awoke to an empty bed but not an empty apartment. My lips still tasted of Jonah's mouth, and my skin was redolent of his smell, which was a little bitter and a little sweet.

He nudged me awake with a cup of coffee. "Wake up, Sleeping Beauty. I have to be back at work soon, and we should talk."

I propped my head on my arm. "I'm a dancer. I talk with my body."

He kissed my shoulder. "And your body is very eloquent. But if you don't cooperate, I'm putting you under house arrest."

I pretended to consider this. "Sounds interesting. Tell me more."

He smiled, and the lines of worry around his eyes cleared. "Believe me, if I thought I could tie you down, I would have done so a year ago."

I wrapped my hands around the steaming cup. "How long has it been since you suspected Nelson?"

He sat down to tie his shoes. "Nelson and Brett were at the top of my list from the beginning. They were at the scene of Eddie's death, as well as Maurice's. Psychologically, their personalities suggested they were capable of murder. Both were more in love with their careers and reputation than with any human being. Brett, of course, had means, motive, and opportunity. But he also had a powerful reason to keep Maurice alive for at least a few months longer, which outweighed any possible benefit that might accrue from his death. The timing was wrong."

I already knew this. *"The Nutcracker.* Brett knew if he could pull off a really extraordinary production, he'd be named resident choreographer. But without Maurice, the whole project was literally on shaky ground."

"Right. With Brett an unlikely candidate, I concentrated on Nelson, trying to find a motive. Nothing recent popped out, so I went back to the first crime, the fire that killed Heather Ford. Maurice was questioned, but nothing linked him to the arson."

I thought again of how Eddie hinted at Nelson's guilt. "Nelson acted as if he was justified in killing Maurice and Eddie. No remorse at all."

"I'll tell you as much as he told me, before his lawyer shut him up. Last summer, Nelson visited Brett and Maurice. Brett pitched the idea of doing a documentary, and he gave Nelson access to all of Maurice's old photos, as well as a stack of paintings Maurice had stowed away. According to Nelson, those prove Maurice's guilt. That's what Olga sent you."

I still didn't understand. "What possible reason could Maurice have had to kill Heather? And how did the paintings link Maurice to the arson?"

Jonah's mouth curled in disgust. "Maurice and Heather were finalists for a major prize in their senior year. It opened doors for Maurice and launched his career. Nelson didn't suspect Maurice was guilty of setting the fire until he saw photos of Maurice's graduation portfolio and identified two of the paintings as Heather's, as well as a photo that appeared to place Maurice in the dorm on the night it went up in flames. Would that have been proof enough to convict Maurice? Doubtful. I'm still not convinced. Nelson probably knew no jury would convict Maurice on such circumstantial evidence."

I couldn't match the artist I knew with this portrait of a cold killer. "I don't believe it. Maurice was wildly competitive, but he couldn't have meant to kill Heather. Maybe he set the fire in order to destroy Heather's paintings, and the blaze got out of control."

I strained to remember the first time Jonah and I discussed the murder case. "You told me about a fight Brett and Maurice had last summer. Did it have anything to do with Brett showing Nelson those pictures?"

Jonah pointed a finger at my head. "Brains and beauty."

I wasn't used to being praised for intelligence. That was my sister's talent, not mine.

Jonah said, "Brett had no idea why Maurice threw out the pictures or why he was so upset that Brett had shown them to Nelson. I believe him."

I wished we could spend the day in bed, but neither Jonah nor I had that luxury. I checked the weather outside. Not enough snow to halt the subway, the daily company class, or the evening performance.

His phone rang. I tested the strength of my injured foot and pretended not to listen.

Jonah ended the call. "That was the chief. The director of the new Broadway musical, *Mad Music,* contacted him. Are you familiar with the show?"

"The whole dance world knows about it. The production has been cursed with one problem after another. The choreographer wanted me and a few others at ABC to join the cast, but *Romeo and Juliet* performances begin right after *The Nutcracker* ends. Why do you ask?"

"The star of the show says someone is trying to kill her. The chief wants me to investigate. And the director of the show asked for you. They're willing to wait."

I grabbed a hat from the dresser and struck a pose, with one arm over my head and the other on my hip, à la *A Chorus Line.* "Do you think I can pull it off?"

He pulled me back onto the bed. "I do."

Acknolwedgements

I want to thank my editor, Shawn Reilly Simmons, for her patience, time, and talent, as well as those other wonderful Dames of Detection, Verena Rose and Harriette Sackler.

I am indebted to my kids, and there are a lot of them. In no particular order: Geoffrey, who offered advice and encouragement throughout multiple iterations of this work; Luke, whose sharp eye and witty edits helped me through the thickets of each draft; Jacob, whose pragmatic perspective is exceeded only by his ironic sense of humor; Gregory, whose artistic sensibility spans a multitude of disciplines; Becky, whose devotion to ballet is equal to mine; Jesse, whose precise recall of every movie we've seen together is the stuff of family legends; Kris, whose support is unstinting; and Emily, who loves talking about poisons and knife wounds as much as I do. And I'm endlessly inspired by the newest generation: Viola, Sophie, Ava, and Alice. Like me, they love a good story.

I owe a lot to my sisters, who are many and various. First, in every way, is the sister I was lucky enough to grow up with, Karyn Boyar. Next are my sisters-in-law: Lisa, Barbara, Jane, Gail, and Lolly. Last, but not least, I want to thank my talented Sisters in Crime.

To my brother Richard: I wish you were here to see the publication of this book.

Much gratitude is due to the many dancer friends who have supported me. Your kindness and talent know no bounds. Thank you, from the bottom of my heart.

To Vladimir (The Duke) Dokoudovsky (1919-1998) His brilliance still shines for generations of dancers who were lucky enough to earn a place at his barre.

This book is dedicated to Glenn, who still thinks—after all these years—that he's the one who got lucky.

About the Author

Lori Robbins began dancing at age 16 and launched her professional career three years later. She studied at the New York Conservatory of Dance and the Martha Graham School and performed with a number of modern dance and classical ballet companies, including Ballet Hispanico and the St. Louis Ballet. Her commercial work included featured spots for Pavlova Perfume. After ten very lean years onstage she became an English teacher and now writes full time.

Lori is the author of the On Pointe and Master Class mysteries. She won the Indie Award for Best Mystery, the Silver Falchion for Best Cozy Mystery, and was a finalist for both a Readers' Choice and Mystery and Mayhem Book Award.

Short stories include "Accidents Happen" in *Murder Most Diabolical* and "Leading Ladies" in *Justice for All*. She's also a contributor to *The Secret Ingredient: A Mystery Writers Cookbook.*

As a dancer, writer, English teacher, and mother of six, Lori is an expert in the homicidal impulses everyday life inspires.

SOCIAL MEDIA HANDLES:

https://linktr.ee/lorirobbinsmysteries
https://www.instagram.com/lorirobbinsmysteries/
https://www.facebook.com/lorirobbinsauthor/
https://www.bookbub.com/profile/lori-robbins
https://www.goodreads.com/author/show/16007362.Lori_Robbins
lorirobbinsauthor@gmail.com
https://twitter.com/lorirobbins99

AUTHOR WEBSITE:

https://www.lorirobbins.com/

Also by Lori Robbins

Murder in First Position

Murder in Second Position

Lesson Plan for Murder